Acclaim for Pamela Ribon's novel
Why Girls Are Weird

"Full and hilarious. . . ."

—*Miami Herald*

"Truly funny. . . . Anna is . . . more real than most chick-lit heroines."

—*Fort Worth Star-Telegram* (TX)

"Light and entertaining."

—*Booklist*

"Witty, wonderful and wise."

—*Maryland Gazette*

"I absolutely loved [it]!"

—Pop Gurls

"Online or offline, this girl is funny."

—*Calgary Herald*

"With wit and spark, Ribon hopscotches through the high-bandwidth dramas of the modern girl's life."

—Pagan Kennedy

"A muscular, sexy ride through the irresistible thrills of online flirting and the all-too-familiar heartaches of real life romance. [The] writing is as moving as it is funny, with a shock and a delight on every page."

—Claire LaZebnik, author of *Same As It Never Was*

"Reading the irresistible *Why Girls Are Weird* is like hanging out with your best friend just when you need to most."

—Melissa Senate, author of *See Jane Date*

Also by Pamela Ribon

Why Girls Are Weird

Available from Downtown Press

Why Moms Are Weird

Pamela Ribon

NEW YORK LONDON TORONTO SYDNEY

An *Original* Publication of POCKET BOOKS

DOWNTOWN PRESS, published by Pocket Books
1230 Avenue of the Americas
New York, NY 10020

Library of Congress Cataloging-in-Publication Data is available.

ISBN-13: 978-1-4165-0385-9
ISBN-10:   1-4165-0385-4

This Downtown Press trade paperback edition August 2006

10   9   8   7   6   5   4   3   2   1

DOWNTOWN PRESS and colophon are
trademarks of Simon & Schuster, Inc.

Manufactured in the United States of America

For information regarding special discounts for bulk purchases,
please contact Simon & Schuster Special Sales at 1-800-456-6798
or business@simonandschuster.com.

For Dad

Acknowledgments

I only get one page and there are too many people to thank, so these are the people who were a part of this book, in countless ways:

The big four: Amy Pierpont, Megan McKeever, Kim Witherspoon, and Alexis Hurley.

The big three: Todd Christopher, Amy Schiffman, and Erin Searcy.

My best man: Daniel J. Blau.

The best people: Adam Blau, Rebecca Russell, Andrew Kamenetzky, Brian Kamenetzky, Steve Skelton, Jessica Kaman, Tyson Heder, AB Chao, Allison Lowe-Huff and Chris Huff, Todd and Hilary Anderson, Sara Morrison, Tom Hargis, Evany Thomas, Frank Stokes, Stephanie Markham, Josh Lanthier-Welch, Jami Anderson, Brently Heilbron, Liz Feldman, Jason Allen, Laura House, Patrick Srail, Maureen Driscoll, Tara Ariano, Dave Cole, Sarah Bunting, Ray Prewitt, Andi Teran, and Jeff Long.

The girl crushes: Kimberly Wright, Kimberley Helms, and Kara Baker.

My first family: Paula Ribon, Natalie Ribon, and Chris and Marcy Kelman.

My second family: Jeff Schimmel, Chris McGuire, Brian Rubenstein, Steve Trevino, David Lucky, Brian Hartt, Cristela Alonzo, Blaine Capatch, Bob Oschack, Ted Sarnowski, Tim Jennings, Robert Morton, and Carlos and Amy Mencia.

My broken home: Suzanne Martin, Andy Gordon, Sebastian Jones, Anne Flett, Chuck Ranberg, Christian McLaughlin, Valerie Ahern, John Davoren, Ken Andrade, Jennifer Shaklan, and Chris Shiple.

Thank you, Richard Breton, John Wolcott, and Florence Clark. Thank you, Swork.

Thank you, pamie.com.

And, as always, everything is because of my sweet stee. I love you.

"I won't be happy till I see you alone again.
Till I'm home again and feeling right."

—CAROLE KING

"Sid and Nancy's relationship forever
illustrates the worst part of being in love
with anyone, which is that people
in love can't be reasoned with."

—CHUCK KLOSTERMAN,
KILLING YOURSELF TO LIVE

Why Moms Are Weird

To Whom It May Concern . . .

I thought I should write this just in case I ever accidentally kill my mother on purpose.

Charles Whitman did this, before he climbed the tower at the University of Texas in Austin and shot all of those people. He wrote a letter, to whoever found it after his death, because he had a feeling he was about to kill his mother and then a whole bunch of other people for good measure.

I'm not as positive as Whitman was. In fact, I think he ended his letter with "P.S.: By the way, I'm pretty sure there's a gigantic tumor pressing against my brain." (Which there was.)

I wanted to write all of this down just in case somehow something horrible happens to my mother. This is for if the coroner says, "It looks like she fell down the stairs. Three times." If the cops all look at each other with stern concern because they know this was a case of accidental matricide (a second- or third-degree offense, I'm sure), this will be something tangible in my defense.

And no, this isn't a confirmation of premeditation. This is anti-premeditation. A preretraction. A remnant from before I went crazy, before I do all of the things the little voice in my head tells me to do. I don't mean "little voice" like Whitman's tumor voice, either. This is the little voice that says, "This isn't how your life is supposed to be! Now go shake your mother!"

Just in case. You understand.

Your honor. Kind jury. Dear reader. Whoever it is holding

this book, wondering what the hell happened to that nice girl Belinda Bernstein. The one with the pretty brown hair and the big, blue eyes. Just in case I have to run away to Mexico after accidentally feeding my mother rat poison.

I'm not going to do it. I'm totally not going to do it.

I'm writing this all down, though.

Just. In. Case.

Exhibit A.

"Hello?"

"Hi, honey, it's just your mom."

This is how my mother starts all of our phone conversations. Actually, I knew it was her long before I said hello. I can tell by the ring. It has a certain *need* to it.

"Hi, Ma."

"You sound busy."

She always says this no matter how I sound. It's so I can say, "No, I'm not busy."

I hear her suck on her front teeth. "I never know what time it is over there."

"I'm three hours back." I once made the mistake of joking that Los Angeles was "in the past" compared to Virginia, and Mom's understanding of time shattered forever. "What's up?"

"Are you sure you've got time?" she asks.

"I do."

"You're not busy?"

I was microwaving a bag of popcorn, ready to watch the entire fourth season of *Mr. Show* on DVD yet again. I was busy according to my own terms, but maybe not by anyone else's.

"What's going on?"

"I think I have chlamydia."

That can't have been what she said. I must have misheard. Bad connection. Terrible reception. Ear infection. Temporary mental retardation. Any and all other explanations are preferable to the possibility that my mother has just told me she has contracted a sexually transmitted disease.

"What? Ma, what?" I'm yelling like I'm actually in the past now, holding a giant horn to my ear while screaming into the machine hardwired to the wall. *Operator! Give me Poughkeepsie 5–472!*

"Boobs? Are you alone?"

That's my nickname. It's short for "Benny Boobenstein," which is what she started calling me when my chest arrived at thirteen. I know; it's fucking hilarious.

And the answer to her question is, of course, "Yes." This is Mom fishing for info on my personal life without coming right out and asking, "Are you dating someone yet?" I swear, sometimes she calls the house and holds the receiver up to a ticking clock. I cannot seem to get through to my mother that I have no desire to get married anytime soon.

I know you're thinking, "She just asked three words. 'Are you alone?' It's a simple question, Benny. I might ask you that myself if I called to discuss chlamydia." But you're new, and you don't know my mother never says three words without five different intentions behind them. You'll see.

Now Mom's saying, "I have this thmurmur?"

She mumbles. She does this a lot. It also often sounds like she's falling, or putting the phone down midsentence. It's as if she gives up, right in the middle of the conversation, the phone too heavy to continue. Or maybe she gets bored with me.

Actually, I think Mom gets distracted. She's probably still talking, but she's remembered she needs to take some clothes out of the dryer. So she's still talking to me, but from down the hall. She hates that I won't let her put me on the speaker-phone.

"Chlamydia? Isn't that how you say it?" She sounds it out, like English is a second language. "Chlam . . . clam . . . clam-mid?"

"Hold on, Ma." I put the phone between my knees and glance at the smirking faces from the DVD on my coffee table. Bob and David seem to be taking great joy in my suffering. I take a breath and put the phone back to my ear.

"Boobs?" she says. I wonder how many times she said that while I put her on hold. I clearly indicated I was going to put the phone down. Why does that not mean anything to her? Why does she have to call out my name like I've abandoned her?

"Ma. I need you to repeat what you just said you had."

"Chlamydia?"

"Now I need you to never say that again." With the heel of my free hand I rub my eyes, one after another. I have to figure this out. There's an explanation for all of this. Perhaps she's finally entered dementia. Is that how you say it? Do you "enter" dementia, or do you "come down" with dementia, or is it more of a "hit with" kind of thing?

Mom's succumbed to dementia.

"I hate bothering you, honey," she says. She goes into the martyr thing pretty easily. "I know you're busy. I'm sorry."

"You're not bothering me, Ma." Not if my mother's vagina is in peril. Holy fucking shit, I have to think about my mother's vagina. There aren't enough curse words to handle this current situation.

I haven't had to think about this place since I left it, since that eviction notice was tacked to the inside of the womb and the tongs pulled me out of there. Mom said I was stubborn— not only was I a week late, she was in labor for thirty-six hours. So long, in fact, that Dad had gone to work. Even my grandparents missed showtime, assuming if I had taken a day and a half, a few hours more weren't going to make a difference. They were at a Denny's, eating breakfast. Gramma wanted to name me after her eggs Benedict, even after she found out I was a girl. Mom had the good sense to name me Belinda. Gramma was stubborn, though, and called me Benny. It stuck. A girl named Benny. Crazy families sure know how to jack up a girl's name, don't they?

I'm Belinda "Benny" Boobenstein Bernstein. Sometimes I'm simply known as "Boobs." Clearly I'm going to kill someone someday. It's just a matter of time before I snap, and everyone will understand.

"I didn't know what else to do," Mom says, referring, I suppose, to her calling me for medical advice.

"Did you ask Jami?" That's my younger sister, who currently lives with my mother in a *Grey Gardens* way. Neither of them has ever seen the documentary, and I hope, for their sake, it stays that way. I don't want them picking up any tips on how to let a hundred cats live in their home.

If my mother mumbles, Jami shouts. She's the opposite of me in many ways. Jami's favorite things include tattoos, cigarettes, and boys who have stood in front of courtrooms pleading "Guilty."

"It doesn't itch," Mom says.

"What doesn't?" I ask, already dreading the answer.

"The bumps. On my legs."

"And the bumps are from that thing you said you had?"

"I don't know. Didn't you say you had it, too?"

"No!" I don't care that I sound insulted at having something in common with my mother. This isn't something I'd like to bond over, and I can't believe she thinks I'm the one to call when bumps appear. "When did I say that? No!"

"From your . . . last . . . boyfriend."

Okay, here's where it'd be so easy to say to Mom that there is no way she has chlamydia, because I'm pretty sure you can't get it without having sex with someone who has chlamydia. I'd like it to be easy as pie to say, "Ma, you can't have it." But the truth is I can't say that, and it's the fact that I can't say it that I hate more than anything on earth.

My father died three years ago. This means my mom is now "entertaining gentlemen." This is how she puts it. It sounds like she's dancing in front of a row of horny men, pulling her clothes off to the sound of a three-piece jazz band.

My mom? Oh, she's a "Gentlemen Entertainer." Yes, it's a real job. She makes her own hours.

She is entertaining gentlemen because legally, morally, and spiritually she's supposed to be "out there" searching for other men who could make her happy. I can't stop using quotation marks when I talk about it because I'd like to keep as much distance as possible from my mother's love life. Unfortunately, my mom doesn't have the same desire. She'd rather have me create her a MySpace page, and then help define the parameters of her sexual interests. I say this only because last year that's exactly what happened. And that's the first time I ever hung up the phone in the middle of a conversation with my mother. And no, I still don't feel guilty about it.

My father died of cancer. There's a long story I don't have to tell, because you get this one word, *cancer,* and everybody can picture it—the hospital visits, the chemo, the sound of machines counting down the moments you have left with the person who brought you into this world (even if he was behind a desk at a mortgage company at the time of my arrival).

He died of cancer, and he died rather quickly. They had air-plane tickets to see Paris for the first time. It was going to be their thirtieth anniversary present to each other. You know how people say, "We'll always have Paris"? Well, my parents won't. As far as I'm concerned, I won't either. Paris is every missed dream, every broken promise. You only have Paris when you didn't get what you actually wanted. *That's* when people say, "We'll always have Paris." When it's over. When everything is ruined.

An Interlude. A Tangent, If You Will, Since My Mom's Still Talking about Her Infected Girl Parts.

Ever have someone say they'll wait for you? And I mean this in the emotional, "We'll always have Paris," kind of way. Has someone ever looked you in the eye and said, "I'll wait for you"?

Don't let it happen. Right there, right when it's said, you should take his or her hand and reply, "Don't."

Waiting for someone is impossible. It can't be done. It's nobody's fault, but eventually the waiting stops. One has to, in order to save face. There might be a spectacular, last minute, desperate attempt right before the supposed waiting period starts or ends where someone makes a grand gesture, probably at an airport before a plane takes off. Well, really that stopped once we weren't allowed to run to the gate any-more. So many grand gestures never happen now that we can't get past the loading zone. On one hand, it's sad, but it's keeping a lot of people from making assholes out of themselves in front of the Cinnabon.

My point is: the waiting won't last. It can't. I've tried. This is why I'm giving you this advice, even though we barely know each other. I'm sure you're a nice person, and I bet all kinds of people like you. I don't want anyone to think you're a dick. So allow me to share my wisdom. I don't know much, but what I know is all yours. Hey, maybe one day you'll say:

"Belinda Bernstein may have killed her mother accidentally on purpose, but she also kept me from pining for Chris Harrison for another month. That guy was never going to love me back."

When someone's waiting on you, it creates a certain amount of resentment. Why should someone have to wait on another person? Wait for what? To be good enough? To be better than all the other options in the world? To be literally the last opportunity?

Waiting on someone, *for* someone, drives you crazy because all you can do is (a) think of all the things you'd be doing together if you weren't waiting; (b) think of all the things you should be doing with your time instead of waiting; and (c) listen to every song that plays on the radio and assume it's being sung just for you.

It's (c) that did me in. When I was waiting for a certain man to realize that we belonged together and he was the one person who made me happy and I didn't want to really live my life without him, there were many minutes, hours, days, weeks when I was alone and stuck with option (c). This is when you hear a dumb-ass song like Samantha Mumba's "Gotta Tell You," with the chorus: *"Don't wanna love you if you don't love me / Don't wanna need you when you won't need me too."* Normally, you wouldn't even notice. You'd probably absentmindedly change the radio station while changing lanes. But if you're waiting on someone, your brain works very differently. The wrong synapses fire, and you find yourself thinking, "I have to find a way that he can hear this song. I wonder if it's on iTunes."

I shouldn't know a single lyric to a single Samantha Mumba song. But that day I ended up listening to the song all the way through, and then I Googled the lyrics, and then I cried all night while I cleaned out my bedroom closet. I had to clean, because it's the only thing that effectively disguises what I was actually doing, which was waiting.

It makes you go crazy. Waiting for someone to love you, to come to you and only you, to choose you like you've already chosen, is the most degrading, debasing, demoralizing . . . and yet, sweet, sweet pain there is. It's as humbling as it is humiliating. But yes, there is a sweet side. You know what'll happen when the choice is made and you're finally together. You know that's when your heart starts beating for real. That's what you think, anyway. That's what you keep telling yourself.

But listen to me. It doesn't happen. You wait, and eventually you realize you've been wasting your time. You lost time making yourself available to something that was never going to happen. You're a sucker and you're the one who did it to yourself.

So. No waiting. I used to be the girl who would wait. When my mom's done talking about her chlamydia, I'll tell you exactly when I realized that not only is love not worth waiting on, about 99 percent of the time, it's probably not really love anyway.

Back to the C Word.

"No, I never had chlamydia," I say to Mom, trying to remain calm and patient. At least, in voice.

"When the doctor told me I had this before, I called you. You said you had it, too."

"What do you mean, you had this before?"

"Remember when I was going out with Ward, the one who worked with computers? We came back from that trip to Atlantic City and I told you how my hips were sore from—"

Here's what my brain does right now to deal with this situation. In order to let her finish this sentence, my head fills with this sound:

BEEEEEEEEEEEEEEEEEEEEEEEEEEEEEEEEEEEEEEE!

But when I listen again, she's saying, "Maybe it's herpes. The rash is starting at my knees, but it's getting closer to . . . other parts. It's moving up. Toward my—

BEEEEEEEEEEEEEEEEEEEEEEEEEEEEEEEEEEEEEEE-EEEEEEEEEEE!

After my small blackout, Mom finishes with, ". . . and the rash is a bunch of little blisters."

"You have blisters on your thighs, but they started at your knees?"

"Yes."

"So why do you think this is a sexually transmitted disease?"

"Well, what else could it be?" Her voice gets really high here, indignant, like I'm insinuating she *doesn't* have a fantastic sex life.

"Seeing as how most people don't have sex with their knees, I'd say the chances of it being an STD are pretty slim."

"What did you tell me I had last time? Wasn't it an STD?"

"Are you talking about the UTI?"

I don't want to bring this particular horrible memory up again, but it is still preferable to the one we're creating right now. About a year ago Mom called at eight in the morning to mumble something about peeing blood, and if I'd know anything about that. I said, "Drink some cranberry juice, go to the doctor, and pee after sex." And then I hung up. The damage had been done, though. I didn't have sex for three weeks after that. I just kept imagining Mom with her cranberry juice and my spine would curl in agony.

Not that I'd be having lots of sex, anyway. Since Mom's busy discussing thigh pustules, I'll use this blackout to tell you that I don't have a steady boyfriend now, and I haven't had one in a little while. They don't stick. And by that I mean they don't stick around. Or I don't stick around. Really, the entire dating thing has been exhausting. I'm just going to go ahead and blame my mom for this one, too. I've got a dead dad and a germy mother. Who wants to take on *this* hottie?

"I guess it's not a UTI," Mom says, sounding a little too disappointed.

"Have you gone to a doctor yet?"

She makes this scoffing sound, as if I've asked if she's planning on shooting porn this weekend. "Now, how am I going to talk to a doctor about this?" she asks.

"Preferably in a voice low enough so that I don't have to hear it anymore."

"Benny, you're smart. Get on the Internet and tell me what's going on with my Aunt Doris."

"Jesus, Ma. If you're old enough to get it sick, you're old enough to call it by its real name."

"I'm not saying that V word."

"You said 'chlamydia' just fine."

This is officially the weirdest conversation I've ever had with my mother.

"Don't start, Benny."

"Ma, did you have sex with someone who has chlamydia?"

"I don't know."

"You don't *know*?"

"It's not like I'm going to ask him."

"Why not?"

"Girls don't ask boys questions like this."

My mother is fifty-three.

"I want you to get off the phone, call the doctor, and go see him today. You tell him what you've told me, because he went to school for a very long time to accurately tell you what he thinks about weird bumps."

Mom sighs. "Fine. I thought you'd be mffwffwa."

"I'd be what?"

"HELPFUL."

It's possible Mom mumbles on purpose so when I make her repeat herself she can yell the word she's pissed about.

"I love you, Ma."

"I love you, too, Boobs."

"Now go get your skanky ass to a doctor."

A Disclaimer.

I don't really have fantasies of killing my mother. I love her more than anyone in the world. She is a fantastic woman.

Here's how fantastic: she has saved no fewer than four lives in this world. Four different people would not be alive if it weren't for my mother's bravery and skill.

A man once had a heart attack on the highway, and his truck swerved across three lanes of traffic before smashing through a fence and rolling to a stop in the parking lot where my mother was loading groceries into her car. She ran over to the truck, crawled into the driver's seat, and performed CPR until the paramedics arrived. He would have died if she hadn't been standing there. If she'd been standing three feet to the left, he would have killed her.

When I was about ten and my sister was seven we had a big family vacation, staying at a bunch of hotels as we drove along the coast of California. (By the way, Mom claims this trip is one of the reasons I now live three thousand miles away and curses this vacation constantly. "I never should have taken you at such an impressionable age," she says.) At one particular hotel they had a small pool. Jami and I were bobbing along the deep end, playing Dolphin—a game where we'd try to flip into the air as high as possible, pretending to catch fish and eat them. We were too busy attempting somersaults to notice a blond toddler slip into the water behind us. She had wandered away from her mother, who had turned around to drape her towel over a lawn chair. That's how quickly the little girl slipped into the water without a splash. But Mom saw. She dove in, got the kid, and brought her to the surface before the little girl had even a moment to realize she was breathing water. My mother is a hero.

The other two lives she's responsible for? Mine and Jami's. We wouldn't be here without her, and while I never forget it, Mom sometimes acts like it was no big deal at all to create us from inside of her body and unleash us on this world. I think it's the most amazing, selfless thing anybody has ever done for me. There's no way I could ever thank her.

So I really hope I don't accidentally kill her.

I don't know what compels her to call me and ask for this advice, opening up this kind of dialogue. I know this isn't normal. There aren't movies where a mother turns to her adult daughter and says, "Can we talk about chlamydia?" Maybe my mother doesn't have enough friends. I don't either, so I can't judge. But I would love to find a way to make her think differently enough about me that she doesn't try to girl-bond over sex. I don't ask to have her treat me like a daughter all that often, but I think here I have every right to be creeped out.

She needs a great girlfriend. I wonder if I can make her a MySpace page for that instead.

Okay. So Back to Me.

I moved to Los Angeles almost four years ago because Brian, my boyfriend at the time, wanted to. We were living in Chapel Hill and I was working at a software company. Marketing. It was my job to set up trade booths for conventions. I ordered giant banners, created pamphlets, sorted name tags. Yeah, it was really smart stuff. Totally using my art history degree to the fullest. Sometimes I'd have to lie down from thinking all those really deep thoughts about PowerPoint presentations.

I thought it would be incredibly romantic to drop everything and move across the country to be with my struggling actor boyfriend. We were young and full of hope. I could already see his Oscar acceptance speech. I'd be stunning in a tight, red gown designed by someone whose name I couldn't accurately pronounce. Tears would be streaming down my face as Brian looked at me from the podium, wrap-it-up music fighting for supremacy as he shouted, "But all of this is because my wife, Belinda, never stopped believing in me! She is the greatest lady who has ever lived! I love you, Boobs!"

It's true; I never stopped believing in him, even six months after we moved here, when every cell in my body was sure he was cheating on me with a girl from his improv class. I believed every excuse he gave me when he didn't have enough money to pay the electric bill, when he pawned our CDs to pay for an audition workshop, when he borrowed my cell phone and never returned it. When he cried at night, telling me he wanted so badly to be able to propose, to give me a ring he was proud of and pay for the wedding of our dreams—I wanted to believe him so much my toes would ache from clenching them in hope. But in the end, I couldn't believe hard enough. In the end, I knew he was just acting.

Then. Then I got stupid. I waited for someone.

I met Kevin at a friend's birthday party. We were both freezing in a courtyard, shuffled off to the side. We started talking, and didn't leave each other for the next two weeks. We had so much in common it was like I'd found part of my own body, something I didn't even know I'd been missing. Kevin had a similar background, also had an art history degree, and his CD collection looked exactly like mine.

The problem was Kevin wasn't living in Los Angeles. He was just in town from New York for a few months, working on a project. And Kevin really liked his life in New York. Having already moved across the country for one boy, I knew I didn't want to do it again for another. Instead I thought I'd handle this maturely.

I threw a small tantrum, and afterward I told Kevin that I'd be here when he was smart enough to realize we belonged together.

I can't really tell you how I knew this. But I did. When I looked at Kevin, I saw my future. Every time he made me laugh, part of me clicked into place. But I wasn't going to give myself up for him. That's what happened with Brian, and why he walked all over me. With Kevin, I wanted to be equal. I wanted him to come to me like I'd come to him. I could already picture him calling me from New York, telling me he was miserable, that any distance from me was the worst pain he'd ever felt.

I semistalked him over the Internet, sending him approximately three hundred emails a minute. Or so. I didn't count. But let's just say there wasn't a way he could write back to me as often as I wrote to him. I had a desk job; he had something that resembled a life.

To his credit, Kevin waited until we were sitting across from each other again to tell me that it wasn't going to work out. In the end, he didn't miss me enough. He didn't say that, not exactly. But that's what it means. I thought he needed me more than he did. I don't know where he is now. I don't even look him up, even in my most depressing moments in the middle of the night when I'm drunk and alone with the Internet. I failed at making someone love me like I loved him, and I don't need a reminder that life goes on for other people. I don't want to think of anyone surviving me.

What I've figured out after Kevin and Brian is that I've never really been in love. Not real love. Not true love. You can be in love with someone, but if it's not returned, then it can't be true love. I refuse to think that real love makes you miserable all the time. If love is supposed to be this painful and difficult, why would people get married, choosing to feel this way forever? There must be a different kind of love, one I haven't felt yet, when someone looks at you just like you're looking at him and you don't have to say anything. You just know. It's got to be rewarding and fun, because the only love I've ever known has always ended up kicking me in the ass.

Does this make me a cynic or a romantic? Both, I guess. I believe in love, I just don't believe it's happened to me. And a small confession here: I don't see it happening for me anytime soon. Not until I'm way older, with some idea of who I am. Lately all I've been able to figure out is who I'm not.

So. Me. I live alone, in an apartment in Hollywood. I've just turned twenty-seven, an age that comes with absolutely no pressure or responsibility, which I enjoy. I'm not in "The Business," or "The Industry," as so many people around here are. While I enjoy the fact that Los Angeles lets me live in a weird dream world where celebrities are sometimes buying groceries in line with me (Hello, cute concierge from *Gilmore Girls*), I don't want to have anything to do with being rich and/or famous. It makes me, in many ways, the famous one among my group of friends. They think my life is like a blissful vacation, free from the daily rejection and self-doubt their world surrounds them in. It also makes them think I'm small-town, even though I'm in the exact same freaky metropolis they live in. I have to watch what I eat and work out just as often as they do. The only difference is I don't lose a guest spot on some prime-time soap if I'm a little bloated.

A typical example of a night out with my friends consists

of us meeting at a restaurant walking distance from my house, but I still take my car and park with the valet. We will say we're meeting at 8:00, but the first person shows up at 8:10. Everybody hugs, and the boys kiss the girls on the cheeks. First we compliment each other's looks, because it's really important to some of them to be told how pretty they are. Then we order a bottle of wine, before we've even cracked the menu. I listen to my friends—both boys and girls—dissect the menu like they're reading the paper, discussing both the price and caloric count of each item, cross-referencing each fact with a complaint about either a lack of money or a lack of a job. They then all order the most expensive item on the menu, the one that has the least amount of food. I listen to their stories of auditions and near brushes with fame, or at the very least, a chance at a few hours of employment.

While I'm happy that I don't have the slightest desire to do what they do, I can't get all high and mighty. What I do to pay the bills is just as depressing as a fifteen-second audition for an unattainable role.

I work at a travel agency, which means my job is very annoying, and not just because seventeen times a week I send someone to Paris. I also send them to Morocco, London, Sydney, and Tokyo. Every day I put someone on a dream trip, to places far away and beautiful, while I sit in the same cramped, leaky, mildew-streaked office on Ventura Boulevard. My dreams do not lie in the travel agency world. My dreams have sort of run dry. I thought by now I'd be working at a gallery, scouring the country for new talent to break into the art world. But when I got out of school, I needed money to live. It would have been easier to learn how to construct a gallery with my own hands than to land a job in one. Then I went to Los Angeles, hoping the atmosphere would be inspir-

ing. Instead, it was overwhelming. Everybody here is suppos-
edly creating something, but usually it's really crappy. And if
everybody I know is creating something crappy, then chances
are I'm doing something crappy, too. I'm no genius, and I
don't have the ambition it takes to be mediocre. It's much easier to stop. Eventually I was disappointing myself enough
that my brain decided it'd be best to lay low for a while. Take
some time off. Wait this part of my life out. I have put myself
on hold.

I know. *Wah.* I live in a beautiful city where it's eighty de-
grees and sunny every day. I'm completely employed and
healthy. I have my own apartment. I own a car. I even have
money in savings because Dad had a great life insurance policy and left a very detailed, very balanced will. There is nothing for me to complain about. I know that.

Then why do I have this horrible feeling in the pit of my
stomach that I'm missing out on something amazing? What's
making me search crowds at movie theaters, wondering if I'm
supposed to bump into someone? How come I get anxious
when I'm down to the last page of the book I'm reading,
upset that I'll be finished and have to find something new to
occupy my time? I get hooked into the strangest things, and
obsess over the smallest distractions.

Here's my latest, and I can't stop myself from doing it. I
search for personal meaning in the music playing over the
loudspeaker at my local supermarket. I'm not even waiting on
someone, so I don't have the excuse, but the practice appears
to have stuck.

I don't like grocery shopping because it always takes much
longer than I think buying food should. My list will have
items that seem very logical when I write them down, but in
order to fetch the items on the page, from eggs to milk to toilet paper, I have to run a haphazard maze across the store. In-

evitably I forget an item or two because I didn't turn down the cereal aisle, or no longer had the energy to wind all the way back to produce. So to keep myself Zen about the entire shopping experience, I find myself sucked into the music they play over the loudspeaker.

I don't know if this is strictly an Albertsons thing, but the music they play—a collection I'd call *NOW That's What I Call Inoffensive!*—is a mix of some of the cheesiest, sappiest, most banal songs that seem to all live deep inside my brain, somewhere near my cerebellum. I am convinced that someone's playing DJ whenever I walk into Albertsons, and all the songs are tiny little messages just for me, like a fortune-teller flipping tarot cards as I push my cart toward the produce section.

Yesterday I went into the store with a list of ten items. I can't remember anything I had to buy, but I remember the songs, because I walked into the store thinking about my last nonboyfriend, Ted. He's a guy I saw for two weeks, until he told me he needed me to tell him I was in love, or he no longer wanted to continue seeing me, because "at his age" it was time either to find someone willing to be his wife, or move on. What kind of girlie breakup is that? He dumped me because I wasn't needy enough. I'd feel bad, except I was trying to figure out how to make that be our last date, anyway. He never washed the sheets on his bed, listened to Tori Amos unapologetically, and called me "Benicita." You do not get to nickname me if you've known me for less than a month.

So, check out what DJ Supermarket had in store for me.

Song one: John Waite's "Missing You." The lyric is actually, "I ain't missing you at all," but it's a song about long distance love. I don't have a long distance love. I'm not removed from anybody. So I took the lyrics at face value, because I ain't missing nobody. And just in case you're wondering if I'm in some kind of denial, let me reiterate: I ain't missing Ted at all.

The next song was Jane Child's "Don't Wanna Fall in Love." See? One song leads to the next. Another song about someone trying to avoid falling in love. This would have been way more painful if there was someone I was trying to avoid. When the song doesn't match my mood, I wonder if it's because I'm supposed to be thinking about something else. If the music wants me to think about love lost, or love never had, is that because I've moved my life in the wrong direction? Yeah, I know that's a bit extreme, but my imagination goes into hyperdrive when I'm bored. When I'm stuck in a doctor's office, waiting on an appointment, I'm able to convince myself that I'm the last person on the planet and everyone else has turned into zombies. I try to figure out where I'm going to live and what people I'd need to resurrect to help fight the zombies with me. The problem is after casting the two Johns (McCain and Depp), I start getting distracted with mental tangents.

I need to keep myself entertained in the Baby and Pet aisle, since I've neither at home depending on me. All I have is my brain to keep me company, and apparently my brain likes making the entire world revolve around me. This means my life has a soundtrack of sorts, and when I'm at the store, everybody is an extra in the "Benny Goes Shopping" scene.

I tried to will the songs into what I'd rather think about, get some girl-power up in the place, and was soon rewarded with En Vogue's "My Lovin' (You're Never Gonna Get It)," which made me shake my booty in a rather embarrassing, yet uncontrollable way as I shimmied down the paper products aisle.

I was still rocking as the loudspeaker changed to Irene Cara's "Flashdance (What a Feelin')," which is just a weakness. The song is fantastic and I couldn't help but sing along until I got busted by a boy staring at me from the magazine section. I had no defense, no comeback, nothing to say for myself other than, "I grew up in the eighties." He didn't say anything. Just slowly nodded. His hair was dark, short, and pushed forward, close to his head. A hint of a goatee outlined his mouth. He wore the hipster uniform: a faded red T-shirt advertising a candy from when we were kids and jeans seemingly dangling from his boxer shorts.

Right on cue, DJ Supermarket kicked into The Clash's "Lost in the Supermarket."

Nice work, Mr. DJ.

I was staring at this guy who just saw me wiggle my butt and the music around us sounded like we were living in a movie trailer and I really had to say something soon or there was no saving myself.

That's when he raised his hand and pointed at the ceiling. "Good song," he said.

"Very good song," I agreed. I took the moment to turn around and make somewhat of a graceful exit.

I was almost at my car when I heard from behind me, "Hey."

I turned to see hipster boy. He was still holding his basket of groceries. I pointed at them. "You're stealing," I said.

He looked down and laughed. "I guess so."

We stared at each other for a second. He's cute. I noticed tattoos peeking underneath the sleeves of his T-shirt.

So, here's where I knew I had a choice. I could ask him his name, give him mine, and we could start the song and dance that would inevitably end—most likely, badly. He was cute enough that it would probably screw up my heart for a couple of days. Ultimately, it wouldn't be worth it. I'd be better off heading home, cooking myself a bowl of pasta, and popping in that DVD.

So I said, "Bye."

He nodded, turned, and headed back into the store.

I got into the car and turned the key. The radio blasted Billy Ocean's "Get Outta My Dreams, Get Into My Car."

See, the DJ always gets the last laugh.

Exhibit B. My Voice Mail.

MESSAGE ONE.

"Hello, honey. It's just your mom. I went to the doctor, like you said. Mmffawma. Poison oak. Can you believe that? Of all things. I guess I got it when I was cleaning out those branches in the backyard because your sister wasn't going to help me. What? No, I'm on the phone. Honey, I'm on the phone. Mmmfwma. Yes, with your sister. Jami says hi, Boobs. Get off the counter. I just washed that. I don't care *how* clean your butt is. I don't know. What? Mmffwama. Make it yourself. The dog wants out. The dog wants out. The dog. The *dog*. The—why is there a knife in my china cabinet? Why would you put a steak knife in my china cabinet, Jami? No, that is not funny. Do you hear something ringing? Is that my cell phone? I can't remember where I put . . . Jami! Can you hear where my cell phone is ringing! Jami! OH, JESUS! Ow. I dropped the knife. Ow. Dammit. Dammit. Well, I guess I cut myself. I'll call you back, honey."

MESSAGE TWO.

"MMMFFEwwwwwwwmmmmmmahhhhhhh. Hmmmmm. Dr. Marcus said go to room three. Please walk down the

FFFWmmmmm. Sssscrrruuuuum. Mmmmmm. Schicki—
Oh, my phone's on."

Message Three.
"Hi, honey. It's just your mom. Bit of a crazy day. Got some
stitches, but I'm all right. Did I tell you I have poison oak? The
doctor gave me some cream. So you were right, I didn't have
chlamydia. I knew I could have just called you. Fifty dollars to
have a doctor tell me to buy some calamine lotion. And your
sister put a knife in my china cabinet because she thought that
would be funny for some reason, and I dropped it and it fell on
my toe. I'm okay, but my toe has some stitches. I miss you,
honey. I wish you could come visit. Hope you're doing well and
not working too hard. I love you. Okay, I'm going to hang up
now. I love you. Miss you. I love you. Bye, honey."

You're beginning to understand why I live three thousand
miles away from my mother, aren't you?

I haven't seen Mom or Jami in almost a year. I visit them
on holidays, and that's about it. They don't come out here, either. They think of Los Angeles as Earthquake City, and are
positive the day they move a single limb into this town the
whole place will fall into rubble.

I used to go home often. I would drive up from North Carolina for the weekend because Dad had invited me. He'd find
concerts or festivals, events he'd clip and mail to me from one
of his weird hobby magazines or the newspaper. The clippings
would be circled in green marker, as if there was any way I'd
think he meant for me to read the other side, the half a coupon
and sales ad for Macy's. We called our weekends together
"Faughters Days," because while they were father/daughter
events, we'd also end up getting into a fight at some point during the weekend. It'd be over things we needed to vent about in

person, like my finances, or childhood stuff that I was finally old enough to bring up with some kind of bravery. It remains the healthiest relationship I've had with a man, and I really miss that. I always knew where I stood with Dad, even when he was mad at me. No matter what, he was always proud of me.

Except. And there's always an *except,* isn't there? With a girl like me, there's inevitably the time you find out what goes in the blank after the words *Father Issues.* So here's mine:

The only thing Dad never said in all the time I had with him before he was gone was that I was beautiful.

And the bitch of it is, he was right.

Quick Confession.

Over the past year I have lost over fifty pounds. This isn't something I'm proud of. While I'm really happy that I learned about portion control and conditioned my body to where I can run five miles and not puke, I don't like telling people the number of pounds I've lost. It makes people do two things.

First they look me over, head to toe, and say, "Really?" It's a tone that implies, "And you decided to stop losing weight right there?"

For the record, I haven't decided to stop, but I can't very well say to everyone I meet, "I'm a work in progress!"

Then the person will squint, trying to picture me before, trying to imagine my short body with many more pounds attached to it. I'm sure they place the weight around my gut, all over my cheeks, splashing me in fat. It was really more of an everywhere fat, and that is disappointing to people. Seeing as how most people didn't even notice that I'd lost weight until I'd lost thirty pounds, I know I carry my weight in every part of my body.

"Hey, Benny. Did you lose weight? Your elbows look so much slimmer. And the backs of your hands! Super skinny."

My weight loss disappoints everyone who asks. They're not disappointed in *me,* they're disappointed I don't have a secret to share. When they ask how I did it, I tell them "math." I counted the calories I ate versus the calories I burned and I kept a dorky notebook about it.

When I tell them about my food journal, their faces fall. "Oh, I was hoping I could buy a book about it or something." I could write a book, I suppose, but it would just have one page and it would say, "Put down the cake and go outside."

So, I've lost weight, and it happened in a nonspectacular way, and I don't like talking about it because I hate admitting that I weighed that much more than I do now, when I'm far from perfect now. I don't want people to imagine me before, or wonder how much more I should lose or anything like that. In fact, I'd rather people weren't thinking about my body in its various forms.

I haven't told my mother I've lost this weight. She saw me last ten months ago, when I'd only lost about twenty pounds. If she noticed it then, she didn't say anything. I still don't want to tell her because there's a very real chance that fifty pounds won't be good enough.

This is a great time to slide in the fact that Jami is my mother's favorite. I'm not looking for sympathy here, and I'm not going to delude myself into thinking Jami isn't my mother's favorite kid. It's human nature to pick favorites. There's no way Mom would put up with Jami's crap, including letting her live in her home, if she didn't favor my younger sister.

I've spent my life being careful, doing the right thing, being responsible and good and all that stuff we grow up being told to do. I've never broken a bone, gotten fired, totaled my car, maxed out a credit card, or hit someone in the face. I'm too worried about the ramifications of my actions. But my sister? She's dealt with all of that and worse. No matter what, she walks away unscathed. I don't know how she does it.

Am I jealous? You bet. Who wouldn't want to live that life, just for a little while, where everything is a blur of escaping danger, running from something? I imagine it makes you feel a heady combination of brilliant and alive. While I'm jealous of what Jami's experienced, I'm not envious enough to go break into someone's house or anything.

Jami's done that, broken into someone's house. Someone she *knew.* Back when she was in high school. She took a Nintendo and some jewelry. And then she got caught. But the charges were dropped and Jami was back at school on Monday like she spent that past Friday night at the movies instead of a holding cell. Is it that easy to be bad? And if so, why didn't they teach us any of that in school?

I'm jealous of my sister's criminal record. This is not a good sign.

Back to My Fantastic Life.

I've recently convinced myself it's healthy for me to celebrate my new ass by covering it in something a little fancier than what I usually wear.

Besides, I'm tired of coveting other women's two-hundred-dollar jeans.

I have never spent that kind of money on denim. There's only one item in my closet that cost two hundred dollars and it's the dress I bought for the three weddings I've been to in the past four months. I should probably wear it more often, like to work, and maybe the gym. I won't be happy until I've worn it two hundred times.

Maybe two-hundred-dollar jeans would last longer, fit better, and not get all baggy after the second wearing. Maybe two-hundred-dollar jeans wouldn't have that damn fading under the ass cheeks that every single pair of jeans I've ever owned get. Maybe they wouldn't look slightly acid washed.

This is what has brought me to a store in Beverly Hills. Displayed on the table in front of me are about thirty pairs of jeans. Each one boasts a sticker price of at least $175. Here are the sizes: 25. 26. 27. And 28.

At first I think, Okay. My waist is that small. No problem. Then I pick up the two-hundred-dollar jeans and see that they are so low-rise they're just about going to clear the pubes. This means that the number now doesn't refer to my waist, but my hips.

MY HIPS.

"Ugh," says Super Skinny Salesgirl as she watches me paw through every single pair of jeans. "You know who's a twenty-four? Nicole Richie."

Twenty-four? A 24-inch hip? How small are her bones? Who's smaller than that? *Nobody.* Starving people. Children. Saplings. A 24-inch hip? What does that make her waist? What does that make her? What *is* she?

The salesladies are convinced that I'm going to pull off a 30 in a hot way. They put me back there with a 30 and a 31.

Okay. Two-hundred-dollar jeans, for all they cost, are seriously lacking in fabric. They only came halfway up my ass, just clearing the crack, creating what can only be described as a "roll" above the waistband. Hipband. Whatever.

"Oh, my God!" I shout from inside the dressing room. I stare at my muffin-top in horror.

You know what a muffin-top is, right? When all of your flesh is hanging over the top of the ultra-restrictive jeans, creating an effect on your torso that resembles the top of a blueberry-filled baked good. A muffin-top.

Somebody kill me.

"Come out! Come on out! Let us see!"

I hate swarming salesladies. Somehow I now have two.

"They look soooooo good on you," one says to me.

"You're a liar," I retort.

"When I first got low-rise jeans? I thought I looked terrible in them, too."

"You can see my ass crack."

"Yeah, but you totally get used to it. Those are super cute on you." Her voice is high-pitched and chirpy, like how I imagine ferrets sound when they chat with each other.

I weakly point to this new square shape my hips have taken in order to find a place to hang over the 30-inch restriction I put on my pelvis. "This is not super cute," I say, trying to hide the new, pudgy part of me with the edge of my shirt.

"Aw, they really do look good on you," one of the skinnies says to me.

The other points at everything from the top of the jeans down. "This all looks really good on you."

Crackheads. My ass is stuffed into a flat surface. And my ass? It likes to be free.

"I'm taking these off," I say. I try to sound normal, but the truth is I feel humiliated. Everything I've done to make myself feel like a healthier, happier person has just gone down the damn drain. I didn't have to try and be another L.A. woman. I'm such a poseur. This city is shouting at me: "You are normal. Go back to the Gap, honey."

The skinny with too much pink lipstick puts a heavy hand on my shoulder. "No, wait," she squeals. "Come look in the big mirror! You have to see how good you look."

I'm now in a full sweat, mortified, and seeing red. Other customers can see me in these jeans, these too-small jeans that would fall to the ankles of Nicole Richie. I look like every Fashion Don't there is, and all I can think is, "I can't believe I ever thought I was hot."

"I look ridiculous."

"No, you really just have to get used to them," that stick of a woman insists.

I'm infuriated with these jeans and these salesladies and this notion of what kind of body is supposed to wear these jeans. I'm mad at myself for being so embarrassed. I'm mad at myself for thinking I'm skinny, when skinny is Nicole Richie, and I am the opposite of Nicole Richie.

I try to remember how good I looked when I wasn't wearing the jeans. I try to remember how I'm wearing clothes in smaller sizes than I wore in high school. I try to remember all of that, but the blood isn't going to my brain because it's all trapped around my ass crack.

"Please let me go change," I ask quietly. I sound like a punished child who feels so much guilt she can't even find her voice anymore.

"Oh," the woman coos, like she's finally getting it. "I know what it is." She puts one hand on her hip and tilts her head to the side. Smirks. "You're not from L.A., are you?" she asks, like she figured out my secret. "Where are you from?"

I'm trying to move my mouth to call her names she'll never forget, but I'm paralyzed with too much emotion. I can feel the fabric of these jeans closing in on me. I worry I'll never be able to peel them off, and the more I struggle, the more they'll become Chinese finger cuffs.

"Where are you from?" the girl asks again, head to the side. "Are you from the Midwest?"

It felt really good to throw the jeans at her as I left the store.

I am not a super-low-rise girl. How wonderful to find out that I don't need to drop hundreds of dollars on jeans. But I have to tell you the best part. The perfect punchline. The name of the store?

Curve.

Personal Calls.

"Hello?"

"Hi, honey. It's just your mom."

"Hi, Ma. What's up?"

"Are you busy?"

I'm working on my paper clip lampshade. It's a beautiful creation I've got going on my desk at work. I took a normal halogen desk lamp and created a lovely twenties-style shade by working all of the paper clips together into a sort of mesh covering. I don't even have to hide it when my boss, Wendy, walks by because she is impressed with "creativity." Wendy likes appliqués and anything made with a glue gun or puffy paint. She wears vests to match her canvas tennis shoes. I don't need to say more than that, do I?

"I'm sort of busy, Ma."

She sighs. "I've got some bad news."

I should have known because Mom called at a normal time. It wasn't six in the morning, or on a Saturday night. She called right when I'd be available, right when she knew she could reach me.

"What's wrong?"

"Your sister and I were in a car accident." She delivers the news like she's disappointed, like she dropped a birthday cake on the floor just before the party was to start.

"What happened? Are you okay?"

"We're okay. We hit our heads, mostly from the side air bag. The car's totaled, though. But we're okay. It was scary. You should have seen it. A huge mess."

"What happened?"

"I swerved to miss something, I think, and then we hit the guardrail. It was dark. We were coming home Friday night from Gregory's house. His daughter made the nicest dinner. Your sister wouldn't eat it, of course, but I thought it was pretty nice, even though it had peas in it."

"Ma."

"What?"

"When did this happen?" I just now realize I'm standing up. Wendy is looking at me, full of concern. She's mouthing something, asking me a question I can't decipher.

"What, honey?" Mom asks.

"The accident. When did it happen?"

"Oh. Last week."

"Last *week*?"

Mom makes this clucking sound. "Well, I didn't want to bother you. I knew you'd be upset."

Of course I'm upset. My mom and sister were in a car accident. I'm supposed to be upset. They're supposed to tell me about it when it happens, preferably before anyone goes to the hospital, and then I can be upset. And I'm supposed to go through this with them because I'm a part of their family, right?

Right?

"But you're both okay?"

"The car is totaled. I don't know how we're going to be able to afford another, what with the fact that I lost my job."

"You lost your job? When?"

"And I *mffrrwawahed.*"

"You *what*? Ma, put your mouth next to the phone."

"I BROKE MY LEG."

I don't know what you're imagining right now, because you've never seen my mother, but all I can picture is my tiny mom in a wheelchair, white plaster cast all the way up to her poison oak bumps. I even picture one of those old-fashioned arm casts that prop on the hip, for good measure. She's talking to me through a little hole in her body cast, the one made specifically for her to give me a guilt trip.

"In the accident?"

"Of course, honey, in the accident. How else would I have broken my leg?"

"Ma, are you okay?"

"Oh, I guess I'm fine. No job. No car. Left leg in a cast. Gregory keeps coming over, but I know he has to work. Your sister's got some new boyfriend, so she's never home."

When Jami gets a boyfriend, she disappears. There is proof she exists in the things she leaves scattered around the house like artifacts, but you rarely see her face, except if she needs something. It's fine for her to pull this when Mom's got two legs, four wheels, and a job, but right now I can't believe Jami's traipsing off with a boy while Mom's in a wheelchair.

Did I just say "traipsing off with a boy"?

"Are you okay, Ma?"

"Why do you keep asking me that? No. Is that what you want me to say?" I don't hear this tone in my mother often. Her voice is shaky, and it's deeper than usual.

She's scared.

"I don't understand how you lost your job because of your leg. They can't do that."

"They didn't. I lost the job two weeks ago because they got rid of my position at the office, and then I got into the car accident. You know how great my timing is."

"Oh, Ma."

"I don't have any money, Benny. Without the car, I can't go get another job. And I can't get one with my leg in this cast. They say it'll be at least six weeks before this thing is off. Six weeks! I only have enough savings for just about that. And then what happens? I have to go live with Gregory? No, thank you. I don't want to live with a man again. I like my house, Benny. I don't want to have to sell the house."

"You'd sell the house?"

"Please stop asking me so many questions. I'm going to go lie down. I'm sorry I bothered you."

I want to cry, but I can't with Wendy looking at me. She's going to want to hug me, and I can't hug my boss. I can't be that girl, the one who cries at work. I'm going to handle my shit and be an adult.

"You didn't bother me, Ma."

"Be good."

There's a pang in my stomach when I hang up the phone. It's pulling me out of my desk, out of this city, out of this state. It's telling me what I already know I have to do. I've got to go home and take care of my mother.

I ask Wendy for time off work. I explain my situation as calmly as possible, but soon she's holding me to her chest, her giant wooden beaded necklace pressing into my face.

My sinuses are swelling from her rose perfume as Wendy kisses the top of my head and rocks me back and forth. "You go home and be a good daughter," she says to me. "You go be a good daughter, understand?"

"Yes. Thank you."

She pulls back and pats my forearms. "But I'm still going to need one week," she says. "To find your replacement."

"You mean like a temp?"

Wendy's got a look in her eyes I really don't like as she says, "If that's what you want to call her, then yes. A temp."

I hate when I can hear the quotation marks in someone's speech. Right now I don't need Wendy's audible punctuation.

Found in the Supermarket.

After work, I head to the grocery store to pick up enough items to survive my last week in town. I enter the store to hear the loudspeaker playing Sheryl Crow's "Leaving Las Vegas." Close enough.

If music controlled my life, the way I like to pretend it does, the perfect song would start right now as I hit aisle three, where they keep the magazines, and I'd see that cute hipster boy standing there waiting for me.

The song changes. It's "Lost in the Supermarket." Well, that's certainly a sign, isn't it? Now I'm really wishing for the hipster boy, not because I want to see him, but because this is such a funny moment. I conjured it somehow, created a reality based on my perception of what should happen. I wish he were here. We wouldn't even have to say anything. We could just lock eyes, lift an eyebrow or two, and go back to our lives. When this rare alignment of coincidence and comedy occurs, it really should happen with that other person. It's too great to waste on just me.

I round the corner and freeze.

Hipster boy in aisle three.

This is crazy, I know. And this is pure coincidence and not fate, because come on. This boy hasn't been hanging out in the magazines, hoping I'd show up again. That would make him a stalker. Maybe I created this moment because I wanted it badly enough. Five minutes ago hipster boy probably wasn't here; he was in his apartment or something. But since I wanted this to happen so badly, maybe he was transported through space and time to the magazine section, right when The Clash started up and—

He looks up, raises one eyebrow, and points at the ceiling. "They're playing our song," he says. He has a nice smile.

"You don't look surprised to see me," I say.

"I was going to say the same thing."

We're standing there, cart to basket, sizing each other up, each one probably wondering if the other is a psycho stalker who fabricated this coincidence, or if this is the moment when we're supposed to become incredibly important to each other. Is this the story we'll tell everyone?

Look, you're the one reading a book about a girl confessing she might one day kill her mother, so you formed your opinion on my stability and mental health long ago. I know I'm not helping it any, thinking the music at Albertsons creates my future like an audible horoscope, but you have to admit this is kind of freaky. I thought about him and now he's here and he's looking at me like he just did the same thing.

He has a small tattoo on the back of his left hand, where the thumb meets his forefinger. I can't tell what it is.

He eases back against the rack, tucking his hands into his front pockets. He asks, "Does this happen to you often? Walking around with your own soundtrack? Bumping into the same people?"

"No. Why?"

"You're acting like it's old hat."

I like a boy who uses the phrase "old hat."

"I kind of thought I'd run into you," I say. "Does that sound weird?"

"The magic of Hollywood," he says. Then he puts out his hand. "It's nice to meet you. What's your name?"

I hesitate, as I always do before I tell someone my name for the first time. "I'm going to tell you," I say, "but then you'll want to break out in song."

Another eyebrow raise. "I can't wait."

"Benny."

He leans his head back and wails. *"Benny! Benny! Ba-ba-ba Benny and the—"*

I interrupt him. "Yep, that's the song."

"I've never met a girl named Benny before."

"Why would you?"

A curvy, too-blond shopper is watching us from further down the aisle, her candle-browsing interrupted. Her eyes are narrowed to slits. She's studying us, but I don't know why. Maybe she's jealous.

"Here's how you're going to feel better," he says. And this near stranger standing next to me touches my wrist with his hand as if he's done it a million times before. There's a spark of something shooting up and down my leg, like he just plugged me into a socket. He says, "I'm going to tell you *my* name, and *you* will break into song."

"I really hope your name is Benny."

"Better." He closes his eyes in preparation. "Mickey."

And I'm singing: *"Oh, Mickey, what a pity, you don't understand!"*

His eyes are still closed. "That's the song."

I'm not done. *"You take me by the heart, when you take me by the hand."*

Mickey does a little choreography with his arms. "Familiar with it," he says.

Every time I look at him I see something new. This time I notice a small scar on his cheek, near his ear. His eyebrows are thick and give him a look of concern even when he's smiling, as he's doing right now. The corners of his mouth turn down when he's grinning, making his cheeks have creases like the way we draw a grin—tiny parentheses on either side of his lips. He appears stuck in a perpetual cheeky smirk.

"Is that a family name, Mickey? Is it short for something?"

"I wish. I'm sort of named after the head mouse."

I take his hand and squeeze. "I'm here for you."

The tattoo by his thumb is of a small star.

"Are you hungry?" he asks, looking like the concept of food just occurred to him.

"Famished," I respond, even though I think it's the first time in my life I've ever said that word.

We leave the store without our groceries.

"Your car or mine?" he asks, wobbling his head, impersonating an old movie star.

"Both," I say. "Let's meet at Birds."

He seems disappointed to leave my side for even the ten minutes it'll take to make it to the restaurant. But he doesn't know why I need to drive to Birds on my own. I can't get into a car with him. Not yet. It's way too soon for me.

The Delicate Art of Vehicular Romance.

All of my most meaningful romantic moments have happened in parking lots.

If I like a boy, and he likes me, he's going to follow me to my car. That's a given. Luckily it's considered gentlemanly, so he's got a good excuse to steal me away for a private moment before we say good night and part, for who knows how long afterward.

If he's following me to the car but I know nothing's going to happen, there will be a decent distance between the two of us. My arms might be crossed. If he's still sussing me out, he'll probably be casual, chatting about everything other than what's not being said: that this is the last time we'll have a private moment. This is the end.

If the connection is good and we both want something to happen, but it can't because he's already got somebody, or I'm not ready for this kind of intensity, or I want to wait until we've known each other longer, then I'll already have my keys in my hand, aimed at the lock, reminding myself to get the fuck out of there before something happens that can't be taken back. He'll stand ten feet away, almost having to shout his final words before I speed away, breathless, narrowly missing certain catastrophe.

Sometimes I'll open the door and prop myself inside. Keep a big, metal object between the two of us. We'll talk to each other as if there isn't a vehicle blocking our bodies from touching, keeping two bodies at rest from going into motion.

This is why we do this in the parking lot; I need the car. I need other bodies randomly entering our space to get into their own cars, halting the conversation before we cannot retrace our steps.

But if everything is right, if that boy and this girl want to spend more time together, he'll sit in the passenger seat. I won't even have to ask. Sure, I'll make an excuse—there's a song I want him to hear, or it's getting cold outside, or there's someone staring at us (the bouncer, another couple lingering by a different car—it doesn't matter; it's just an excuse). We'll close the doors and lock ourselves into the tiniest world. Only the two of us matter now. Everything else doesn't exist. We've created our own universe.

This is when love happens.

We're sitting closer than we could at a restaurant. It's much quieter than in a bar. The slightest shift of movement is picked up, translated, understood. He can touch my hand and it's no longer casual.

Fuck seat belts.

We turn to face each other, letting the windows fog around us, and really talk. For the first time, it seems, we can truly hear each other. Because there are no distractions. When he tells me I'm beautiful, it's as if nobody has ever said those words to me before. Not like *that*. He's looking at me and talking to me and I can hear his breath and see his foot wiggling from fright and I am everything in that moment.

This is when we make our confessions. This is when we both stop playing games. It's serious now. We're in the car, in a quickly emptying parking lot. We should be home by now, but we aren't going anywhere. We stifle every yawn. We fight every impulse to go home because this moment, however fleeting, feels tangible and malleable. This is when my heart can fall hopelessly, seemingly effortlessly, in love. It is because of those moments of weakness when my heart has been on display that I have learned to be wary of love, to understand that just because I can give myself over to someone doesn't mean a happy ending is to follow.

I started learning these lessons my junior year of high school, which was the first time I invited a boy to move to the backseat of my car. That's where I told Troy Matthews (sixteen and trembling like I was about to light him on fire) that I'd never found a love as pure as the one I felt for him. I told him I would die for him. At the time I felt I'd invented the very concept. I wanted to throw myself in front of an oncoming train if it meant he'd never live a day of his life unhappy. I needed him to know that. Troy reciprocated the sentiment in the only way he knew how at that age—by sucking an enormous hickey on my neck that made me look like I'd been mauled by a cougar. We had one hot, sticky, spit-drenched evening of wrestling each other in the back of my car, and the next week he was gone. I'd scared him off with my intensity, my vehicular aggression. I learned a good lesson through Troy: there is nothing more terrifying to a boy under the age of twenty than a woman who knows exactly what she wants.

It wasn't until my senior year of high school that I learned how heartbreaking a backseat conversation could be when I said good-bye to the next love of my life, Tom Castle, who was getting shipped all the way to Oregon to live with his dad. A bomb had gone off in my heart, and I needed Tom to know that I was never going to fall in love again. We'd been dating for six months, and I let him take my virginity under the biggest moon I've ever seen, listening to our song—The Doors' "The Crystal Ship"—on repeat. It was only much later when I looked up the lyrics that I learned the song was about a heroin addiction. I suppose Tom was like heroin for me.

In college I upgraded my car to a newer Honda, but I downgraded the boy to a stoner named Guy. He enjoyed making pipes out of clay, working for a pizza joint, and—as I was able to deduce after just one night in the front seat of my car—boys. Guy would never kiss below my neck. One night I purposefully drove him to a parking lot, one that was almost deserted, just to work a little Honda magic on him, to get him to at least take off my shirt. When he didn't respond to any of my approaches, I asked him if he loved me. Guy said that he did, but that it was all "too heavy" for him. I pressed him, assuming he was being shy. Guy broke into tears and told me he was only dating me to make his parents happy, because he was in love with a boy from his dorm. I had rivers of tears rushing down my face as I pathetically asked, "Does this mean you want to break up?"

The boys have become somewhat smarter as I've grown older. Now they know how to work their way into the car, and have little games designed as excuses to linger. Some guys go right for the glove compartment, taking out each object like they're clues to solving the mystery of me. Others pretend to be fascinated with my iPod, the water bottles that clutter the backseat, or find a way to tell me the longest stories they know.

We take our time, in the dark, in the car, testing each other, looking deep into each other's eyes, wondering what the other one has in store. I've been romanced, dumped, caressed, fondled, and destroyed in the confines of my car. It's the shell that protects me when the rest of the world can seem so infinite. When everything in love becomes too chaotic, I can take a man to the smallest place that can contain us, force him to look at me and tell me the truth.

Chicken?

Birds is a small, dark, mostly red restaurant that serves up rotisserie chicken in about thirteen different ways. It has an Alfred Hitchcock theme (thus the *Birds*), and is located directly across from the Scientology Celebrity Centre, a mansion that I like to think at any moment holds both Tom Cruise and John Travolta as they keep their eyes on me, waiting for the moment they want to flank me and carry me away with them. What's worrisome is that I'm pretty sure I wouldn't put up much of a struggle.

Mickey sits across from me sipping his black and tan. A little foam sticks to his upper lip and I watch his tongue dart out to catch it before he chases it with a wipe of his sleeve. "This is where we do the song and dance," he says.

"The First Date Shuffle," I reply, nodding. "I kind of hate it."

"I don't," he says. "I love the first few days."

"Really?"

"Well, I love them after this first hour. This first hour sucks. All small talk and basic facts. 'Where are you from? Where do you work?' Not the good stuff. I'd rather know the good stuff."

I feel the same way. I want people to come with portfolios I can read before we meet, so I don't have to ask the boring questions. I've just figured out the secret of online dating.

"I have an idea," I say. "Let's get the dumb stuff taken care of as succinctly as possible."

Mickey grins and tugs at an earlobe, intrigued. "How so?"

"You have to tell me your logline."

He scrunches his nose, exposing his front teeth. "Are you a screenwriter?"

"No, I dated one once, though. Picked up some lingo." I don't tell Mickey that the screenwriter went absolutely crazy and one day I went to his apartment to find him standing in his underwear, holding an electric fan, convinced that he was able to make the blades stop spinning with his mind. I'm not going to tell Mickey this story, even though it's probably exactly the kind of story he's craving, because I worry he'll think I have the potential to date people who get naked with their fans. Because I did.

"Can I use a pen?" he asks. "I want to get it right."

I dig one out of my purse.

Mickey pulls a movie ticket out of his back pocket and holds it up. "I like knowing the last time I wore these jeans by the movie I saw." After a second he adds, "I know that means I haven't washed them since."

"That's okay," I say, rooting through my bag. "You don't want to know the last time I washed this bra."

I can't believe I just said that. I'm relieved to see Mickey is laughing. His head is down in thought as he taps his pen against the dark wood of the table. The swirls of his close-cropped hair are endearing.

I know that's the first sign of trouble, if I'm finding sweetness in someone's scalp. I force my focus onto my own logline.

Mickey's ready first, but he waits for me. "I'm too nervous," he admits.

I read my writing, leaning close to the candlelight to see better. "Single girl who hates her job at a travel agency must fly to the other side of the country to take care of her unemployed mother and sometimes outlaw sister. Hilarity ensues. Your turn."

Mickey tilts his head. "But I have so many questions."

"Read yours first. Then we can ask questions."

Mickey lifts his movie ticket. "Music store employee who lives alone in Hollywood and is tired of finding everyone around him to be an idiot is shocked to find an actual interesting female in the sea of plastic he surfs daily to avoid drowning in his own paranoid delusions." He drops the ticket to the table and adds, "Or something like that."

I can feel my face flush as I stammer, "You're better at this than I am." I add, "Your handwritting must be tiny."

"You're leaving," he says.

"Yes. Soon. I'm sorry." I tell him about my mother and why I have to go, how I know it's what my father would have wanted. Then I find myself telling him about Dad, and how he worked for a mortgage company for years, but I never really found out what he did there. I know he had something to do with helping people get loans.

Mickey nods. "My dad worked for a law firm, but I never knew what he did when he went into the office. It's weird, because I knew everything about my mom's day, but Dad would just go somewhere else, and nobody thought to ask him what he was doing all that time."

"The mysterious fathers," I say.

"I guess."

"Your father. He's past tense, then."

Mickey grabs his fork and plays with it. "What?"

"You used past tense when you were talking about him just now."

He keeps his gaze on his fork as he says, "Yeah, he's past tense."

The food arrives and we lean back to allow the waiter

between us. It's quiet as we take little stabs at the vegetables. Mickey looks up about a minute later. "You pay attention," he says. "I didn't even notice I used past tense."

"I find you interesting," I confess.

"See? The early parts of the date. They don't have to be horrible. Right now you and I are nothing but possibilities."

"I never thought of it that way."

He waits until I've put a forkful of chicken into my mouth and then he says, "You're very pretty."

As I'm blushing around my mouthful, waiting to be able to thank him, I realize this is the first time I've had a man tell me I'm pretty without having the impulse to correct him.

Hey, Mickey!

We're making out in Mickey's bed. His hand slides down my side.

"Why do you do that?" he asks, pulling away from my face for the first time in half an hour.

"Do what?"

"Suck in your stomach like that. Like it's trying to escape."

"I didn't realize." I don't know how to tell him it's an involuntary reflex whenever someone goes near my stomach; I want to make it as skinny as possible.

Mickey laughs as he goes back to kissing me.

"What?" I ask.

"Nothing. I just thought of a terrible joke. I'm not telling you."

"Tell me."

"No, it's mean."

"Tell me."

"It's really mean, Benny. I'll tell you, but you have to know I'm completely kidding and I don't mean anything cruel by it."

"What?"

"You make out like a fat chick."

I push myself out from under Mickey and let my feet find the floor.

"You promised," he says.

"I didn't," I say.

"Oh, God." Mickey rolls onto his back. "Tell me you're not one of those skinny girls who always thinks she's fat."

"I'm not."

"And no matter where we go or what day it is you need me to remind you how thin and beautiful you are."

"I don't!"

"Because you really don't seem like that kind of girl, Benny, which is why I thought I could crack that joke. I love women, all kinds of women. Even fat women."

I don't say anything.

"It's a joke!" He's on his back, hands in the air, eyes open wide. "I thought you'd find it funny. You're pulling in your stomach when I go to touch you. You put the covers over your hips like you're hiding something. I even saw you curve your back to make your torso look longer."

I'm caught. "How did you know I was doing that?"

"I've dated other women. *Cosmo.* I pick up a few things. And while I've certainly been with a few women who benefited from those tricks and contortions, you don't need to hide yourself." He reaches out and slides his knuckles down my forearm. "You are absolutely beautiful. Stunning. Perfect."

"What if I weren't?"

"I don't understand the question. What issue of *Cosmo* is that one from?"

I don't want to ask the real question, which is, *"What if you met me a year ago?"*

Mickey rolls off the bed and crawls in front of me, naked, on all fours. He rests his head on my thighs. I place my palm over the tattoo on his shoulder, a symbol that sort of resembles the Partridge Family emblem.

"I am very sorry," he says.

I pet his head, sliding my fingers through his short, soft hair. "I know. I'm not mad."

"I told you it was a terrible joke."

"It was."

"I really wish you weren't leaving on Monday."

"Me either."

He rests his cheek on my knee. Looking up at my naked body, he says, "This is a nice view."

We spend the entire next day in bed. When I leave his apartment, it is only because I absolutely have to. There's a stranger coming over to get a copy of my keys.

I can't believe I'm going to have a stranger living in my apartment, even though I'm sure the subletter is a very nice girl. She is a friend of Wendy's daughter. She just moved to Los Angeles right out of college and needs a place to stay for a little while as she figures out where she's going to live and how she's going to make a living. I figured it'd be good Karma for me. She has the very pretty name of Grace. It's a name that doesn't describe me at all. I'm never full of grace. I'm Benny, full of klutz.

Standing in the doorway of his apartment, Mickey kisses me good-bye for so long it feels like he's pressed the reset button on my life.

Suitcase, Full of Grace.

Grace is tall. She's about a foot taller than I am, and it makes me feel like a child to stand next to her. As I give her the nanosecond-long tour of my apartment, I come up to just above her elbows. When she pulls back the shower curtain, I almost take a joint to the eye.

"This place is nice," she says.

I instantly hate my apartment. I'm seeing it through Grace's eyes. There's mildew on the edges of the tub. There's a weird brown spot on the living room ceiling from a leak in the upstairs apartment. The faucet in the kitchen drips. My bedroom looks like a place I never visit—just a mattress on the floor, a few sheets, and a side table. After moving out of Brian's place, I never got around to making my bedroom into anything other than a sleep receptacle. What does it mean to Grace that I don't have cable? Or that my kitchen appliances amount to a microwave, a coffee maker, and a blackened, crumb-filled toaster oven? Does she think it's weird that I don't have any vases or prints on the wall like real girls are supposed to have? Maybe Grace can sense I've hidden my vibrator in a shoe box wrapped in a blanket stuffed in a pillowcase in the top corner of my bedroom closet. And if so, I hope she never tells me what happens after she finds it.

"So, here are the keys," I say as Grace stretches her French-manicured fingers my way to take the jumble of metal. "The round one is for the top lock. The square one's for the bottom. Little key's for the mail."

"Got it." She's still looking around, mentally giving my place the *Queer Eye*. She's got deep-set brown eyes with a hint of dark circles underneath them. Long lashes curl up to kiss her carefully plucked eyebrows. Her dark hair is in a hasty ponytail; the strands that have freed themselves look so effortlessly cool that I'm jealous. When I wear my hair like she's got hers, I look homeless.

"You'll be okay here?" I ask.

"Oh, yeah. Thanks again so much for this," she says. "You're saving my ass."

She has just one suitcase. It is at least four feet tall, and stuffed with her belongings. It took the two of us to lug it from her car into the apartment. I imagine all kinds of things in there. Pillows. Bookshelves. Grandfather clocks. What else does one girl fresh out of college need in a fully furnished apartment? It can't be a suitcase full of ramen, can it? Maybe a girl that tall needs an enormous suitcase to hold all her big clothes, long coats, and huge shoes.

"You leave soon," she notes. Everyone keeps reminding me I'm on my way out of here.

"Yep."

"Are you excited?"

I tell her the truth. "Not exactly."

Mickey Has a Plan.

"Here's the plan," Mickey says as we walk to his apartment sipping Jamba Juices. "We'll keep seeing each other."

I wait for him to continue, but that appears to be all he has to say. "That's the plan?"

"It's simple. But it just might work."

"I've known you for less than a week, and now we're making promises to each other?"

Mickey stops walking suddenly. I have to go back for him.

"I'm sorry," I say.

He shrugs his shoulders. "I didn't mean to be such a woman."

"You're not a woman."

"I am. I just got my period."

"I'm sorry. If I explain my mother to you, do you think you'd understand why I have to leave?"

"Is this going to be one of those stories where when it's over I can't quite look at you without wanting to break into tears?"

"Now that you're such a woman, I suppose so."

We go back to his apartment and I tell him more about my mom and sister, how Jami moved back in not too long ago, but it somehow seems like they've always lived together. He asks if we're close.

"We all love each other," I say.

"Well, that's not the same thing, is it?"

"They're close. And they care about me. I see them when I can, but they seem to keep a distance from me."

"Do they?" he asks. "Or are you the one keeping the distance?"

I admit I'm not sure.

Mickey grabs my foot by the ankle and pulls it into his lap. His thumb traces circles on my skin as he stares at my leg. "I've got a brother," he says.

"Older or younger?"

"Older by three years. He used to pretend he was a dog. He'd sometimes stop talking and start barking. He'd jump to the floor and crawl around. It was great when I was little, because I always had this big pet dog and he'd let me ride on his back. But as we got older, it got weirder. Once he was thirteen, it was getting embarrassing."

"What did your parents do?" I ask.

"They bought him a dog and he stopped pretending to be one."

"Smart parents."

He plays with the cuff of my jeans as he nods. "Smarter brother. Jesse's a genius. He really is. Test scores off the charts. He became a doctor. Everybody thought he was going to cure cancer. But then something snapped. I don't know what did it. Nobody does, actually. He was around for Christmas and then he wasn't, and then a few weeks later we got this call that Jesse had locked himself in one of the trauma rooms at the hospital and wouldn't stop barking."

I take Mickey's hand.

"He lives in a facility now, which is weird. And my mom calls all the time because she thinks she failed at being a mother. I sell CDs and my brother thinks he's a Doberman. She can't even show her face at church, you know? She's always reminding me that it's not too late to go back to med school. But it is." Mickey leans his head back against the couch and closes his eyes. "I don't ever want to bark," he says.

"I'm sorry," I say.

"Yeah, well, there's no such thing as a happy family, right?"

"Maybe not."

Mickey leans over and kisses me, pulling my bottom lip into his mouth for just a second. It tastes like oranges from his Jamba Juice. "So you'll be changing the subject . . . now."

I try. "How come your brother didn't get named after a Disney character?"

"He wasn't conceived in the happiest place on earth. But you think it's bad having everyone sing Elton John to you? Jesse's had girls break up with him because they couldn't stand getting Rick Springfield lyrics shouted at them wherever they went."

"Yikes."

"Yeah. Change the subject better."

"We could get naked."

"Miss Bernstein, I do believe I'm falling in love with you."

I'd be nervous if I thought he wasn't kidding. But he's grinning and yanking at my jeans and I'm too busy thinking about his body on top of mine to bother wondering what's going on past this second.

She Takes a Swing, but She Can't Hit.

I see Jane about once a month, but when I do, we climb right into each other's lives like we were never absent. We buy two bottles of wine and sit out on her small porch, staring at the lights of Mid-Wilshire, and pretend we have a home high in the Hollywood Hills, the kind that's so difficult to find up the windy roads that people would rather just leave us alone.

Her hair is longer than I've ever seen it before, hanging in thick tangles down to the middle of her back. A thin, metal barrette holds her bangs back at a hasty angle, like Jane can't be bothered with how beautiful her hair is. I watch her open the bottle of wine, her slender fingers turning white as they grip the bottle against her small frame. Her entire face goes into yanking the cork. When it's finally out, she relaxes and shoots me a huge smile. "Yes," she says. "I already feel better."

Jane's a social worker. Her hours are long and her patients are more than distraught. She often jokes that she gets the people Hollywood chews up. While she's not allowed to tell me the details of her work, I am always proud of her for being able to be beside someone at a moment of absolute crisis.

After Jane tells me about the renovations she's doing to her kitchen, she grabs my arm. "I said that as quickly as I could," she says, "so you can tell me all about going to Virginia. Start talking, and don't stop until I'm done with this glass of wine."

Instead of telling her about my mother and sister, I find myself talking about Mickey, and how I'm frustrated to have met someone interesting right when I'm out the door.

"It doesn't have to be over," she says. "You're not going for forever."

"But I don't know how long I'll be gone, and it's not fair to ask him to wait on me. We just met."

She touches her thumb to her fingers, one by one. "Cell phones. Computers. Mail."

"What are you doing?"

"Just thinking of all the ways we communicate with someone we can't see every day. When's the last time you saw me?"

"Almost six weeks ago."

"Do you love me less?" She drops her head to my shoulder.

"No."

"See?"

I'm shaking my head. "This is different."

Jane sits up and claps her hands, bouncing in her seat. "Let's make a list!"

"No, Jane. We aren't making a list."

She pouts. "Lists are important. We'll find out if you love him."

I refill my glass. "First of all, I'm not in love with him. We don't need a list for that. And second, lists are too girly. I don't need to make a list."

"I just want some of his pros and cons. List them off, and then I'll tell you what you want to know."

"What do I want to know?"

Jane sighs. "You want to know if he's worth it. That's what you always say when you meet a guy." She frowns and lowers her voice. " 'He's not worth it.' "

She just did a pretty accurate impression of me, but I don't want to give her the compliment.

"I'm not making a list with you," I repeat.

Jane shakes her head, beautiful brown hair falling all over her shoulders, her arms. I wish I could look like that, gorgeous when I have no awareness that anyone is even noticing. "I want flaws," she says. "I need to hear some of Mickey's flaws or I will go find him and date him while you're gone."

"You could," I say. "He's not mine."

Jane nudges me, so I start thinking. I try to decide what's keeping Mickey single. He said he hasn't had a steady girlfriend in almost a year. It could be that he makes fat jokes, or because his bedroom smells faintly of the end of a chewed pen. In his bathroom there's a towel stiff with dirt that I'm pretty sure he uses to wipe his mouth after he brushes his teeth. One of his tattoos is of a girl's name, but he won't tell me what it means.

After hearing all of this, Jane concludes, "You're an idiot. Those aren't flaws. Those are descriptions of men. Tell me the good stuff, then."

"I'm still not making a list."

"Tell me."

"I don't know. Owns a car. Rents an apartment."

Jane makes a buzzing sound. "Try again, Benny."

"The other day Mickey took me on a tour of his Los Angeles, showing me his old apartments, restaurants where he had conversations with celebrities. He brought me to the elevator he was standing in when he learned that Hunter S. Thompson had killed himself. He showed me the parking lot where he slept in his car the first night he moved to Los Angeles from Boston, when he wasn't sure how he was going to break it to his mother that he'd just dropped out of med school and didn't want to be anything like the person he'd been planning on becoming."

Once I start naming things for Jane's dumb list, I can't stop. I tell her how Mickey makes stupid jokes so surprisingly funny they make me snort. He touches the small of my back for emphasis when he's telling me something he likes about me. His left eye squints more than the right when he laughs. He ends stories by hunching his shoulders, turning his palms face up as if to ask, "Can you blame me?"

He lives five blocks from my apartment.

He has abs I could climb like a ladder.

No matter what I do or say, he's still interested. He looks at me unlike anyone else ever has, like he's constantly discovering me. He makes me feel fascinating. I have no idea how to handle that.

Jane laughs. "Yeah. Sounds like you hate him."

"I don't love him."

"How's the sex?"

"Very good. In fact, I'll get to have some when I leave here."

"And then you're going to break up with him?"

"It's because I care, Jane, that I'm going to."

"Wow," Jane says. "You really are an idiot."

Saying Good-bye.

In the time it takes for me to get ready, I talk myself into and out of seeing Mickey seriously no fewer than ten times. This is when I should say good-bye, pull myself away before things get weird. I like him a lot, but it's silly to think we can be any more than this when I'm about to go out of town and he's . . . well, he's got his own life to live.

This night calls for the Fuck Me/Leave Me Alone dress. It's black, clingy, short, and has magical powers. Every time I give the Final Talk to a man while wearing this dress, I know he won't feel bad about it until I'm long out of his sight. This dress keeps a man solely focused on what it'll feel like when he's pulling it off my body. I'm not proud of the power of the FM/LMA dress, but I appreciate the clean getaway it often affords me.

I answer the door to find Mickey wearing the male counterpart of my superdress. When he smiles, all I can do is tuck my tongue into the corner of my mouth to keep the grin from growing too goofy.

"So," he says. "Let's do this thing."

"Yep."

Maybe tonight it'll stay just a dress.

* * *

We're leaning toward each other at a table in the near dark.

"You ever been here before?" he asks.

"No. I'm a fan of candlelight, but I'm a little scared to eat sushi in the dark."

"You'll be safe," he says.

I sip my sake, the tiny cup in my hands making me feel awkwardly monstrous.

"You look amazing," Mickey says.

"Thank you. So do you."

I let him order. This is something I never do, but when Mickey looked over the long, skinny menu, I saw his eyes searching, occasionally widening in surprise. I knew he'd order things I've never tried before. I'm normally the one who decides what I eat and in what order, but this time whatever comes to the table will be something he wants to eat, and something he wants to share with me. I won't have many more moments of this. I will have many more nights of ordering my own sushi. How weird that it matters to me, right now, that I want him to choose our menu. Even weirder that I recognize when I'm a different person around him. He makes me feel like it's okay to try something incredibly risky for me: relinquishing control.

A small plate of food arrives. As I go through the soy sauce, wasabi, and chopsticks ritual, Mickey watches. "You have nice fingers," he says. My instinct is to pull them back immediately, hide them from his view before he sees he's mistaken, but my hands are occupied. I thank him again.

We eat quietly. I concentrate on putting large amounts of fish and rice into my mouth without looking like Cookie Monster on a bender. It's difficult to look sexy while eating hunks of tuna, so I end up holding my hand in front of my mouth like a giggling Japanese schoolgirl as I chew.

"I wanted to take you to dinner because I didn't want you leaving without us having a proper date," Mickey says, sounding like he's been having a conversation in his head for a few minutes that has just now started to become audible.

I nod, sticky rice making my mouth dry.

Mickey gives a quick sigh and rests his hands on the table, arms straight. His mouth is working as he thinks, like he's still chewing on the words he's about to deliver. "I think you're a wonderful woman," he starts. "But . . ."

Oh, my God. He's dumping me.

My chopsticks make a tiny *plink-plink!* as I lower them to my plate.

I say, "Uh-huh."

"But you're about to go out of town, and I just met you, and as much as I like you and this . . . it's probably best if you're not having to worry about me, or think about me while you're taking care of your family. I don't want to be a burden."

He's giving me the "burden" line. I *invented* that line!

"You're not a burden," I say, sounding like the other side of the script. I'm delivering the boy's lines. This is backward.

"I don't mean a burden, I guess," he says. "From thousands of miles away it can look pretty pathetic. So for your own good, and for my own good, I'm cutting you loose. Setting you free like a pretty butterfly."

He's doing exactly what I would have asked of him. It's like I'm writing his words.

"You're looking at me like I'm crazy," he says. "Are you okay?"

"What you just said to me, people don't say that."

He places his hands on his face. "I'm lousy at relationships," he says. "I make girls want to kill me." Then he shrugs, hands facing upward, innocent. "I get wrapped up, but as soon as I have her, I get distracted. I get insanely fo-cused on something that isn't her."

"Why are you telling me all of this?"

"Because I want you to know what you're dealing with. Look, when you get back, if you miss me and I miss you, then we'll just pick up where we left off. But for now there's nothing I can do. Nothing you can do. You've got to go home. And I'm going to lie on my couch a lot and pretend I don't miss you." He spears a piece of salmon sashimi and drops it into his mouth. "For reals," he says around the fish, grinning.

"Don't wait too long," I say. "I'm not worth it."

He nods, and I can barely hear him say, "I'll bet."

"I'm sorry."

"There's another option. I wasn't going to bring it up, be-cause it's something I can do regardless of what you're doing. But I figure you should know."

As I nibble on a piece of ginger, it feels like someone froze my stomach. "What is it?" I ask, helpless.

Mickey says, "I tell you I love you and we deal with it."

"Oh." I try not to close my eyes, to keep my blood circu-lating. I don't want him to see I've been knocked over. This is too soon. I'm not ready for this. This isn't how I want it all to go. I'm getting dumped while he's telling me he's in love with me. I have the entire range of a relationship here, and he's asking me to choose, to handpick, exactly what I want from him.

"You can stick with the first option," I say, hoping he un-derstands both what I'm saying, and why.

Mickey nods. "I thought so," he says.

It's quiet for a little while. We poke at the remaining pieces of fish.

"It's good that you said that, though," he says.

"I'm sorry."

"No, no, it's good. Because if I had said . . . the other thing, then I'd have to prove it. Because it's way too early to say something like that and have you believe me. I'd have to wait for you."

"I don't want you to wait for me."

"Right, I can see that."

"I have a no-waiting policy."

"I think you have a lot of policies."

"I'm sorry."

He looks away, stares at another couple at another table. They are sitting diagonally from each other instead of across, sharing a bowl of some kind of salad. She's leaning into his shoulder as he talks. They look like the same person— skinny, with dark hair slicked and waxed into structured messes.

Mickey finally takes a deep breath, looks at me with his eyebrows raised, and forces a smile. "This isn't what I thought would happen," he says.

"Why? Most girls pick the other thing?"

I see him wince. He wasn't joking with me.

There's no game here anymore. I'm looking at Mickey, and he's changed. The mystery of a man who might be more has faded into the guy who isn't going to be. And suddenly I want to tell him everything that's wrong with me. I feel absolutely compelled to justify his decision to drop me here, and my decision to let him.

"I'm not worth it," I repeat. "I suck at dating. I don't want anyone around for very long."

"Well, I'm not very good at having someone need me," he says. "Always makes me feel like there's something wrong with her. If she thinks I'm going to be able to save her? Lady, you aren't nearly as smart as I require in a woman." Then

Mickey leans back. "Look how mature we are, discussing our insecurities as we break up."

"Yes, we're great examples of humanity and decency."

He's said all that and I've said all this, but he's still looking at me with those eyes and the sake is making me feel really warm. We've just said we don't need or want each other, but I can feel the pull between our bodies right now, so strong it's amazing I don't fly across this table and land in his lap.

"You know what would make this even better?" he asks, raising a hand to wipe his chin.

"Breakup sex."

He reaches across the table and takes my hand, giving it a brief squeeze. "Dammit, Benny," he says. "You make me want to marry you. Good thing I don't love you. Then you'd really be in trouble."

Later, in bed, in the dark, with sweat cooling against my skin, I kiss the soft side of his chest. I already miss him. "I'll tell you your biggest flaw," I say.

"What's that, love?"

"Your timing sucks."

"Right back atcha, pretty thing."

Departures.

Mickey pulls the car over three times on the highway to kiss me. His hands are large and warm. They are everywhere. My seat belt is cutting into the skin on my neck. I don't care.

We reach LAX. Mickey merges the car into the lane underneath the sign that says Departures. I watch him reach over and silence the radio, which is playing Queen's "We Are the Champions." Mickey shakes his head like he's disappointed in the radio gods. I can't help but grin.

We're standing at the curb, suitcase by my feet, Mickey's arms tight around me. The sound of buses, car alarms, and jet engines is muffled by his skin against my ears.

Mickey says, "I was just starting to get used to you." His voice cracks slightly on the last word, his mouth against my ear.

"I'm kind of used to you, too," I say. "That's weird, right?"

"I think it only takes a week," he says.

"What takes a week?"

He pulls back and smiles, lips clamped shut. He's blushing.

"What takes a week, Mickey?" I don't want to let go of his hand.

"Don't push me to say the other thing if you don't want to hear it," he warns.

"You're right."

"God, you're such a woman. 'Love me, but don't love me. But love me!'"

We're swinging each other's hands, like little girls at recess. We're playful even in our last good-bye. It's different from what I'm used to, and I hate this nagging feeling that this is what it's supposed to be like.

"Do you believe in signs?" he asks. "Like, fate telling you things?"

I haven't told him about the supermarket music. There are lots of things I haven't gotten to tell him. Why do I want to stay and keep talking?

"I don't know," I say. "It's nice to think it's possible."

A security guard motions for Mickey to move his car. Mickey nods, but then goes right back to me without moving a muscle toward the direction of leaving. "I don't really believe in fate," he says, "but sometimes I'll let something else make the choice for me. When I had to pick where I was going to live in Los Angeles once I moved here, I threw a dart at a map of the city. It hit Hollywood."

"You're so lucky."

"I know. What if I'd tossed that thing into Compton?"

Mickey checks his watch and then looks over my shoulder, as if he can see the plane I'm supposed to be on. "Anyway, before I set you free to live your life, and I go back to Hollywood and talk a few desperate, sad actresses into having sex with me, I wanted to give you a sign that means I'm thinking of you."

"Okay."

"A red car. Whenever you see a red car, that means wherever I am, I'm thinking about you."

I must be looking at him like he's crazy, because he keeps talking.

"We didn't get enough time to have any proof we were together. The only thing I've ever bought you, you ate."

"I'll keep looking for the red cars," I say. "I promise."

"Have a good flight, Benny." He leans in and gives me one last kiss.

I take the handle of my suitcase and step up onto the curb. "This is the weirdest breakup I've ever had," I say.

"Yes, we should break up more often." He runs a hand along the top of his head like he's holding back more words. Then he turns on his heels and gets into his car without another glance toward me.

Unlimited Minutes.

"We're so excited you're coming," Mom says. "Jami even broke plans with Charles tomorrow so she can see you."

"Charles?" I'm sitting on my carry-on suitcase, waiting at the gate. I have about ten minutes before my group is boarding. My mother has been on the phone with me since I was in the security line. I've heard all about her job search, her last date with her boyfriend, Gregory, the constant phone calls she's been getting from her ex-boyfriend, Michael, who either would like to start dating her again or thinks they *are* still dating, and the way her foot has been itching inside her cast.

Mom has been talking to me for over an hour. My ear is almost as hot as the cell phone pressing against my head. I worry briefly if this is the call that's going to set me over the edge, and cause the cancerous tumor to begin forming in my brain. Well, I suppose that's one step closer to being Whitman. Look out, clock tower.

"Jami's boyfriend," Mom says. "I don't like him. You won't, either. I don't know where she finds these guys. This one drinks. A lot. He has weird hair. And he calls me 'The Moms.' Always plural. I am not more than one person. It sounds like one of those weird rap people they listen to."

"Uh-huh." I shuffle to the line forming at the gate. I press my free hand to my other ear to block out the loudspeaker announcement.

"When you get here, promise you won't say anything about the house."

"What's wrong with the house?"

"You're going to be mad."

"Why, Ma?"

"Just don't say anything. I know it's a mess."

"Well, you're injured. It's okay if the house is a little messy. I'll clean it."

Mom's quiet for so long I think the phone has cut out.

"Hello?" I ask.

"I miss you, Boobs. I'm glad you're coming home."

"We're not going to have anything to talk about if I don't get off the phone now."

The gate opens. People are filing in.

"Fly safely," Mom says. "And make sure you wash your hands when you get off the plane. That thing is filled with germs."

"Love you."

I close my phone and shove it into my pocket. I know she'll call again before we depart, so I don't bother turning off the power.

Cue the Violins.

I thought I'd give you a rundown of some of the more humiliating moments in my life that involve my mother and my weight.

She did not allow me to partake in Halloween one year, saying I didn't need any candy. Jami and I had to give out chocolate bars and M&M's to trick-or-treaters because "there was no reason to punish the neighborhood just because Benny's so fat."

When I was thirteen she gave me an Overeaters Anonymous book. She assigned homework.

I once found her crying in her bedroom. She was sitting at the foot of her bed in just her underwear. When I asked her what was wrong, she said, "I'm fat and ugly. None of my clothes fit me. I wish I could be like you and not care what I look like." I was eighteen.

For a few days in high school, I stopped eating. I would only drink water and eat one piece of toast a day. I thought my mother would beg me to eat again. I expected her to apologize profusely, clench her hands together in agony, crawl on her hands and knees and serve gigantic bowls of mac and cheese—anything to get her precious daughter to eat again. I lost ten pounds very quickly. My mother considers it to be one of her finest triumphs in parenting.

College. Mom and I had a late meal at a Chili's. I realized the girl seated a few tables over had gone to high school with me. We had a very messy falling-out over a boy. I couldn't remember which one of us stole the other's boyfriend, which means I probably did the taking. When she was leaving, she stared at me and loudly proclaimed, "She still looks like a fat shit to me!" She walked out before I could come up with a great comeback. Mom said, "That's a terrible thing to say to someone." Before I could commiserate, Mom followed up with, "I wish you didn't give anyone the ammo."

I haven't been thinner than my mother at any point in my life. When I see Mom in a few hours, the first thing she's going to say is how thin I am and how fantastic I look and how proud of me she is. Then she'll tell me how right she's always been—I am really pretty without all that fat.

I never thought of myself as a fat girl, never even consciously tried to be a skinnier person. In fact, once I got out of my mother's house I never even said the word *diet*. So the absolute worst of all of this is the fact I know that Mom's right. I look better now. I'm healthier now. I like myself more than when I was heavier and unable to run for an hour or wear a swimsuit without pulling a T-shirt over it to cover myself.

I know it's my mother's voice in my head, telling me I'm better now that I'm thinner. I hate that voice. I hate that part of me.

There Was a Storm of Cats and Dogs . . .

. . . located directly over my mother's house. I don't know how else to explain what I'm seeing.

The small white house with blue trim now has a large, imposing dog tied to the oak tree out front. As I approach the house, the brown mutt—part boxer, part killer—leaps toward me, fangs foamy and exposed. Around the front steps there's a chicken-wire fence cordoning off the area like police tape. Penned inside the structure are several small yippy dogs of various breeds. They wiggle and bark, announcing my arrival.

There are cats lazing around any area of the yard unprotected by canines. A few glance in my direction, ears pointing away, eyes half-raised in apathy.

I stand with my suitcase, taking this in. At what point did my mother's house become an animal shelter?

Maybe I'm somehow standing in front of the wrong house. Perhaps the one behind me is clean and pretty and has my mother standing on the porch, holding a tray of fresh-baked cookies.

No dice. Across the street are two red cars, parked bumper to bumper.

Inside, my mom's house is a pigsty.

That's the word Mom used to use when my bedroom was a mess. "Clean this pigsty," she'd say. I had no idea what that word meant, so it became even more confusing when I got a stye in my eye, which led to an embarrassing trip to the school nurse to announce I was sure I had caught "pig eye."

First I must address the smell. It's like cats have been mating over a heating vent. It's so thick I can feel it permeating the fibers of my T-shirt. I'm wearing the smell of this house— ammonia and urine and mildew. Ever forget to throw away a vase of flowers before you go out of town and when you come home you find a jar of rotten, moldy brown stems? That's the smell. Like something's *wrong*.

There are piles of newspapers and magazines stacked to the ceiling. Bookshelves are stuffed with so many knick-knacks and paperbacks there's no place for my eye to rest. I cannot see the carpeting underneath the empty paper bags, plastic bags, discarded mail, and mobs of dirty laundry littering the floor.

There is a difference between a house that's gone a little messy and cluttered and this. My mother's house looks like the inside of a disturbed mind. This is beyond unsettling.

My mother is a woman who used to walk around her house Saturday mornings with gym socks on her hands, dusting every wooden surface. Her idea of a relaxing day was settling down with a good junk drawer and getting it inventoried.

I'm standing beside a bowl of mushy, fuzzy fruit when I hear my mother's voice echo down the hallway.

"Is that my Benny? My Benny's home?"

There's a clunk-*clunk!* in her approach. Mom's walking with a cane. She looks smaller, shorter, and her hair has

grown out longer than she usually keeps it. Her hair is thinning around her temples, and the curl is tired. She's wearing
thick eyeglasses that cartoonishly magnify her eyes. There is a
frailty I've never seen in my mother before that sends a jolt
through me, a reminder that one day she will be gone, too,
and all this time I waste thinking about how much she drives
me crazy will come back to haunt me.

Well. Most likely it'll be my mother who'll come back to
haunt me.

"You're not in a wheelchair," I say.

"What made you think I was in a wheelchair?" She cocks
her eyebrows and smirks. She then raises the bottom of her
sweatpants to show off a purple cast on her left leg that ends
just below the knee. It looks like a sturdy, thick sock.

"On the phone, I thought maybe you were incapacitated.
You said you couldn't work."

"Couldn't *find* work," she says. "I've been looking for a
while, but there just aren't any jobs out there." She leans her
cane against the wall. "I'm only using this today because it
was raining this morning and I'm feeling a little achy. Normally I walk around on this thing all the time."

"So you're fine?"

"I'm unemployed and have no car. Does that sound fine
to you?"

I avoid the tone, jumping over the invitation for a fight.
Instead, I go to Mom and hug her for a long time. The familiar smell from her sweater, of stolen cigarettes and cups of tea,
soothes my head. I nuzzle my chin into her neck. I could be
anywhere; I am home.

"My Benny," Mom sighs. "I missed you."

"I missed you, too. Ma, the animals—" I start.

Mom leans back against the stove. Her hands look thin,
the skin crinkled over deep blue veins. "Your sister can't stop

bringing them home. They find her like she's Saint Francis."

"They're all strays?"

"A vet down the street gives her a discount on their shots. She keeps saying she's going to find them all homes, but we average a new animal around here at least once a week. The cats keep multiplying themselves."

It is at this point I see a birdcage hanging near the refrigerator. There are two small green birds inside, chirping merrily. I point wearily in their direction.

"Ernie and Bert," Mom responds.

There's a metal antique advertisement hanging on the wall over the stove. It's a little black girl with her hair in cotton rags. She's frozen over a bowl of oatmeal, her eyes wide and her mouth open in shock. The cursive writing over her head reads, "These oats is GOOD!"

"Ma," I say. "You have to take that down immediately."

"What's wrong now?" she asks, sounding completely exhausted with me.

"That," I say, pointing. "You can't have that hanging in your kitchen."

"My pickaninny?" she asks. "I think she's cute."

"It's offensive. And don't use that word."

"Pickaninny?"

"Stop, Ma. That's racist."

"Since when?"

"Since always." I'm blushing with shame, wondering how many people have come into this kitchen and thought my mother was a member of the Klan. "How long has that been up in your kitchen?"

"I don't know. I got it off eBay. How is it offensive?"

"Ma. She's saying 'These oats is *good*!'"

"Now *you're* the one making that voice. *That's* what's racist. You're making it racist."

"The man who made the sign made it racist. Please take it down."

I scan the kitchen for other antique ads featuring bankers with long, hooked noses, or Asian men with giant straw hats, dancing with slit-eyed glee. Thankfully, there's nothing but a few ads for Morton salt. Suddenly even "When It Rains, It Pours" sounds offensive.

Mom walks past me toward the refrigerator. "Do you want something to eat? You must be hungry after your long flight."

"Where's Jami? I thought you said she'd be here."

"She knew when you were getting here. She went out last night and said she'd be back early, but she hasn't come home. I couldn't fall asleep, thinking she was dead."

Mom says this offhandedly, but it's the truth. Jami has a tendency to disappear for long stretches of time. When she comes back she sometimes has a new hair color, sometimes a new tattoo, but she rarely gives up any information as to her recent whereabouts. Sometimes she's in a new car. Sometimes she has a new boyfriend. Once she had a court hearing she wouldn't talk about. I am not convinced she hasn't spent at least one night in jail. Jami gets herself wrapped up in the drama of the moment, even when it comes with dangerous consequences. She told me about a time she was in a car full of friends who were buying drugs. The deal went sour and someone pulled a gun. Let me interrupt myself here to tell you that Jami told me this story as if she was relaying a time she went to the store for a box of cereal—it was that casual. Just in the car and there's a gun to her head and somehow they got out of it with nobody dead and that made the story hilarious to her, just another story of her *vida loca*.

I move a stack of unopened mail off a chair and sit down. I realize I've been tensing all of the muscles in my back, waiting for something, like a defensive crouch.

Mom slides a cup of tea and a plate of cookies in front of me. "I don't like your hair like that," she says. "You don't look good in layers."

Welcome home.

My Sister's Nipples.

Jami and I have never looked alike. We're about the same height, although she's just a bit taller and usually in something with a heel. Her natural chestnut hair color is often coated in a shocking pink or purple. Her ears are pierced in places most people would never jam a needle. She has a post in her tongue and one underneath her bottom lip. This leads me to think she's pierced in places only my mother discusses with me. I hope I'm never close enough to my sister's nipples to learn such personal facts about my sibling.

(*My Sister's Nipples* will be the name of the Lifetime movie they will make about me when I one day accidentally kill my mother on purpose.)

On this day, when Jami bounds into the house, it's like staring into a mirror. A mirror that's really into S and M, but a mirror nonetheless.

She sees it, too. "Holy shit," she says, approaching me with her arms open. "Look who's here. And when did she start looking like she's not adopted?"

Jami leaps into my arms and I hold her, just like we did when we were kids. She thinks this is hilarious now that she's taller than I am, how I still instinctively grab her under her butt and hold her to my chest like she's a little monkey. She marvels at the fact that I've never dropped her. This is one of my favorite things. No matter how old we get, no matter where in our lives we are, when we see each other for the first time in months, she jumps and I catch her. Nobody else in the world could understand why we need to do it. We just do.

"How do you like Mom's shithole?" Jami asks as she untangles herself from me. She pulls her dark purple hair back with two hands, holding it at the nape of her neck while she looks me over. Her face is fuller than the last time I saw her. Her T-shirt is riding up on her waist, revealing more flesh than she normally carries around. I notice with a twinge of evil glee that I might be thinner than my sister for the first time since we were ages with a single-digit number. However, it is only now that she's heavier that I can see just how much we look alike. I decide not to say anything about it.

"Don't you live here, too?" I ask. "Isn't this partly your shithole?"

"Don't remind me. I'm trying to get out of here, but Mom won't let me."

"Mm-hmm."

"Honestly. She cries whenever I talk about finding my own place."

"So you're trashing hers, turning it into an actual animal planet, hoping she kicks you out?"

"Now how come you can figure that out in three minutes, but Mom still hasn't gotten it after almost a year?" She pops a Coke and takes a sip, her tongue clicking against the can. "Sit down, Sis," she says. "Catch me up on your glamorous Hollywood lifestyle." A cat, skinny and almost silver, appears from seemingly nowhere. He perches on Jami's lap, purring with glee.

"It's not glamorous," I say as I yawn. I crave a nap. It's been a very long day.

"Are you living with Mom?" Jami asks. "Because I am. And I have to tell you something." She leans in, her eyes darting toward the living room, where we can hear Mom watching television. I notice a new tattoo on Jami's neck—a little yellow flower just above her left collarbone. "I might end up living with Mom forever," she says. "And when that happens, I need you to shoot me in the head."

My Bedroom.

I've never lived in this house. Mom bought this place after Dad died. This means the house holds no warm feeling for me. I don't wander the hallways kicking up memories. I don't have any sense of belonging to the walls and floors. There isn't a place that calls to me, that fills me with safety.

This means there is no place that is mine.

Mom has me sleeping in the videotape room. This is a spare bedroom used to hold roughly three hundred VHS tapes, mostly recorded from television programs. There is an exercise bike in the corner. A computer monitor rests on a small wooden desk. There's no hard drive. There's a large stuffed giraffe on a rocking chair, its neck broken so he looks profoundly depressed. A mirror leans against one wall. Taking up the rest of the space in the room is a white metal daybed—the only remnant I can find of my high school years. I'll be sleeping on a more-than-decade-old mattress that's about five inches thick, in a bed frame that reminds me of just how dorky and lonely my teenage years were.

After checking for animals, I shut the bedroom door and

sit on the bare, squeaky mattress. I close my eyes and let it be as close to quiet in my head as it can be. Downstairs, I hear Mom and Jami yelling over the television about where my sister has been since yesterday. I can hear dogs barking and cats chasing each other through the hallway. It sounds like seventeen people live here, and I don't understand how even one person can take it for more than ten minutes. I already want to go home.

There's an iguana sitting next to me. I jump, screaming, as instinct dictates.

"She found Lars," I hear my mother say before Jami erupts in riotous giggles.

I am home again. Except this time home is filled with so much trash I can't seem to find anything in it that resembles a house. This place is a zoo. My mother has become a hoarder, she's unemployed, wearing a leg cast, and without a car. My sister is dating another gangbanger and seems to find nothing wrong with the fact that she's almost halfway through her twenties and just as far along in her life as if she were eighteen.

Beyond all that, why the fuck haven't they told me I'm skinny?

SOS.

I'm trying to find a dab of toothpaste in a basket filled with empty, rolled-up tubes when my cell phone rings. I almost break a finger wrestling it out of my pocket. I know it's a call from somewhere not inside this house, so it feels like a lifeboat.

It's Mickey.

"Benny? I just wanted to make sure you were okay. I don't know why, but I hoped you'd call when you got in, and I didn't hear from you yesterday and—"

I am so happy to hear his voice I launch right in. "My mother's house has a weird angle to it. The only time it doesn't feel like I'm falling is when I'm standing at the kitchen sink with a glass of water. That's when it feels like I'm tipping my head back to drink."

"You're not mad I'm calling?"

"I found a tiny razor in the shower. When I asked my sister what it was for, she said, 'My pubes.' I had to take another shower just to get clean from holding that thing."

"I miss you. Keep talking."

I walk through the house, trying to keep phone reception, as I tell Mickey all the weird things I've seen in the short time since I left his side.

"Mom doesn't have sheets for this twin mattress I'm sleeping on. It's the twin mattress from when we all lived in the old house. Mom got rid of all my yearbooks, all of my stuffed animals, every stitch of clothing I ever wore, but she kept this ugly-ass bed. I think she wanted to torture me. My back is killing me and I'm sleeping on a bare mattress with my old Strawberry Shortcake sleeping bag."

"See any red cars?"

"A few."

"You should have," he says. "I've been thinking about you."

Then it's quiet. I'm staring at the pattern in the raggedy floor rug underneath the old armchair where Dad used to take his naps. I'm surprised Mom saved this chair, too. I trace my toe along the lilies and listen to Mickey's breath as he listens to mine. I hear the phone shift. He sighs.

"How many days have you been gone?" he asks.

"Two."

He groans. "Wow."

I try to hide in my mother's sewing room. I open the door to find a tiny Chihuahua standing on a footstool. He unleashes an angry tirade of yippy yelps. It makes the other dogs in the house respond until the walls seem to be vibrating in animal rhythms.

"Sorry," I say to the dog. Then, to Mickey, "Sorry."

"What the hell's going on over there?"

"I'm still trying to figure that out," I tell him. "So, how's all the actress-fucking going?"

"Awesome. Had to buy a BlackBerry to keep track of all the appointments."

"Yeah, it's pretty crazy here in Virginia. Lots of men, all over the place."

Then he surprises me. "I do have a date tonight, actually."

"Oh."

What a dick.

"I don't know why I'm telling you this. I don't have to, but it felt like lying not telling you."

I wish I didn't want to ask him her name, if she's pretty, how he met a girl and scheduled a date mere hours after I left his arms, his bed. I wonder if she's someone who was in the wings while he was with me. I want to know why he's telling me about his planned evening, almost as if he's asking for permission. But really I'd just like to know why men fuck up any moment where things are going nicely.

"Well, you have fun, then," I say, chipper as can be. "I'm going to go clean the lizard shit off my pillow."

"Is that a figure of speech?"

"If only it were."

"You don't have to get off the phone yet."

The mood's killed. He's got plans. I'm not in them. No point in prolonging this. I tell him, "Yeah, Mickey, I really do."

See?

Not worth it.

Waiting for Gregory.

Apparently my mother's boyfriend is going to make some kind of feast tonight.

"Gregory's at the store right now," Mom says, her plastered foot propped on the kitchen table as she flips through a decorating magazine. "You're going to love his cooking. He's why I've gotten so fat."

At the mention of the word my ears start to burn. I know it's coming. Here's where she compliments me, or asks me for my secret. Maybe she's waiting until I ask to borrow some of her clothes, and then we'll stand in her closet in our underwear, complimenting each other's tiny waists. I've seen her do it with my sister so many times, and while I never thought I wanted that bond with my mom before, now I can see it happening. It could be a lot of fun.

"You're not fat, Ma," I say. "You're beautiful."

She smacks at her thighs, making a popping sound. "I'm enormous," she says. "And wait until you see your cousin Tracy. Jesus, she ballooned."

"Didn't she just have twins?" I ask.

Mom looks at me like I asked if Tracy enrolled in clown school. "She had those kids six months ago," she says. "If anything, you'd think the twins would make her skinny, running around after them."

"They're not walking yet, are they?" I ask.

Mom flips a page in her magazine to end the conversation. Too much logic for her.

I spend five minutes trying to find a clean mug for a cup of coffee. Then I spend another ten attempting to locate the coffee maker before I give up and ask. Mom points to a closet down the hall. "With the napkins," she says.

The coffee maker is in the linen closet, tucked behind a stack of board games. I try to determine a secret order to all of this—maybe alphabetical, or by decade of invention. My brain needs to understand why a bag of cotton balls rests on a box of trash bags and both are in the hall closet next to my mother's rain boots. Does she buy things, take them into her home, and then promptly forget about them before they get put away? I wish she'd talk about the house and how this happened, but I don't know how to approach the subject.

I hear a horn outside. Five long beeps, as if Mom lives on a farm and there's nobody else around for miles.

"That's Gregory!" Mom says, pushing herself up from the table. She hobbles toward the bathroom. "I need to freshen my face."

Here's all I know about Gregory:

He used to have a mustache. I've only seen one picture, one from a few years ago. He had red, curly hair and a very red mustache that covered his top lip in a way that made him look like he was from the Old West. Jami and I referred to him as "Ye Olde Gregory" until Mom made us stop. She says his hair is darker now, and thinner.

He is divorced. Three times. When he got together with my mother he told her he'd never met a woman who made him feel as good as she does. This makes me trust him about as much as I trust a man who feeds a woman that kind of line to excuse three failed marriages.

He has a daughter named Amber, who once called my mom boring. Mom doesn't know this. Jami heard it from Gregory. Jami uses it as blackmail to get Gregory to let her occasionally borrow one of his sports cars.

Gregory is into sports cars and motorcycles. Must be a mustache thing.

He has sex with my mother. I hate that I know this. I really hate how much I know this. If they could invent some kind of soldering iron that could melt memories out of your brain, I'd take that right to the Mom Has Sex part of my head, even if it were in my temporal lobe. I'd be willing to lose at least two thousand vocabulary words if it meant I never pictured my mom's legs wrapped around Ye Olde Gregory's old-timey hips.

Ugh, I just grossed myself out.

Meet Mom's Boyfriend.

He's tall, wearing a blue baseball cap. No mustache. He bends deep at the knees to lift a heavy bag of groceries out of the trunk. I walk outside to help him, jumping down the porch steps like a little girl. I feel small, too young. I've regressed right here in front of my mother's house. *Let's go meet Mommy's boyfriend! How fun!*

"Gregory?" I ask, my hand already extended, avoiding any other bodily contact.

He turns, a smile already on his face. He's very tan, with

deep-set worry lines around his mouth and eyes. The hair curling around his cap is a dark, rusty color that reminds me of an old horse.

"The famous Benny," he says, taking my hand. "You're the one who lives with movie stars."

"That's me." I don't know what to say back.

You're the one who sleeps with my mom.

"You look like your mother," he says.

"No, I don't."

"Okay."

He continues unloading the groceries without another word. I help him carry bags, but I am not holding up my end of the conversation, either.

At one point I hold the screen door open for him as he backs into the house, carrying a case of soda. He dips his head at me in gratitude. I nod back.

I try again. "So you've been married a few times?"

I swear that's not what I meant to ask. It just happened.

"It's kind of my hobby," Gregory replies. And then he winks. Is he serious, or teasing me for asking the question?

I stand there, openmouthed and silent, until Gregory finishes unloading the groceries and heads deeper into the house.

That went well.

Armwarmers.

Jami brings a friend to dinner, I guess because it wasn't weird enough. I haven't asked her name because she's wearing leg warmers on her arms.

I can't stop staring at them. They're striped, red and green, and they are bunched around her forearms. She's wearing a T-shirt tight across her chest that reads "Ask Me About My Blow Jobs." Her hair is in two pigtails high on her head. Her skin is a warm olive, and her blue eyes are enormous. In her outfit, I would look more than ridiculous. I'd look like a melting Punky Brewster. But on this girl it's right. It's driving me crazy, and I can't stop staring at her as she helps Jami chop vegetables for a salad.

"What do you think of Gregory?" Jami asks, her voice not quiet enough. Mom and Gregory are in the dining room, setting the table. I can hear them discussing something about his daughter. I wonder if she's coming, too.

"I don't know yet," I say. "He's only said about two words to me."

"Were they nice words?"

"He said I look like Mom."

Jami laughs, and clicks her tongue piercing against her upper teeth. "That's a first."

"I know. I think he was reaching."

We have the same hands, Mom and I. That's it. We both have wide palms and short, stubby fingers that look funny in nail polish or rings. Thanks, Ma.

"He's funny," Jami says. "He makes Mom laugh." She turns to Armwarmers and asks, "Don't you think so?"

Armwarmers nods, and clicks her gum with her molars.

I can no longer resist. "How do you get away with wearing that?"

She examines her wardrobe, as if for the first time. "This?"

"Benny," Jami scolds.

"I think she looks great," I say. "But if I tried to wear that, I'd look enormous. Like the Michelin man." I point at her red, low-riding, flared corduroy pants. "If the lower half of his body was on fire."

Jami rolls her eyes. "That's because you don't know how to dress for your emotional age. She dresses like an eight-year-old."

Armwarmers agrees. "Because I'm actually an eight-year-old girl."

"I'm emotionally sixteen," Jami says. "That's why my tattoos look so good."

"Sure," I say, unable to stop my eyes from retreating to the back of my head.

"Oh," Armwarmers moans. "Benny's a grown-up."

They both stare at me, sizing up my emotional age. "That's why she has to dress like an adult," Jami says.

"I don't dress like an adult. I can rock a T-shirt," I say.

"In an old-school way," Jami says. "Ironically. Like a grown-up playing retro. Your clothes have quotation marks around them. You're so 'aware' of your 'outfit.' "

"I'm no longer having this conversation," I say.

"Grown-up!" Armwarmers shouts, like she just won a game show.

Gregory enters the kitchen, wearing oven gloves shaped like fish. "Leave her alone, Amber," he says.

"I'm just teasing her, Dad. I'm trying to form some kind of sisterly bond. Fake-sisterly, I guess." Amber reaches out her hand to shake mine. "Nice to meet you, semisister."

Jami is watching me, enjoying my shock.

"I'm not an adult," are all the words I can find to say.

Vedrai, Carino.

Gregory listens to opera during dinner.

Mom and Jami are acting like every night we sit down to steak au poivre and *Don Giovanni*. They cut through their steaks, swirling the meat in the spicy sauce, bobbing their heads in a solemn, reverent beat. Eventually my mother scolds me. "Eat your food, dear."

"She's not into eating," Jami says. "Nobody in Hollywood eats, right?"

"Maybe we should all move to Hollywood if we want to be as skinny as Benny."

They decided to wait until there are others in the room. They want an audience.

"I think you look great," Amber says, her arm warmers shoved halfway up her forearms. "Atkins?"

I stammer for a second before answering. "No. I didn't do Atkins."

Gregory has his gaze firmly fixed to his plate. I can see the top of his scalp; his hair is thinning. A dog plops down onto my feet, waiting for scraps.

"What did you do, Benny?" Jami asks. "South Beach? Personal trainer? Cocaine addiction?"

Mom laughs. "She probably heard we'd gotten heavy and did this on purpose."

"I know!" Jami leans back, lifts up her shirt, and grabs her stomach. She can barely grab a handful. "Can you believe all this?" she asks. "Gregory's not allowed to make food for us anymore."

"I think you both look beautiful," Gregory says, still staring at his plate.

Amber's watching all of this with transfixed glee. "Can I come over every night?" she asks. She looks at my mom. "You may have heard I thought you were boring. I take it all back. You and your family are fascinating."

"Thanks, Amber. I used to think you were dumb." Mom turns her attention back to me. "Answer the question."

My tongue feels swollen in my mouth. I shift in my seat, wishing I were wearing more clothes. I can't believe they're making me feel guilty about this. "I started running," I said. "And watched what I ate."

"Uh-huh," Jami says, talking around the wad of meat in her mouth. "I bet you kept a food journal." She turns to Amber to explain. "The only way she'd lose weight was if there was some sort of reward system."

I also gave myself gold stars every week whenever I stayed within my allotted calories.

"Eat less and exercise more," Mom says. "Too bad you didn't figure that out earlier."

It Gets Worse.

Way worse.

This is the night I overhear my mom and Gregory having sex.

Can't a girl get a drink of water in the middle of the night without shattering the last pieces of her mother-daughter bond?

I woke up with my mouth feeling like the surface of a tennis ball. I rarely eat steak anymore, and it was wreaking havoc on my insides. I knew leaving the videotape room was going to be tricky, not just because it's a maze of objects that could fall on me at any time, but because I had to pass both my mother's bedroom and Amber, who was sleeping on the couch by the stairs.

See? I was trying to be *nice,* by walking carefully down the hallway so as not to wake the *near stranger* who thinks she's part of *my family,* and I'm rewarded with the sound of my mother's moans.

MY MOTHER'S.

MOANS.

Have you ever heard your mother moaning in pleasure? Let me tell you what it does to you.

First, little sparks appear behind your eyes. Tiny white dots flood in, kind of like you're about to faint, or like you stood up too quickly. There's a swirling sound in your ears. And then you have this rapid-fire montage of memories— your mother holding you over her head with maternal pride, your first tottering steps into her arms, the first day of kindergarten as she said a tearful good-bye, singing on road trips, buying prom dresses, teaching you to drive a car, and then she's naked and her legs are spread and there's this other body down there and he's eating steak au poivre off her thighs and *you never sleep, ever again.*

This Is Why They Say You Can't Go Home Again.

This morning I have to go outside and run for a very long time. I feel like my ass, legs, and stomach have already begun expanding in the short time I've been here. Any moment I'm not sneezing or wheezing from animal hair, I seem to be stuffing my face with something from the pantry. I don't know what else to do. It's difficult to find a place to sit, much less relax. Maybe if I run until I'm exhausted, I won't be so picky about which pile of crap I choose for resting my weary body.

Deciding to stretch out in the backyard, I grab a bottle of water and head out onto the porch. I haven't been back here, so this is the first time I've seen a large gate that runs through the center of the yard. There's essentially a series of gates and metal poles that bisect the lawn, turning the backyard into a multicaged pen. On one side are more dogs, maybe some from the front yard. They don't keep still long enough for me to count them accurately. The other side has a large, scary, monster dog. This one is black and—thankfully—asleep.

There's a shed in the back of the property. I can see cats on the roof, lounging in the windowsills, stretching their fuzzy legs over the stone pavers that lead to the front door, which is open. Even from here I can see the clutter that reaches the ceiling—papers and boxes and what looks like a year's worth of daily newspapers.

I make my way to the front of the house, tiptoeing around landmines of animal shit, and open the side door of the garage. It's worse. It smells like mold and paint cans. There are bicycle wheels leaning against piles of clothing. Rugs rolled up and stacked against the wall tower over milk crates stacked in makeshift storage areas. Inside the milk crates are stacks of plates, bowls, pots, and pans.

This is not a good feeling, the one I have right now. And as I look over the tonnage of useless objects my mother has stuffed into this house I feel like Jennifer Connelly in *A Beautiful Mind,* wandering into that back shed to discover her husband's newspaper clippings and scribblings—proof of a brain gone nutso. This isn't normal. This isn't what a mother's house is supposed to look like. It's scary. I find myself having the same impulse that I had when I was a kid, at bedtime. Once I turned off my bedroom light, in order to find my bed through the terrifying dark, I needed to run.

I hit the pavement and go. I run until my legs won't hold me up anymore, until my stomach is cramping from my breath fighting to keep me alive. The wind blocks out all other sound in my ears. Sweat rolls down my neck, into the curves of my collarbones. My arms are heavy and my feet are numb. When I finally let myself slow down to a walk, hands jammed under my ribcage to keep from imploding, I find I have no idea where I am. I wander back toward the direction I think might be what I'm supposed to call home.

Every time I pass a red car I give it the finger.

When I find the house an hour later, Mom's in the kitchen making a sandwich. Upon seeing me, she immediately pulls out another two pieces of bread to make one for me. I'm covered in sweat, red-faced and gasping, trying to get through a glass of water without choking. It doesn't matter; Mom thinks I should eat.

I wait until I can breathe evenly, until I no longer hear my pulse in my ears. I sit at the table, untouched sandwich in front of me.

"Where did you go?" she asks.

"I don't know. That way." I point behind me.

"I don't like the idea of you running all by yourself in this neighborhood. There are some real wackos living around here."

"I'm a big girl. I can take them."

Mom opens a cabinet to return the bag of bread. One of the shelves is jammed thick with telephone books. I spot one for the Chicago area and close my eyes.

"Ma, the house," I say. My voice sounds raspy, like I've been gulping glass.

"I know," she says. She limps to the table and joins me. She cups her hands around her fresh mug of tea. "I don't know what else to say."

"I'm going to clean it."

"No, that's okay." She waves a hand in the air as if she's clearing a cobweb. "I can do it later."

"You can't do this alone. There's so much stuff."

"I would rather you just spend time with me. I want your company."

"Ma, I have to do something. I came here to help."

"There's not much for you to do."

The house is a junkyard, there's no real income, my sister's dating another parolee-of-the-week, and my mom still has a cast on her leg. If there's one thing I'm supposed to do it's stay here and take care of things until everybody starts living what can be considered a normal life. At the very least they need someone to get rid of all these animals. I can't even imagine all the germs inside the property line.

"I can't leave when everything's like this," I say.

Mom looks at me quickly, and I see the hurt in her eyes. "We're fine," she says.

"You're not fine."

Mom stands up and immediately catches herself on the table before falling. I stand, too, instinct taking over, and grab her arm. She wrenches it out of my grip.

"I'm *fine*," she says, and walks out of the room.

An Impartial Witness.

I cannot clean this house by myself. I decide to hire some help. And because I'm a red-blooded, American girl, I hire a cute boy.

If you're going to be doing lots of heavy lifting, yard work, and sorting through random piles of semitrash, the only way it can be enjoyable is if there's the constant possibility of an attractive man taking off his T-shirt.

This is how I come to meet Zack. He's tan and strong and blond and muscle-y and has this side-grin that kills me. He's just a little taller than I am. His teeth are perfect and his nose turns up a little at the bottom where there's a family of freckles having a little picnic. He wears jeans that are slightly torn on one knee and a yellow T-shirt that rises up his back whenever he bends over.

So I hired myself some eye candy. Come on. I'm not going to touch the boy. But my eyes will do filthy, filthy things.

Okay, so I've always wanted a tanned, blond boy to be at my command. I don't care how shallow I sound right now. A stable boy. A pool boy. Someone who turns when I walk into the room and looks at me like . . . I don't know, like I'm his future. His way out of this mess. It's backward and stupid, and I know it's eight kinds of wrong, but when I was a little girl I wanted a little boy who was *mine.* I was going to let him go when he was old enough, after I taught him everything he needed to know about women. But for five glorious years we'd belong to each other, even though he technically belonged to me. At lunches we'd sneak away to our secret field of dandelions to be naked, learning how our bodies worked with each other. A pregnancy scare would have him crushing dandelions with one knee as he did the honorable thing. For one week we would think our lives were forever entwined. But then when my period came, we'd realize it was time for our love affair to end. I would go to college; he would start his own horse farm in a small Kentucky town. We'd see each other just one more time, at my father's funeral, where we'd have passionate cemetery sex in the rain, and I'd learn he named his eldest daughter after me.

Don't look at me like that. As if *you* didn't have the same fantasy.

Whatever.

Zack Is No Stable Boy.

"I'm not going to pick up cat shit," he says to me. His voice drawls on the vowels, but I can't place the Southern state it's from. "I don't mind shoveling dog shit, but cat shit's nasty."

I've got my face in a mug of coffee, trying to wake up. It's seven in the morning. Zack's an early riser. Our romance is also tempered by the fact that I'm still in pajamas. My hair looks like I'm a member of Poison. My eyes are puffy because I haven't been getting much sleep, on account of the Mom Moans. The dogs yip and howl around us. They announced Zack's arrival with such frenzy I'm surprised there isn't someone from the neighborhood here, offering to euthanize an animal or two.

Zack and I are standing on the one part of the lawn that isn't owned by the dogs. It's piled high with leaves from the large oak trees that are taking over the space above the house. I only recently learned that there's a giant ditch just beyond this wall of fallen foliage. I learned this when I fell into it trying to find the property line.

"I don't see the difference," I say, my voice the unsexy version of husky. "Isn't cat shit smaller? And . . . I don't know, easier to pick up?"

"Cats don't have to shit where they do," Zack explains. "Dogs don't have litter boxes. But cats are assholes. They look for places where you're going to see it. They shit to make you clean it up."

"Zack, are you saying it'll be *my* job to clean up the cat shit?"

"I don't care whose job it is. I'm not touching mother-fucking cat shit."

I shuffle back inside the house as Zack resumes raking the lake of yellow orange leaves into piles.

Jami is in the kitchen, pouting over a bowl of oatmeal, her eyelids heavy with exhaustion. The dogs announced her arrival at around five in the morning. I can't believe she got herself out of bed after so little sleep. "The new boy is hot," she says.

I start tackling the pile of dishes in the sink, watching Zack work from the window. "That's the idea," I say.

"Are you happy you came home?" Jami's not looking at me as she asks this. She's staring at her spoon, like she just asked herself the question, but she accidentally did it out loud.

"I missed you guys."

"I can't believe I live here."

"There are too many animals. You have to get rid of them. It's gross."

"I will."

"What happened to this place?" I ask. I feel like I keep trying to get this conversation started.

"Mom's been going through some stuff," she says. "And me, too, I guess. Charles and I are in a fight."

"Oh," I say, not wanting her to shift the subject to a guy I hope never to meet. "Are you okay?"

"My life sucks."

"You won't always live here," I say. "Everything is temporary."

"You don't understand, Benny. I think I am. I think I'm going to live with Mom forever." She drops her head back, slumping in her chair. "Forever," she repeats, her eyes closed. "Twenty-four and living with my mother."

I join her at the table, still holding a dirty bowl. "Lots of people move back in with their parents."

"I'm not lots of people."

"You've been here for a year. It's just now getting to you?"

"No. This is the first time I've had someone listen to my complaints."

"How about you help me clean the place, get rid of the animals, and give Mom a hand? I could use a little assistance. Besides the new hot boy, I mean."

Jami pushes her chair back from the table. "I don't have time to help Mom," she says. "I'm too busy trying to figure out how to leave her."

In Charge of Our Days and Our Nights.

I can tell from Jami's side of the near-constant cell phone conversations she has with Charles that he's a bully. She spends at least half the time she's on the phone apologizing. The other half she's listening with a pained look on her face, like she's being told the worst news and she's not sure how she's going to deal with it. I've seen her hang up on him more than once. There was a time she slammed her cell phone shut, opened the front door, and threw the phone out onto the lawn. She curses at him, calls him names, and swears she never wants to talk to him again. Then, in the middle of the night, I can hear one half of their reconciliation. This happens so often I've come to loathe the sound of his name.

Charles.

It's just not a great name. I don't trust it. My sister's a

pierced semipunk who dresses like a teenager because that's all she can emotionally handle. What the hell does a boy named Charles look like? I imagine him with pink chunks of hair, safety pins down both legs of his jeans, an unplayed guitar always strapped to his back.

The next time I see Jami after she hangs out with Charles, there are angry welts of purple streaking down her neck. Hickeys.

"We made up," is all she says.

In the Garage.

From the door of the garage, Mom watches me clean. In less than two days, I've emptied out a small path that runs along the middle of the garage, just wide enough for me to walk through. It's an amazing accomplishment.

Mom eases herself into a rocking chair I've uncovered. "I've never noticed this before," she says, "but now that you've lost all that weight, I can see how much you look like your Aunt Ellen."

My father's sister. The anorexic. See what she's doing here?

I keep myself focused on cleaning. "We have the same hair color," I say. "That's about it."

"And big chin," she notes. "Just don't take after Aunt Ellen *too* much."

I take a moment before opening a sealed trash bag to pray for nonperishable items. I'm lucky this time; it's filled with gym socks.

"How much more weight are you going to lose?"

Another tricky question. Is she saying I need to lose more, or does she want me to admit I need to lose more, or is she again implying that I have some kind of eating disorder?

"I don't know," I say carefully. "I'm going to see where my body wants to stop losing weight, I guess. I'm trying not to make it a big deal. I know I still have more to go."

"Huh," she says. Then: "Are you seeing anybody?"

Mickey flashes into my head. He hasn't called since his big date. I don't care. No, really. Okay, I care a little. Only because I want him to care. I'd rather be the one who ended up better off.

I say I'm not really seeing anyone seriously. I'm turned away and can't see my mother, but I know she's shaking her head.

"Well, you might want to try a little harder to get out there," she says. "When you lose weight like you did, it's hard to keep all of it off. Odds are you'll pack some of it back on. Don't want to waste your skinniest days."

The words hit me in waves as I dissect layers of passive-aggressive, backhanded complimenting. I can chip away and chip away, but I'll never stop finding additional ways to be humiliated back into the fetal position.

"You really don't have to do this," she says, referring to my cleaning.

"I know." I dump a pile of shoes that appear to have no match into an empty box.

"Don't get rid of that," she says, pointing to a broken child's scooter in the corner of the room I've designated as the trash section. She has figured out that a third of this stuff is going to charity and more than half of the rest is going straight to the trash. Every day I have to move the piles around and lie about which one is to keep, or she'll pull things back out and move them to different piles. I've had to kick her out of the room I'm cleaning no fewer than five times already. "And that stays, too," she says, pointing at an empty box.

"Ma, it's from my Big Wheel. Dad accidentally ran over that thing when I was six. We no longer need the box."

"It's a good-sized box. For wrapping gifts at Christmas."

I am more frustrated with this mess when I realize how much of it Mom hauled here from the old house. I can't find any of my old *Sweet Valley High* books, but this empty box that held a toy from my early childhood—this needs to be preserved.

"It's going in the trash," I say. "Say good-bye to the box, Ma."

"You don't have to be so mean," she pouts. "And I wish you'd let me help you."

I sit down on a stack of *Family Circle* magazines. "I'm not letting you anywhere near this stuff. This is just like the time you didn't let me sell Girl Scout cookies."

Mom sighs with her entire body, shoulders slumping toward her hands. "What horrible thing did I do to you now?"

"You know exactly what you did," I say, scraping dirt out from underneath a thumbnail. "I wanted to sell Girl Scout cookies with my friends in front of the grocery store, but you said someone like me couldn't be trusted around all those cookies."

"That never happened." Mom's voice is getting louder. She rocks backward on her cast a bit, her indignant reaction knocking her off balance. "You make everything sound so much worse than it was."

"Did you let me sell Girl Scout cookies?"

"Yes!"

"Not that year."

"You had a cold!"

"No! You said I was too fat!"

Our fights quickly escalate into yelling. I don't know how she can get me so angry so quickly. When I feel slighted by my mother, when she accuses me of being wrong when I know I'm right, there isn't a decibel loud enough to make me feel relief.

"You make everything into this big sob story," she says. "Poor Benny. Her mom thought she was fat."

"You *did* think I was fat!"

"You were fat! People made fun of you! I didn't want you to live that way."

"You didn't want other people to see me that way."

"Think what you want," she says. "You always do, anyway. I'm sick of defending myself when you turn the truth into lies that make you sound pitiful."

I try taking a deep breath before asking, "What do you mean?"

"Remember when you told my Tupperware party that we were so poor we had to eat fried bologna sandwiches?"

"We did eat fried bologna sandwiches!"

"Because you loved them! You asked for them! For an entire month, I couldn't get you to eat anything else!"

"That's not true."

"It's not the truth you choose to remember." Mom wiggles herself back into the kitchen. "Just like why you're here."

"What?" I'm calling to her because I can't see her. She's left the room to deliver her closing argument from a safe distance, apparently the official Bernstein way to get the last word. "What's that, Ma?"

From somewhere in the house I hear her shout, "You came back here so you'd have another horrible story in the continuing saga of how your mother has ruined your life. Well, have fun!"

A door slams. It's the closest she can get to grounding me these days. It still feels like punishment.

It's Guys Like You, Mickey.

My cell phone says I have one missed call from Mickey.

I call him back. He answers, "Hi."

"You called?"

"Yeah, but I didn't leave a message."

"I see that."

"I was being evasive. I thought it would let you hate me more easily."

I'm not in the mood to play around with Mickey. If he has something to tell me, I'll listen. But I already feel myself detaching. "What's up, Mickey?"

"I don't know if this is going to make any sense, but I thought if I tried to be a halfway decent friend to you, you'd forget that I was going to be a really shitty boyfriend." Then Mickey makes this loud exhale into the phone.

"Did you read that off something?" I ask.

"I practiced it a few times," he admits. "Did you buy it?"

"Not at all."

"Me either. I'm sorry. I just haven't gotten around to calling anyone. It's not about you. I dropped out a little. I do that. No real excuse."

I don't want him to need me any more than I need him, but maybe it's okay to have him call once in a while, just so I have someone always on my side. That could be a good thing.

I tell Mickey about the clutter I'm cleaning, about finding stacks of chair legs in a box, as if at some point over the past year my mother decided she was going to make chairs, or find chairs that needed legs replacing. It's been bothering me for days, trying to come up with an excuse as to why Mom needed chair parts, and why they were worth keeping in storage. I tell Mickey about Jami, and how I don't know what to say to her to make her feel like I want to listen. Whenever I approach my sister, she makes a joke and then pulls away.

"Sounds like me," Mickey says.

"How's your new girlfriend?" I ask.

"She was boring, so I stopped seeing her. Also, she wouldn't answer the phone when I called, so I figured it was time to dump her."

"Yeah, why keep around the girlfriend who won't let you see her?"

"It's why I dumped you."

"Why did you call me, Mickey?" The joke is getting old. I get it; we're not dating. It's *hilarious*. "I haven't heard from you in over a week."

"Feels like longer than that."

It does. It feels like I've been at my mother's house for about a year, when in reality it's been less than half a month. Maybe it's the fact that I'm in a town that actually has seasons instead of the daily perfection of Los Angeles that reinforces the notion that time has passed.

"I miss you, Benny. Is that weird?"

"Yes."

"I know. But there it is. You don't have to do anything about it, but I don't usually miss girls. I miss you. I thought you should know that."

"Thanks."

Maybe Mickey's onto something, and I could make him become my guy friend in a John Hughes–movie sort of way. He'd be my best buddy who once had a fling with me, who cares about me, but never wants to get into a romantic mess again. Granted, this has never worked for me before, because eventually someone breaks down and admits he stayed in love the entire time, or I stayed in love the entire time, and cannot handle the platonic nature of the relationship anymore. Now that I think about it, that's how it goes in those John Hughes movies, too.

"So how's the cleaning going?" he asks.

I suddenly don't want to talk to Mickey about the mundane, the trivial, or anything else. If I keep talking to him, I'll come to depend on him. And over the past week he's shown he's anything but reliable. If I'm being really honest, I don't want him to need me right now, either. I've got enough going on already; I don't need a man on the other side of the country wondering where I am all the time. I shouldn't have called him back. I should have let him be alone.

"I'm still in the middle of all the cleaning," I answer. "I should probably get back to it, actually."

"Sure, right. Bye." Mickey hangs up so quickly I don't know if he heard me reciprocate his good-bye.

Lost.

"Well, since you're here, and you're already cleaning, I need your help."

I can tell by her voice Mom's been crafting that sentence for days now, and she's very happy she got past that part. No mention of our last argument. There won't be, either. Mom doesn't like to rehash.

"What's wrong?" I ask.

We're standing in the garage, which I've yet to make a major dent in because Mom still keeps salvaging half of what I've determined worthy to throw away. I'm now staring down a pile of baby clothes, clothes I don't think were either mine or Jami's, which introduces a whole new set of questions about exactly what baby Mom was holding on to these clothes for.

"I've lost something, and since you're digging around in my stuff, I thought you might come across it."

"What is it?"

Mom opens her mouth and closes it. She bites on her thumbnail. She looks at me and gives a weak smile. "My engagement ring."

"From Dad?"

"Yes, from Dad. What other engagement ring do I have?"

"Well, I don't know."

"Benny, don't make this difficult," she says, her face turning red. "It's bad enough I've lost it."

"How did you lose it?"

She sighs impatiently. "I took it off because I didn't feel right wearing it when I was with Gregory, and I put it somewhere safe, and now I don't remember where that was."

Jesus Christ. It could be literally anywhere. Go check under your bed. Mom might have put her ring there for safekeeping. I'm serious.

"Did you ask Jami?"

"I'm not going to tell Jami, because she'll find it and keep it."

"Did you tell Gregory where you put it? Maybe he knows."

"If I tell Gregory I took off your father's ring, he's going to take it as a sign and it's not."

"You don't think he hasn't noticed you're not wearing it?"

"We don't talk about these things. This isn't therapy, Benny. This is a lost ring."

When I think about the enormity of the stuff in this house and then how small my mother's ring is inside it, I want to cry. Actually, I want to cry for lots of reasons right now, mostly because there was a moment when my mother wanted to take off her beautiful diamond ring, the one that represents her link to my father. She wanted to because of a man who might be reminded that there was once a man who was my father.

"What room do you think you hid it in?" I ask. "Because it'd be easier to start somewhere."

"Honestly, Benny, I did a lot of looking and now with the leg I can't look anymore. I turned my bedroom inside out."

"Do you think it's here in the garage?"

It must have been something in my tone, because Mom gives me the evil eye. "I don't think I put it in the garage, Belinda."

"Sorry."

"Please just find it. I know you can do it. You're good at these things."

"What things?"

"Fixing problems."

Mom hobbles back into the house. I scoop up the baby clothes and toss them into the donate pile. I follow her, deciding to start looking for my mother's engagement ring somewhere she'd never think to look: on her damn left hand.

If my father were alive, everything would be so much simpler. Mom would have someone taking care of her. The bills would be paid. The house would be clean. Dad might not have been an active part of our household, but he made sure things stayed in line. In fact, my father's role in the house was often more like a patrolman; he'd wander the hallways from room to room, checking in to make sure all the homework was finished, the chores were done, and my mom was cleaning something.

It used to make me frustrated, how our house felt stifling under the amount of rules and regulations. It wasn't that my father was strict; he just made sure the house was a place where he'd come home to find peace. I know it doesn't sound loving, but compared to this chaos my family now lives in, remembering the sense of rigid order feels like an escape.

Tsk.

I find Jami sitting on the back porch, smoking a cigarette. She's watching Zack feed the dogs. I sit down next to her. I rest the side of my leg against hers. She doesn't pull away.

"Do you think Zack is happy?" she asks me.

"I don't know. I don't know much about Zack."

"I tried talking to him, but he's kind of an asshole."

"Which means you're now in love with him."

Jami shoves my leg with hers. "You're funny."

"How is he an asshole?"

"He's always got some snarky comment on whatever it is I say to him. Like he thinks I'm stupid. I asked him if he wanted anything, and he told me he'd like peace in the Middle East, a bottle of Jack Daniels, and a hooker who lets him give it to her up the butt."

"Well, you asked. And why are you bothering him, anyway? He's working."

"He's cute. And I hate Charles."

I had a feeling it was leading up to this. "What happened?"

"He borrowed my cell phone and used up all my minutes and didn't tell me so I got jacked on my bill and he won't give me any money." Jami's sentences flood out of her, a stream of words without punctuation or enunciation. Sometimes her mouth barely moves, and the only way you know she's finished with her statement is a pissed-off little *tsk* sound she makes in the corner of her cheek. When that happens all I can do is provide a couple of words to keep her talking.

"Well, that sucks. What're you going to do?"

"I'm gonna be pissed at him until he apologizes, which he probably won't do but he'll, like, buy me something or take me somewhere and that's supposed to be good enough because as long as he's not fucking somebody else, then he thinks he's the best boyfriend in the world. *Tsk.*"

"Right."

"Hey, did I tell you I picked out my baby name?"

My brain sends a jolt of white-hot fear through my entire skull. *Baby.* I tread carefully through my response, sounding like I've just learned the words. "For what?"

"For a *baby.* Duh. Charles and I are gonna name our baby Nelly."

"What baby?" *Pleaseohpleaseohplease no baby. Please no baby. Please no baby.*

"The baby we will have eventually."

Everything in me drains clockwise, through my toes. From the side of the yard, Zack shouts a curse word and pulls his hand away from the big black dog, the one he's named Menace.

"You're going to have a baby with a man you hate?"

"I only hate him today."

And finally I actually hear the question she was asking in the first place.

"You want to name a baby Nelly?"

"Isn't that cute? A little baby named Nelly. And then when he gets older it'll be hilarious, because he'll be this tough white kid named Nelly. That'll be so funny."

"You're naming your kid a joke name on purpose?"

"He's my kid. I can name him what I want." She gives another *tsk* before she stands up, collecting her cigarette box and lighter. She's done talking.

I ask Jami to do me a favor: "Leave Zack alone."

"If you want dibs, Boobs, just be a man and call dibs."

I swat her on the behind. Jami wiggles it at me, daring me to do it again. Zack watches us, shaking his head.

Sugar Daddy.

Gregory wants to give me one of his cars. He drove it over here. It's a tiny, beat-up sports car kind of thing. And, of course, it's red.

I don't know much about cars. This looks like something that was once a sweet little car, but is now an old little car, one of those that drive thousands of miles past what anyone ever expected of them. Gregory is leaning against the driver's side door with his arms folded proudly over his chest.

"It's one I rarely use anyway," he says. "I keep telling myself I'm going to get around to fixing it up, but I haven't. In any event, I figured you could use a car while you're out here. You know, to tool around." He mimes driving a steering wheel like a crazy person when he says that last part. I hope that's not how he envisions my driving.

"I suppose I do need a car. How much can I give you a month to rent it?"

"You're not renting it. You're borrowing it."

"Thanks."

"Don't mention it." Gregory is still leaning against the car. His ability to stay still for long periods of time is admirable. "I appreciate you out here, helping your mother," he says.

"I don't know how much good I'm doing."

"It's doing her good just having you here, even if you weren't lifting a finger. She likes having both her kids at home."

"Most moms want the opposite," I try to joke. It doesn't work.

"The best day of my life was the day Amber told me she wanted to live out the rest of her life here in Oaktown."

"That's nice," I say, because I honestly don't know what else he's expecting to hear. Is he saying I'm not a good daughter for going to California? I ask him, "Did my mother ask you to convince me to move here?"

Mom would welcome a horrific accident that would render me incapacitated so she has to spoon-feed me for months on end, just to have her daughter back at home. Like a living doll. She never hides the fact that she's hurt I moved all the way to California so soon after graduating from college. "All the way to California" is how she puts it, like I hitched a wagon and Joad-ed across the country. I didn't live near her for college—I was down in North Carolina—but I was close enough that she could have visited on weekends. She didn't. Apparently distance does make the heart grow fonder, in a direct correlation with the amount of distance. If I moved to Tokyo, Mom would never stop crying.

"She didn't ask me to do anything," Gregory says. He spits on the ground in front of him and drives the glob into the dirt with his toe. "Your mother is the best woman I've ever met." And with that, he walks past me and into the house.

I slide into the driver's seat of my new car and take it for a spin. It's been so long since I've been behind the wheel of a car, I had no idea how much I'd missed it. One of my favorite things about Los Angeles is the absolute need to own a car. You have to periodically shut yourself off from the rest of the world to get anywhere. The car is your bubble. Your sanctuary. And luckily this sanctuary has a working radio and speakers that can handle the volume I need to feel sane.

I don't even care that the one rock station I can find is blasting Coldplay. I've missed music and solitude this much that I'll even buy into the faux-emotion Chris Martin's trying to sell me. I buy into it so hard-core I don't even feel bad about these tears falling out of my eyes.

Fucking Coldplay.

Watching Paint Dry.

Zack just repainted the front of my mother's garage, so I bought a six-pack of beer and brought it out to him.

"The good news is they're already cold," I say, crouching down to the driveway to open two bottles.

"They would have been anyway. It's freezing out here." He bangs together his hands. "I would've brought something warmer if I had known the temperature was gonna drop like this. I can't believe I'm gonna sit here through another Yankee winter. Damn, it's times like this when I really miss Texas."

"Where in Texas?"

"East. No place you've ever heard of. Small town, baby. I'm small town and proud." He pretends to put on a pair of sunglasses. "Hell, yeah," he whispers.

"Do you want something warm to wear or what?"

"Whatever, darlin'."

I run inside and bring back my dark blue hoodie. He puts it on and turns in a circle, modeling. "Is this a big turn-on for you?" he asks. "Having me wear your clothes?"

I toss off a breezy "Oh, yeah." But also? Sort of. He looks really good in that way pretty boys can make everything look sexier just by touching it. He pulls back his blond hair with one hand and I note how soft his forehead looks. I've never admired someone's forehead before. But Zack's staring at me with his side-grin and intense green eyes, and I find myself searching for something on the ground to focus on, so I don't break out in a blush.

We squat down together on a pair of paint cans and watch the garage door. After someone paints something as big as a wall or a room, the object needs a certain amount of time just being stared at, getting admired for the enormity of the task. I don't know why people do it, but it occurs to me that whenever I've painted something, I needed to sit and look at it for a while, just to set in my mind the new color of the thing.

"So what's happening?" Zack asks.

"Nothing."

"Fantastic."

"You?"

"I painted a garage."

Lately I've been finding reasons to take breaks in my cleaning to come outside and check on Zack. He doesn't seem to mind my company. A couple of days ago we had lunch together, debating which of the dogs in the yard is the ugliest.

"What else?" he asks.

"What else what?"

"What else is happening?"

"I don't know."

He tells me everything he's done in the yard—raking, shoveling, "kicking cat shit into the neighbor's yard"—and everything he's planning to do, including getting a garden started as soon as Jami gets rid of at least five of the eight dogs who call the backyard their permanent home.

Zack opens two more bottles and hands one to me. "Do you miss Los Angeles?" he asks.

"Not like I thought I would."

He takes a swallow of his beer, clears his throat, and announces, "I have a master's degree."

"Are you bragging, Zack?"

"Yes. I think you think I'm just an errand boy. I want you to know I'm highly intelligent."

"What do you care what I think? You made Jami think you're an asshole."

"Your sister wants to ruin my life. She'd love nothing more than to get me naked and against that shed over there, and then make me her baby's daddy."

I can't even find a way to convincingly deny that statement. Zack waits for me to try. When I don't, he gives his side-grin again. This time he seems to be impressed with my reserve.

He continues. "Anyway, I look at you and think, 'This girl is smart.' And today it hits me. 'She thinks you're a moron who paints garages and kicks cat shit. An actual shit-kicker.'"

"I don't, though." Why he cares what I think about him is beyond me. Sure, we've shared a few lunches together, talking about movies and things we have in common. We've swapped a few songs from our iPods, because our musical tastes have almost nothing in common and still seem to complement each other. Last week I made him put on sunscreen, despite his protests. Regardless, I couldn't have made any kind of impression on him that would cause him to wonder what I think of him.

"I don't think of you as an errand boy," I tell him. I want to let him know that I don't judge him for what he's been hired to do, and that when I see Zack and hang out with him, I don't think about the work he's doing. I just think of him as Zack. Nothing more. But when all those words jumble in my head, they unfortunately come out as this sentence, which I say to Zack: "I don't think of you at all."

"You're not very good at giving compliments," he says.

"I'm even worse at taking them."

"Good. Then let me be the first to tell you that I no longer find you to be as ugly as I first thought you were."

He's caught me so off-guard, my throat makes this little clicking noise in response. "Did you just call me ugly?"

"No. I said I used to think you were ugly. See the difference?"

"Is that a compliment?"

"No. It's a fact." He's teasing me. I know he's teasing me, but I can tell there's a kernel of truth in there. Zack just admitted he noticed me, despite having no interest in even looking in my direction. With the slightest insult, he just gave me his highest compliment.

"Then I should probably tell you that now that I've seen you in my clothes, I find you slightly less exciting."

"I can dig that, baby," he says, leaning back on his elbows, pretending to smoke a cigarette.

"So, I'm not as ugly and you aren't as cool," I say.

"Sounds like the start of an amazing relationship," Zack jokes.

It's nice to finally have a memory associated with this house. Now this garage, this color, will always make me think of sitting here drinking beer with Zack.

"Hey, is Zack short for something?"

"Why do you care?" he asks. "You think nothing of me."

"That's not what I meant. And I'm making conversation. We talk about things like the weather, schools we went to, our full names."

"I see. Well, it's short for something, but it's also my middle name. I'm not going to tell you my full name."

"Why not?"

"Because I don't like it."

"Can I guess?"

"Whatever floats your boat, darlin'. Be my guest." That's twice he's called me "darlin'." Yes, I noticed. And yes, I kind of like it.

"Is it short for Zachary?"

"You'll never get it."

"Zack . . . aham."

"No, but I like your creativity."

"Come on, Zack. Tell me your real name."

"I'm never going to tell you because my mother is evil and named me something stupid."

I put my hand out. "Hi. I'm Benny. Have we met?"

Zack takes my hand and shakes it. "Yeah, I believe we just did. Finally."

I Think I'm Goin' Out of My Head.

I'm trying to sleep, but a song has been playing, loudly, downstairs in the living room. At its fourth repetition, I can no longer pretend it will soon be over.

"Well, I think I'm goin' out of my head . . ."

Appropriate, because I am going to lose it. My body aches from days of uninterrupted work, and the few hours of sleep I do score a night are so precious to me that this musical assault makes me want to find the source and kill it. There's a good chance that either a cat or a lizard has stepped on a button somewhere downstairs, tripping the stereo to blast this oldie. I don't understand why it hasn't been turned off yet. Jami must be out, because this is exactly the kind of thing that would have her screaming from the top of the stairs. Where's my mother?

"And I think I'm goin' out of my head . . . 'cause I can't explain the tears that I shed . . ."

It takes all of my strength to drag myself out of the videotape bedroom. I make my way through the dark hallway to the stairs. I only make it halfway down.

My mother is dancing with a man who is not Gregory. He's much shorter than Gregory, just slightly taller than my mom, and I can see the large patch of pink scalp on the top of his head popping through a few strings of gray hair. This man is humming along with the song, his arms around my mother, holding her tight, rocking her back and forth. Mom's got her broken leg kicked up behind her, so she's leaning into this man, letting him hold her upright to sway her back and forth. She's giggling into his neck.

There's an open bottle of wine on the coffee table, which has been pushed off to the side. My mother is in a pretty purple dress that catches sparkles from the nearby candlelight.

I have walked into a romantic moment between my mother and one of her gentleman callers. I wasn't aware she was still entertaining others that weren't Gregory. I wonder if Gregory knows.

If only I'd lived in this house at least once in my life, I might have known about the squeaky stair. But I didn't, so I set it off trying to climb back up the stairs without anyone seeing me. It triggers a growl and yelp from the once-sleeping Pekingese at the top of the steps.

"Benny!" my mother calls, still giggling. "Benny, come meet Paul."

For the next hour I'm curled up into a ball on the corner of the couch, mentally willing my pajamas to become larger and less pajamalike as I meet my mother's man-friend.

Paul is nearing sixty. He barely looks at me while we're talking because he is head-over-heels smitten with every molecule of my mother. He gazes at her like he just discovered love. I swear I can see his heart beating in his chest. Every time Mom says something he laughs this charmed laugh, like we're at a wonderful dinner party. Mom tells me she met Paul at a ballroom dancing class she took last year. He is her favorite dance partner, and she is, as far as he's concerned, his *only* dance partner. Paul tells me this while keeping his eyes firmly fixed on my mother's face. They both have the same pink glow to their cheeks. Mom can't meet his gaze for more than a few seconds before she looks to her lap, a grin exploding across her face.

"I could go back to bed," I offer, wanting to give them

even more privacy than they're probably expecting. I want to walk out the door and keep going. I know this is nice, all the goofy love smiles and sweet talk, but it's still my mom, and this guy is so quiet and singularly focused on my mother's every breath that I'd much rather be somewhere far away while this is going on. Not right upstairs. It's just way too close to the proximity of where my mother will soon be canoodling.

Yes, *canoodling*. People in their fifties canoodle. They do not make out. They do not tongue-kiss. They cavort and canoodle, and you're not going to talk me out of this notion.

I can't leave the house and my sister isn't home and it's so late but I'm not going to fall asleep as long as there's dancing going on downstairs. Mom doesn't seem to mind that she's blasting a Beatles ballad so loudly I feel like I'm living inside the stereo. I suppose that's still preferable to the sound of her giggling. And that's even better than the sound of nothing, which means that downstairs, mouths are touching.

I can't take it. I can't sit here and picture my mother with a man. The only place I know where I can be right now is in the past.

The past. Los Angeles.

I check the clock. It's almost two. Mickey would still be up.

I pause for a moment to think of red cars, and then reach for my cell.

Long Distance.

"Hey, you." I can hear the caution in his voice, approaching me like I'm a crazy girl. I haven't spoken to him in a while. He's probably wondering if I'm calling this late to dump him, drunk-style, or confess undying love.

"This may sound odd," I say, "but I really need you to talk to me and keep talking until I can sleep."

"You want me to be boring, so I'm like a sleeping pill?"

"I want you to be a fantastic distraction." I tell him about my mother's date and its current proximity to my head.

"That's not fun," Mickey says.

"No, sir."

"I was just about to make myself a late-night snack of a tuna fish sandwich and beer. I could talk you through this process."

I appreciate that he doesn't want to talk about us, or why we haven't spoken. He seems to understand I just need to hear his voice and have it take me far away from my present reality.

"That sounds perfect," I tell him.

I'm on my daybed with the phone, the cord stretching across the room. In the thousands of things I've uncovered since I got here, you'd think there'd be a cordless phone by now. Three different fax machines, a working mimeograph machine, and five pagers, but not one cordless phone.

I hear a clattering on Mickey's end of the phone. "Okay, I've got all of my ingredients on the counter. I'm about to open the jar of mayonnaise."

"What kind of mayonnaise?"

"Are you crazy? Best Foods. The only kind."

"You know out here it's called Hellmann's?"

"Wow," Mickey deadpans. "That's fascinating."

"I bet you didn't know that."

"I didn't *need* to know that. Virginia is making you *bor-ring.*"

"You're the one describing a sandwich, dude."

Which he then does, before going on to describe the taste of his beer. Mickey tells me about the view of Los Angeles from his porch, and how the air has turned colder earlier than usual. I tell him about all of the dogs, and how I've found myself talking to them, sometimes. It concerns me, because I fear it means I'm starting to accept them. We talk about whether it's time for him to get a dog, if he's mature enough and responsible enough to have a living creature depend on him for survival. He plans on naming the dog after a Quentin Tarantino character.

I tell him about my sister's baby, Nelly. When he finally stops laughing, he tells me about a recent horrible date with a girl who dragged him to a hip-hop bar and then had an asthma attack in front of the fog machine. This time when Mickey tells me about seeing a new girl, I don't feel jealous. I don't feel like I'm in second place. I'm interested because not only do I want him to be happy, I want him to stay my friend.

It's almost five in the morning when I hear Mickey yawn.

"I should let you go," I whisper. My house is dark and quiet. I'm glad I wasn't on a cordless after all; I'm not sure the battery would have made it.

"I don't normally stay on the phone this long with a woman if I'm not going to at least get some phone sex."

"Oh, here we go."

"Nah, I'm not going to make you talk dirty to me. You had a rough night already."

"Hey, Mickey?"

"You're not singing the song, are you?"

"No. I'm genuinely trying to get your attention."

He pauses here, refraining from commenting on how much of his attention I got. Instead he asks, "Then what is it, Benny?"

"Thanks," I say.

"No problem. What are friends for?"

More Fun Facts.

In the morning, Mom wants to know what I think of Paul. I'd love to finish one mug of coffee before falling into a potential fight with a family member.

"I don't know anything about Paul," I tell her.

"He liked you," she says. "He says you have a nice smile."

I don't remember smiling anywhere near him. "He likes you," I say, which is a huge understatement.

"Oh, yes," Mom says, using this tone that makes me uncomfortable, one that implies he likes her in ways I don't want to imagine. "He has a son, you know."

"No, I don't know."

Mom clacks her fingernails on the kitchen table, changing her strategy. "Paul's son is very attractive. He's a teacher. Algebra."

"I'm not dating your boyfriend's son."

Mom clacks her fingernails again. "Well, you're in no

mood to be a nice person today, so let me just tell you: Paul thinks I stopped seeing Dave, and Dave knows about Gregory, but Gregory doesn't know about Paul or Dave, and I'd like to keep it that way for now, okay?"

"Is this one of Paul's son's logic charts? Because I sucked at algebra. And who's Dave?"

Mom folds her arms defensively. "He lives in Philly. He comes here to visit his parents. You'll like Dave. He does impressions."

So my mom has three boyfriends, right now. *Three.* And not that it matters, but I don't even have one.

Even keeping one boy interested can take so much energy, but she's got three men attracted to her, and is even able to hide some of them from the others? The ones who know about each other—how are they okay with this? Perhaps it's a generational thing; people who grew up in the sixties all still believe in free love.

I go out back to find Zack, because I know he'll have some interesting thoughts on this.

"Your mom's kinda slutty," is all he concludes.

Maybe Zack doesn't have all the answers.

Places Where You Will Not Find My Mother's Diamond Ring (A List That Would Make Jane Proud).

1. Her bedroom. Anywhere in her bedroom.

2. Okay, maybe it could be in the small drawer next to her bed, but you'll have to pay me millions of dollars to open that thing. I have suffered enough traumas for one lifetime, so I'm not opening my mother's private bedroom drawer.

3. In her bathroom.

4. Okay, maybe it could be on the top shelf of her linen closet in the bathroom. Again, I'm not going to put my hand anywhere where I might find something that has to do with my mother at her most intimate. Whatever is behind that box of douche, I don't want to know what it is. If it's my mother's ring, she deserves to never find it again, hiding it back there.

5. In the kitchen cabinets.

6. In any of the nineteen sugar canisters I found inside my mother's cabinets.

7. Behind the couch.

8. Under the couch cushions.

9. In my mother's jewelry box.

10. On my mother's left hand. (I was really hoping it'd be there.)

Say Cheese.

In the back of the garage, I find a box of pictures. I have found six of these boxes already while cleaning. One was in the kitchen, underneath a box of cookbooks, containing wedding pictures of family members I've never seen before. Two were of people I learned weren't even relatives. Apparently my grandmother was into collecting photos of *other people's* families. She'd find them at a garage sale or on the side of the curb ready for the trash. All these people, long dead now, still living on in a box that hadn't been opened in decades, made me feel responsible for them, as if I should find their families and give them back their memories.

This box just holds pictures of me. At first I'm insulted it was way in the back of the garage, underneath a milk crate filled with soup cans. But I'm quickly over it when I lift the lid to find a collection of some of my worst moments, preserved with a matte finish.

I don't know that I've ever had a good haircut. I know everybody says this when they look back on old pictures, but really my hair was just shameful. It looks like I'm constantly wrestling with an animal, and I've chosen to wear my latest trophy pelt right above my forehead for everyone to admire. In the fifth grade I had a "flop" haircut—a skater cut that meant my bangs hung over my right eye, giving me the nonchalant head-flip so totally rad back in the day. When pictures came around that year they wouldn't let me wear my hair in my face. Instead I've got it sprayed back in a horrendous wing that looks like an eagle is trying to shelter me from danger overhead.

It only takes a few minutes for me to realize what all these pictures have in common. In every single one, I look thin. If you had stumbled upon this box, right now, you'd wonder why anybody would have ever made a single comment to me about my weight. I look like every other kid with an ordinary childhood. If anything, you'd wonder if someone used to torture me weekly with a Flowbee.

This means one of two things: either I never really had a fat past, and my mom made me think I was a big kid when I wasn't, or Mom has gotten rid of all my fat pictures. Which one is better? There is no right answer to this question. I'm screwed either way. I don't know whether to feel sorry for myself or angry with my mother or just roll my eyes and know this is how she is, and there's probably another box around here that's filled with all of my fat pictures. Maybe it's this one underneath the skinny pictures.

The box is small and red. Using my keys, I slice through the masking tape that seals it shut.

It's not filled with pictures.

They are letters, handwritten, to my mother, from a man. They are in one stack, without envelopes, bound together with a rubber band. They're dated from fifteen years ago.

In these letters, someone is telling my mother how fantastic she is, how he can't believe how lucky he is to have met her, and how heartbreaking he finds her face, her skin, the way she walks into a room.

These letters are not from my father. They are signed "G."

Gregory?

The last letter in the bundle tells her how he can't take any of this anymore, how he knows he'll never be truly happy in his life because he'll always want the other life, the one where every decision was different, the one where they could have been together.

It's when I'm reading that last letter that my stomach drops its bottom, and a thousand questions flood my head.

So the Next Time I See My Mother, It Goes a Little Something Like This:

She's in Dad's old recliner, reading a romance-mystery novel, the kind that pretends to be about history, but is really about people getting it on during a time period that involves corsets or—even better—muskets. She's wearing glasses. A stack of pillows on the edge of the chair keeps her casted leg elevated. I try to walk past without her noticing. It doesn't work. She moves her book to the side and gives me the once-over. "That's not the shirt you're going to wear to Gregory's, is it?" she mothers. My hands immediately go to the fabric, patting to make sure it's still there.

"I don't think I'm going to Gregory's tonight," I say. We're supposed to have dinner and a movie with Amber, but I don't think I'd be able to sit in his house for more than an hour without needing to ransack his closets, looking for old letters in my mother's handwriting. "I'm not feeling well," I say, holding my head and my stomach at the same time.

I'm not a very good liar when I'm on the spot. I need to have the lie's backstory, enough details to truly believe in the lie, almost convincing myself it's what's really happening. Since I didn't know I wanted to skip out on Gregory's until a few minutes ago, I hadn't had enough time to decide which part of me was ailing. But then again, the truth is both my head and my stomach feel like someone's jamming broomsticks through them.

"Maybe you should eat something," she says, lifting her book to resume reading.

"Hey, Ma?" I say, feeling brave for a moment. "I found something in the garage."

"What's that?"

If I ask her this right now, I'm going to know the answer. But I don't know if I'm ready to find out my mother wasn't faithful to my father. I don't want to know that Gregory has been around much longer than I ever could have imagined.

I chicken out, picking the lesser of two evils. "I found all these pictures of me from when I was little."

"Oh, good. Will you bring them in? I want to make decent family photo albums, finally. Now that I'm all laid up, might as well."

"Do you have another box of mine with photos that are . . . less flattering?"

Mom shuts the book and places it in her lap. "Where is this going, Belinda?"

"They were just all skinny pictures of me. No fat ones. Did you hide the fat ones? Did you throw them away?"

Mom tries to rise dramatically from her reclined position, but nobody can get out of a recliner easily, much less a woman with the use of only one of her legs. She wiggles and thrusts, flailing in the chair like a gasping fish. Wow, it's funny. I take a moment to study a nearby plant leaf.

"I'm sorry," I say. "Ma, I'm sorry."

She finally gets herself out of the chair, her lip curled in a sneer. "Honestly, Benny," she says. "What you must think of me."

"I don't," I say. It's a sentence that means nothing, I realize, but I don't know what else to say. "I don't think anything bad, Ma."

"Why do you stay here, anyway? If we're such horrible people. Why would you ever want to stay here with us?"

Mom doesn't wait for an answer. She hobbles out of the room, staggering on her cast looking like she's had too much to drink.

Saying "Grace." Repeatedly. Into Voice Mail.

I cannot get my subletter on the phone. Grace doesn't answer when I call my house phone. She doesn't respond to email. I even tried reaching Wendy, who admitted she hasn't seen Grace for some time, while still attempting to assure me that everything is fine.

It's not an irrational need, to know that your apartment still exists and that the person living in it hasn't gone completely crazy. I wish I'd been smart enough to remember to take my building manager's phone number with me. Grace had promised to drop off rent payments in the box in the lobby, as I wasn't technically allowed to sublet in the first place. I've basically given my home and all of my belongings over to a broke college student who just moved to Los Angeles. Perhaps I've made a mistake.

I call Mickey again, but get his voice mail. I leave this message: "Hi, I know you're busy, because you haven't been calling me back. Maybe I used up all of your time the other night. Is that it? You only have so many hours for me? I'm not saying that to be mean. I honestly wonder if I just freaked you out by needing you. I don't need you. Really. Except I need you right now. Maybe you don't care. I hope you care a little, because I sort of have a favor to ask. It's a big favor, but it won't take you long or anything. Can you please call me back?"

Jami runs into my room. The pursed grin on my sister's face lets me know that she's up to something. I realize it's been about three days since I've seen her last. Does she miss us when she's gone, or does she think of us as paused, waiting for her to return and pick up right where she left off? She never says hello or hugs me as if time has passed in the slightest.

"You have to come see this," she says. "Mom's talking in her sleep."

Downstairs, Mom's upright in Dad's recliner; the romance-mystery-history-sex novel has fallen to the space between the chair's arm and her lap.

"Her eyes are open," I say.

"It's really creepy," Jami warns me. "But so worth it. Ask her a question. She's like an oracle."

"Ma?"

Her sapphire eyes are fixed on mine. Her hair floats around her face like she's looking down a gust of wind. Arms folded across her chest, leg propped on the recliner's footstool—she resembles a broken genie.

"What is it?" Mom sounds more than a little irritated.

"You okay?"

She gives a huge sigh, followed by an angry glance at the wall beside her, as if she was asking our home audience if they could believe how stupid her child is. "I'm fine," she says.

"Ma," Jami says. "Tell her about the waffles." Then Jami turns around, her hand jammed over her mouth, holding in giggles.

"Waffles!" Mom scoffs. "Don't you start with me about the fucking waffles." Her face is flushed. She's shaking her head, snarling. "All day long I have to deal with your bullshit, and then you get fucking started with me about fucking *waffles*?"

Jami squats down, her head between her knees. I can hear her shuddery laughter.

Mom's turned her fury to me, so I cannot even break a smile. It's unnerving, seeing my mom so angry in her dream state. Are you supposed to wake someone up when she's like this? Are you supposed to leave her alone? Let her talk it out? I have no idea.

"I'm sorry," I say, hoping that's enough.

"I'll bet you're fucking sorry. What the hell is in a waffle, Benny?"

Who knew there'd be a question-and-answer period in Crazyland? "Eggs and milk?"

"Exactly."

She's so smug and justified in this answer that I can't help it. I have to laugh. I try opening my mouth and setting my jaw, so it doesn't *look* like I'm laughing. Maybe Mom doesn't understand laughter in her current condition, anyway.

She's not done. "And I know you touched the clocks, Benny."

"What clocks?"

"Oh, God," Jami roars, still on the floor beside me.

"The clocks in my bedroom," Mom says. "The ones with the ghosts. Jesus Christ, Benny, I said not to touch them because the ghosts would be mad and then you go and touch them and now the ghosts are all flying around."

Jami stands up, jumps, and clasps her hands together. "Caught one, Ma!"

"You're grounded," Mom says back, one finger pointed in the wrong direction. "I have to pee."

Jami grabs my arm. "What if she pees right there on the chair? I won't be able to take it!"

"Don't let her pee."

"Is this all the lasagna you're going to give me?" Mom shouts, calling out toward the kitchen. "I ordered Chinese."

Jami is practically hyperventilating, doubled over. She gasps between her words, repeating, *"I . . . ordered . . . Chinese!"*

This is starting to make me a little nervous. What if we're staring down the future of our mother? Mom loses her keys seemingly every six hours. She forgets movies she's seen and books she's read, only remembering halfway through that she's heard the story before. Sometimes she'll forget whom she's called once the person answers the phone. Mom jokes all the time that she's slowly succumbing to Alzheimer's. What if this is what it's going to look like?

"We should leave her alone," I say.

"No way." Jami twirls her tongue ring between her teeth as she plots her next move. "Hey, Ma. Which one of us is your favorite?"

Mom looks up to the ceiling. "Your father," she says.

"No, of me and Benny. Who do you love more? It's me, right?"

Mom's eyes have gone soft. "Go get your father," she says. "He should be here."

It's that moment where it's too late, when your eyes close and your neck involuntarily twists your head back to protect you from the now, because everything went too far and it's not going to be funny anymore.

"I miss him," she says, looking right at me. Her eyes seem so clear and focused.

"I miss him, too, Ma," Jami says immediately.

"Why hasn't he come home? I'm so tired, and he said he'd be here by ten. I'm starting to worry."

Jami kneels down next to my mom and takes her hand. "He'll be here," she says. She looks at me and dips her head. My turn.

I say, "He called a few minutes ago and said he's on his way."

"Oh, good." Mom's lips are trembling in the corners. "He works so late, sometimes I get worried when he's driving home at night." She asks me, "Did he say if he ate?"

"He said he would pick up Burger King."

Mom sighs, resigned. "Now the car's going to smell like fries."

I can't believe how long she's been asleep and awake. "Help me get her up," I say to Jami.

We grab under her arms and ease her to standing. Mom looks at me, but her eyes are vacant again. "Dad should get a cell phone," she says. "Maybe we could buy him one for Father's Day, if we all pool together."

"That's a good idea, Ma," I say. "He'd like that."

"He would. I think he would."

Once we get Mom to her own bed, her eyes close. Jami takes my hand, like when we were little, when we were about to cross the street.

"I'm sorry," she says. "I didn't expect that."

"It's okay. It was nice to have him back for a few minutes."

Jami turns to me, smiling, eyes loaded with tears. "It really was."

Looking for a Signal.

My cell phone's reception hates this house, so I'm standing on the back porch, bending myself into different positions, trying to keep four bars going long enough to leave messages for both Grace and Mickey. I'm past being polite with Grace. I'm now ordering her to call me back. I only wish it sounded as threatening as I want it to. What's that thing about possession being nine-tenths of the law? She's living in my place, paying my rent and bills, avoiding my calls. Am I down to a single tenth now?

I show more restraint leaving Mickey's message. I'm still asking him for a favor. "Hey, Mickey. Benny here. Still need you to swing by my place, if you could. Just let me know if it smells like dead girl, or if you find the hallway littered with heroin junkies. You don't even have to go into the building. Just let me know it hasn't burned to the ground. But if you wanted to, knock on my door, just five blocks from your apartment, remember? You could hit it on your way to get a Jamba Juice. Not that I'm asking you to do anything, or trying to plan your day. Hey, it's starting to look like you're mad at me. I'm hanging up now."

"You have excellent communication skills." I whip around to find Zack leaning against the porch rail, enjoying himself.

I jam my cell phone into my pocket. "It's a gift," I say.

He points at my chest. "You should be wearing a sweater. It's cold today."

"I was only going to be a minute."

"Can it be more minutes? I've got something I want to show you." Zack is holding on to the back of his neck with one hand, a pose I thought worked only for models in magazines. It's pretty damn irresistible.

Fifteen minutes later—and please don't judge me—I'm sitting in the front seat of Zack's truck, listening to a country song he wanted me to hear. The song is really good. And look, it's not vehicular romance if the boy invites *me* into his car. It doesn't work the other way around.

Zack fiddles with the gearshift, staring out the windshield at the barking dogs. "You know how in movies and books they always use five-five-five when they're giving out someone's phone number?" he asks.

"Yeah. I hate that."

"I'm always happy when someone doesn't do that, when they use a real number."

"Me, too," I say. "But then I really, really want to call it."

"Yes! That's what I was just about to say. And that's why they use the five-five-five in the first place, to keep us from calling. But it's because they don't want me to do it that I want to do it." Zack shakes his head like he's figured out one of life's mysteries. Then he lurches forward to turn up the volume. "Okay, shh," he says. "Here's the part I want you to hear."

I'm only telling you this other thing because I know you're wondering, so: Zack's truck is red. But that means nothing because Mickey is either dead or no longer wants to talk to me. Either of which means the red vehicles now mean nothing. Red is just a color. Paris is just a city.

"What's wrong?" Zack asks. He points at his face. "You're all like . . ." He pulls the corners of his mouth down and scowls.

"Sorry. I was thinking about Paris."

"Yeah, fuck that place. But how come?"

I explain my theories on Paris, and how my parents didn't get to go there. "It's the city that represents everything that never happened," I conclude.

Zack takes this in. "That's one way to look at it," he says. He's pulled a toothpick out of a small box on his dashboard, and he's now working it around in his mouth. "Want to hear another?"

"Okay."

"Paris is always going to be there. Longer than either of us will be alive, there will be Paris. It can mean that, too. Paris exists to represent all of the things you didn't get to have with someone. 'We'll always have Paris' doesn't mean 'Yippee! You're the best thing that's ever happened to me.' It means 'We didn't get a fair shot. We didn't get to do everything, but I'm grateful for what I got with you.'"

I lean back, my head against the passenger window. "Look at you, using that master's degree."

"I'm brainy. I've also watched *Casablanca* a lot."

"Wouldn't have pegged you for a Bogie fan."

Zack pulls another CD from the case strapped to his sun visor. "You don't know much about me, sweetheart."

"What else, then?"

He punches a few buttons on the stereo. An R.E.M. song fills the silence as Zack appears to be mulling over which tidbit of information he wants to give out. "I've got one, but you're not going to like it."

"A scandal!"

Zack side-grins, his eyes meeting mine. "Pay attention. Ready?"

"This must be good, if you're asking me to prep myself."

He's chuckling, grinning wider now. "It's a doozy," he says. "It'll change everything. Are you sure you want to know?"

Now I have to know. I turn down Michael Stipe and lean in toward Zack. "Hit me."

"I'm gonna tell you, and then you'll want to hit me," Zack says.

"Quit stalling."

"I'm not single."

I sit back. "Oh."

"I didn't think I needed to tell you, but lately we've been so chummy—"

There's a great word. *Chummy.* Like I'm made of shark bait. I hold up my hand. "I get it," I say.

"I like you, Benny. But I can't like you. So I thought you should know that I'm not likable. Don't be wasting your time."

"Wasting my time on what?"

He puffs up his chest, comically, acting like this is all a big joke. "Pining for me."

"I am not pining for you."

"I'm flattered you're interested in me."

"I'm not. You brought this up. I was just sitting here."

"And I already told you that I don't think you're as ugly as I used to think."

"Zack. Stop it. I don't like you."

I don't. I'm only disappointed because now we have to change our dynamic. He can't be the guy I hang out with most of the day. Or can he? I don't know. We're not doing anything other than talking. It's not my responsibility to monitor our time together. He's the one with someone to answer to.

"I'm glad we had this talk," he says.

"It was completely unnecessary. You're my hired hand."

"You can't use my hand, either, honey." He kills the car battery and opens his door. "Besides," he says, "it sounds like you've got a boy back in La-La Land."

"I don't." In fact, every boy I know these days is finding a way to get the hell out of my general vicinity.

For the record, I'd like to point out that I wasn't even trying to approach Zack and he found a way to turn me into someone who needed to be dumped. I'm getting really tired of other people deciding to make me just as single as I've been all along.

Seriously.

Not worth it.

Going Out. In Public. With My Family.

Eating at a restaurant. It seems like such a simple thing. Families do it every day. But not my family. When my family goes out to eat, it's always a disaster.

We've never talked about this. I've never asked Mom, "Hey, ever notice that on the ten or so times we've all gone to dinner as a family, someone cries during the drive home?"

My parents almost got a divorce at an Italian restaurant. The fight began over the complimentary garlic bread they brought to the table. Dad asked for seconds. Mom thought it was inappropriate to ask for more of something that was "a gift" in the first place. Dad thought Mom was trying to keep Jami and me from eating the cheesy, buttery bread. Mom, knowing Dad was right, countered that Dad was trying to control her and the entire restaurant, by having everyone cater to his whims. I don't remember all of the fight, but I have a vivid memory of Jami, who was eight years old at the time, screaming across the table, *"I don't want the fucking calamari!"*

We tried going out as a family for my graduation. I had to be at the ceremony hall by seven, but Dad was enjoying himself, bragging that his eldest was about to go to college. He kept ordering drinks for people—strangers—who were seated nearby, and I remember he was trying to smoke a cigar for the first time. Mom was mortified with Dad's newly found bravado, and Jami was mortified to be seen with her family— a by-product of having recently turned fifteen. It gets a little fuzzy here, but I remember that I was crying because we were half an hour late to my graduation. I had to sneak through the ceremony after it had already started to find my seat, which ended up being taken because everybody had filed in. I had to squat on the floor, pretending to be seated in a chair where there was none. My thighs were screaming from exhaustion by the time my name was called, and I almost fell trying to walk up the stairs. My family was forced to watch the ceremony from backstage, too late to score a seat. There are no photos of my graduation. The security guards wouldn't let Dad take pictures from behind the podium.

Okay, so you get the point. I don't have to tell another ten stories. I don't have to make it any clearer that it's always a bad idea when my family enters a restaurant together, right?

So. Mom wants us all to go to Benihana. There is no talking her out of this. "We haven't all gone out as a family," she says. "Not since you got home. Gregory likes this place we've all gone to a few times. I'd like you to come."

This means that Mom, Jami, Gregory, and probably Amber have gone out as a faux family. I know it's perfectly normal for people who know each other to eat in public restaurants, but it makes me so furious. How come the four of them can pretend to be a normal, functioning family unit, but the four of us couldn't get it together enough to make it through one trip to the salad bar at Sizzler without someone freaking out next to the croutons? Is it because they're *not* a family that everybody's so cool they don't need to eat in front of a television to distract them from each other? I had to find out.

Bring it on, Benihana. Give me a normal night. Let's see if you can do it. But first, you should know the rules.

Jami doesn't like foods with colors, textures, consistencies, sharp edges, wiggly parts, things with eyes, things with legs, things with tendons, things that are pinker on the inside than the outside, prickly parts, things you have to open and eat the insides, food that isn't covered in cheese, food that isn't white, food that requires dipping or ripping or dunking. At this restaurant, Jami will eat a bowl of white rice with salt and pepper on it. She may allow a small sprinkling of soy sauce. She will eat two pot stickers, plain, but will insist on calling them egg rolls, even when they clearly aren't, because the phrase *pot stickers,* to her, sounds like an exotic animal and, therefore, gross.

Mom has no internal volume control. She gets louder the more inappropriate the comment. She is flabbergasted when people are offended, because she assumes the thought in her head is the exact same thing everyone else is thinking. Then she gets upset if you ask her to tone it down. She thinks *you're* the one with the problem.

Now let's go have some fun!

Waiting for the table-stove to warm up, Jami is staring at our chef. The man, dressed in white with a tall chef hat, wearing a name tag that declares him as Heio, seems to be purposefully keeping his eyes from meeting any of ours.

"I bet he's not even Japanese," Jami mutters.

Heio shoots a quick glance in Jami's direction. She immediately studies her menu.

I watch Mom and Gregory hunch together, talking. They

look like a set of parentheses, keeping the rest of the world out of their conversation. It's as if they're on a game show, debating their final answer, and everything is riding on what they order to drink. It's not that I want to know what they're talking about, but I wonder why it has to be so intensely secret. I get it: you like each other. Now straighten up and include us.

Does Mom turn into punctuation marks with Dave or Paul? How is she able to keep all of these men in her life without any guilt? If she and Gregory were writing letters to each other while Dad was alive, how many more men has Mom been seeing over the years?

I can't think about this because it's starting to make me feel sick. I order a beer and ask Jami about her latest job interview.

"They said I sounded like the perfect fit," she tells me, "but then this morning I got a letter in the mail. Who sends a rejection letter in the mail?"

"Maybe they interviewed lots of people."

"Maybe they never wanted to talk to me ever again. I just wanted to answer their phones. It's not like they're the government or anything."

Heio drops a few flecks of water onto the stainless steel stove before us. The drops sizzle and wiggle in the heat. Satisfied, the chef goes into his knife acrobatics, clanking the blades against the metal appliance before flipping them into the air.

All of us watch the floor show, happy to have something to hold our attention. My mom narrates, because something inside of her needs to hear the English language spoken at all times. "Look how he does that," she says. "Up! And then he catches it."

I close my eyes and listen to Mom tell the story of our

Japanese dinner. "He's moving the rice around the skillet so it browns evenly. I like fried rice, do you? I know Gregory doesn't like the fried egg, but that's my favorite part. Look how he's using soy sauce there. And up! Goes the knife. Ha! He caught it again. And the shrimp. There goes the shrimp. Look how fast he's cutting. Up!"

Something wet and warm smacks the center of my forehead. I open my eyes. My family is laughing at me. Heio is giving me the smallest of smirks.

"Did you just hit me in the face with a shrimp?" I ask. But Heio keeps his attention focused squarely on his routine. More knives and food fly through the air. He gestures for Jami to open her mouth. She does, and Heio flips a slice of carrot between her lips. Mom cheers. Gregory watches, quietly, smiling. It's a proud smile he's wearing, like he choreographed this entire evening, and it couldn't have gone any better for him.

He catches me staring at him. "Do you like Oriental food?" he asks.

I nod and lean forward on my elbows toward him. The beer is working and now I'm feeling braver. Let's amp this dinner up a notch, shall we? Let's really *bond.*

I say, "I was wondering how you and Mom met." I might not get him to admit to writing any letters here tonight, but maybe I could get a time frame that would place them in the same city back when someone named "G" was heartsick in love with my happily married mother.

Gregory sucks his lower lip into his mouth as he stares at the flying food. I can't tell at first if he's going to answer me. "That's a long story," he finally says.

"I'd love to hear it," I say. "Mom hasn't mentioned."

"What's going on?" Mom barges in. "What'd she ask you?"

Gregory leans away, back into his parenthetical aside with my mother. I can no longer hear them.

Heio serves our food in small bowls, bows quickly, and then takes a break. It's quieter with the table-stove off.

"Your mother and I knew each other a long time ago," Gregory says.

"We met at a job," she says. "When your father wasn't working."

Then it all flooded back, that weird period in my childhood when Dad was home and Mom was seemingly always working. Dad couldn't find a job for the better part of a year. He grew a beard, took long walks, and developed an odd addiction to cooking shows. That was the year Jami and I always tried to find a friend's house for dinner or sleepovers, so we didn't have to be home when Mom and Dad fought about money.

"You remember I worked for that bank?" she asks.

"Vaguely," I say. "You didn't work there for long." I'm trying to sound dismissive, but my legs have turned to jelly. The letters were written exactly when she was working for that bank. So there it is. Mom and Gregory were in love when I was a little girl, when I was home with Dad, when he was unemployed. My dad was home and my mom was carrying on some kind of something I don't want to think about with this man who pretends he just happened to become part of my mother's life. And suddenly I'm grateful for Paul and Dave, and I hope there's a Jake and a Travis and a Carl, and I want to watch Gregory find out about all of these other men and I want him to hurt.

Dad was home, unable to find employment and depressed about his future, while Mom was with Gregory. I wonder how much he knew, and if that's why they were fighting all the time. Maybe he'd found some of the letters.

I force myself to remain calm. I don't want them to see my

face starting to burn. This isn't the time, this isn't the place, and this isn't how I want everyone to find out what I know. I use all of my strength to become very, very cool.

"I was terrible at that job," Mom says. "But Gregory worked in a different department. We used to see each other in the break room."

"You were always running late," he says.

They're smiling as they eat their food, stealing little glances at each other. I want to take Gregory's hand and mash it to the sizzling skillet. I want to watch his skin melt and stick to the metal, flecking off and curling next to the little shrimp legs that remain on the table-stove.

"So you were just friends?" Jami asks, teasing. She kicks me gently under the table, thinking I'll find this as amusing as she does. I stare at the inside of my glass to keep from giving anything away.

"Your mother was the nicest woman at that bank," Gregory says. "They were wrong to fire her."

"You got fired?" Jami asks, excited to have yet another thing in common with our mom. "What'd you do?"

Mom shakes her head. "I left one of the doors unlocked. Nothing happened, but when I did it the second time, they said I wasn't handling the responsibility well."

"They overworked you," Gregory says, massaging Mom's back with one hand. My brain is screaming, *Hands off, buddy. Haven't you done enough?*

But Gregory keeps going. "Your mom talked about you two girls all the time."

"I never saw you kids that whole year," Mom says. "It was so hard. I think I must have sabotaged that job subconsciously, just so I could go back home. I was jealous of Ray, getting to be with you."

That year it felt like Jami and I were completely on our

own, fending for ourselves in a little fort, like all the fantasies we'd enact when we played "Grown-Up" in our basement playroom. Those months have morphed into a memory of the two of us eating cake for dinner, watching television way past our bedtime, and finding a bottle of sherry underneath a cabinet and taking turns sipping it, pretending we were at a dinner party.

"That was when Dad took a lot of naps," Jami says, and I wonder if she has the same memories I have of that time. "Every night we'd try to wake him up to make dinner, but he'd say he was too tired and we should cook—"

"Spaghetti," I finished.

"Yes!" Jami picks another piece of shrimp out of her bowl with a fork before scooping rice into her mouth. She talks through the food. "Every night he was going to make spaghetti. He never did."

"I still regret being gone that year."

Gregory takes Mom's hand. "I'm glad you were."

Jami and I both look up at Gregory then, because it's inappropriate to appreciate our malnourished childhoods just because it let him eventually hook up with our mother. He doesn't seem to notice how awkward he has just made it.

Jami changes the subject entirely. "I hope Heio comes back with some chicken." She pronounces it "Hee-yo." "I'm starving."

"How'd you know how to say his name?" Gregory asks. "Is that right?"

"I took a guess," Jami says, fingering the condensation on her water glass.

"Orientals have some crazy names," Gregory says.

"Asian," I correct immediately, loudly, like a reflex.

"What?" Gregory leans over, touching the back of his ear.

"Asian. Say 'Asian.' Not 'Oriental.'" I can feel my face

flaming with shame. I look around, but I don't see Heio or anyone else within earshot.

"Why?"

" 'Oriental' describes objects. The people are 'Asian.'"

"So why aren't the names Oriental?"

"I don't know. But you weren't talking about the names, you were talking about the people."

"I was talking about the people who have those weird names. Hee-yo. That's a weird name, even if he was from Rhode Island."

"Please, he's coming back."

Gregory turns to my mother. "When did 'Oriental' turn bad? I didn't say 'Chink.'"

And on that word, Heio returns to make the next round of food. Silently, he spills oil onto the skillet, sending it sizzling to life. The word *Chink* is practically echoing off the heavy, sharp knives dangling overhead.

Do it, Heio. Kill him. Fling a knife between his eyes. I'll totally vouch for you. Occupational hazard. Happens to the best of us.

"Did you bring chicken?" Jami asks.

Heio doesn't answer. He doesn't flip the food, or play with the knives. He simply cooks and serves without any fanfare. Someone else delivers the check.

I rest my head in my hands, wishing that this family had some kind of governmental intervention legally blocking them from leaving the house.

Not Too Good.

The drive home is quiet. I keep thinking of words I'd like to say, but swallowing them. Nothing will change or fix anything. I opt for a sigh.

"What's wrong with you?" Mom asks. She's in the passenger seat. I'm sitting diagonally behind her. Beside me, I can feel my sister tense up. Gregory glances at me briefly in the rearview mirror, then trains his eyes back on the road.

"Nothing," I say, letting the end of the word stress that, in fact, it's *everything*.

"If you have something to say, just say it."

"I don't have anything to say."

The road hums under us, and the quiet murmur of talk radio keeps the car from utter silence.

"That man didn't hear us talking," Mom says.

"Right. That's why he served us pink chicken he hoped would kill us and then had someone else take over."

"We didn't say anything wrong."

Gregory looks at me again in the mirror. "I'm sorry, Benny," he says. "I honestly didn't know they don't want you calling them Orientals anymore. It's not like they sent out a memo."

Mom laughs.

Gregory enjoys cracking my mom up, so he continues. "Is there a book you get in college or something, or a web page with alerts that I can read, so I can follow one politically correct phrase to the next?"

"I don't think so," I say, trying to control my voice, making it sound even and levelheaded.

"Because I don't like offending people," he says. "I stopped saying 'coloreds' when we were supposed to, too."

Coloreds? What fucking year is this?

"Let's stop talking about this," I say.

Mom cranes herself around in her seat, and I know I'm about to be in serious trouble. Mom only turns herself around when she's had enough. "Well, *thank you* for deciding our conversation is over," she says. "And I suppose you've decided we've been sufficiently *chastised* as well."

"I'm not—"

Mom holds up a hand, closing her eyes. She's in full speechifying mode now. "It's one thing to inform us when we're using terms from our generation that your generation has deemed unacceptable. That's fine. That's important. But for you to sit there and judge us when we've done nothing wrong—"

"He said 'Chink'!"

"He was making a *point.*"

"That he wasn't nearly as racist as he could have been?"

"You were looking for a fight, and you found it. You waited and pounced, and then made a big production out of a simple question."

"I didn't do anything!" I sound like such a baby.

"You wanted to make us feel stupid."

"I'm sorry I embarrassed you," Gregory says.

"I'm not looking for an apology," I reply, to which Gregory shrugs, I guess having exhausted all his options.

Mom is staring out her passenger window like she's talking to someone in the next lane. "Miss Los Angeles. Knows how to be so perfect."

Anything I say now will just be taken the wrong way.

Mom says, "Here in the real world we say what we mean. So forgive me for being blunt, but you've been behaving like a real snob ever since you got here."

In the dark, in the quiet, Jami takes my right hand and holds it. She doesn't squeeze, or even move. Her hand is there, reminding me that there are others in this car, and this moment can end as soon as I want it to.

I say nothing for the rest of the drive, letting Mom have the last word. When Gregory drops the three of us off, only Jami thanks him for treating us to dinner.

I don't help Mom into the house, or up to her room. I let her drag that gimp leg behind her the entire way. If she thinks I think I'm too good for this family, then she can pretend I'm not a part of it.

Going Mental.

"Are you going home, then?" Zack asks. I'm helping him clean out a patch of branches and dead leaves way in the back of my mother's property. Neighborhood kids keep climbing the fence and building small forts that they seem to be using to practice spray painting.

"No. I'd feel guilty for leaving them like this."

"And you'd miss me too much," he says, giving me a teasing smile.

"That's mostly the reason," I joke back.

"Are you ashamed of them?" Zack stops piling boards of wood long enough to stretch his arms overhead. I see a peek of tanned flesh, curved hipbones, and smooth skin, just above the waistband of his jeans. I have to ask him to repeat the question.

"I'm not ashamed," I answer. "I don't know why they have to be so . . ." I stop, because there is no word for how I feel. I want them to be different, but exactly the same.

"Unsophisticated?" Zack offers.

"Obnoxious, but that's still not the right word."

"This one really bothers you," Zack says. "I can tell."

"How's that?" I find an empty beer bottle jammed into the crook of a tree branch. I have to jump to free it, dropping it into a trash bag.

"You haven't done nearly as much staring at my ass." He gives his rump a little shake, like an apathetic hula dancer.

"You need a haircut," I tell him.

"Did you learn that one from your mother?"

"I did, as a matter of fact. Now let me call you a redneck."

Zack isn't finished. "You're a smart girl. I bet you already know what's going on here." He drops to a pile of wood, elbows on knees, and proceeds to diagnose. "You like being needed," he says.

"Brilliant conclusion, Zack. Next you'll tell me I enjoy breathing and sleep."

I feel like he's trying to trap me into some kind of confession. "I am not the problem here," I say.

"Neither am I, Sugar Hips."

"When was this conversation even about you? And that's a lousy nickname. Give me a different one."

"I can go back to calling you Ugly."

"Keep trying."

Then Zack says, "I want you to know that I've decided I'm cool with us flirting, because it's not going to go anywhere. Plus, I know you can't help it."

"Really."

"Look at me, Benny. I'm a fucking Abercrombie & Fitch model over here."

He's right. But *still*. "I'm managing."

"For now."

I want to go over there, slap him, kiss him, and fuck him. I can't explain this. I just know it's what I'd like to happen right now. It's a weird way to feel lust, but there's something about our banter combined with the boredom of menial labor that makes the little voice in my head play "What if?" We'd fool around on these wooden boards full of rusty nails until we're exhausted and covered in tetanus. In the silence of this minute, I can tell we're both thinking it. We're living it in our heads—naked and sweaty and breathless. It's perfect up here, in the fantasy. There are no weird body parts, or limbs getting tangled up in each other. Our mouths open just right and our tongues touch in that way they're supposed to. It's not spit or drool, or spastic dry humping without an ounce of dignity; it's the movie version of bodies combining.

Zack snaps his fingers. "Earth to Benny. Quit fucking me with your eyes."

I jump, having been caught. "I wasn't." The skin on my face betrays me.

Zack crosses his arms in front of his chest, demurely. "Then why do I feel so violated?" he asks, in a girlish voice.

"Shut up," I say.

"Man, you are one messed up little girl." He clucks his tongue. "The things I'd do to you."

"To my head?"

"That, too."

Our semi-inappropriate banter continues through the afternoon, as we lug large panels of wood out to a nearby Dumpster.

It's late and getting dark when he asks, "Does it make you sad that we'll never have sex?"

"Not as sad as it should make you."

He suddenly gets incredibly serious. "No, really, Benny," he says. "It is much sadder for you."

I bite. "How so?"

"I'm so good at fucking that if I fucked you, I'd ruin fucking for you for the rest of your life."

I hope he didn't see that my left foot just tripped over my right. I concentrate on rooting my feet to the ground.

"Quit looking at me like that," he says. "You're giving yourself way too much credit."

"You don't know what I'm thinking."

"You're thinking for someone who's in a relationship, I've been pretty inappropriate."

"You just said you'd fuck me so good I wouldn't want to fuck anymore."

"I was joking, Ugly. Pay attention."

My head's all mixed up and I feel like everything I say he turns into either something dirty or incriminating. So I tell him, "You're an asshole," and storm back into the house, his laughter echoing behind me.

Just before I slam the back door I hear him shout, "Was it something I said?"

Making Up.

I don't hear Mom enter my room, which must mean I've become accustomed to the rhythmic clonking of her cast, like a little pirate hobbling around.

She touches my shoulder. "Are you awake?"

It's dark, and I could easily pretend I'm not. This could be her way of continuing the Benihana argument, waiting until I'm dazed and twilight-y from near sleep so she could close in for the kill. But there's something about having Mom check on me in bed, just like when I was little, that sets me at ease.

"I am, Ma," I say. "You okay?"

"Do you want to cuddle?"

She snuggles into my bed headfirst, wriggling her way into the covers like a puppy.

Her cast is noticeably heavy on top of the comforter, but the rest of Mom is under the covers, her curly hair in my face. She's wearing a jogging suit that still smells like the lemon chicken we had for dinner. She rests her head next to mine and sighs. I reach out my hand and rub her shoulder. Mom takes this as a signal, and moves closer to me. She rests her head on my shoulder. We are cuddling, but I'm the one holding my mom.

It's very, very weird.

I don't want it to be. I'm sure all kinds of moms and daughters spoon, right? Normal families get together and cuddle, right? We used to share a bed all the time. This is exactly what happens in every other home in America at this hour, I'm sure.

I'm spooning my mother. Maybe I should Google that, find out how many other women find themselves in bed with their moms.

"I can't find your ring, Ma."

"You will."

"I hope so."

While I know this can't be what most people do, and it's probably illegal in at least three states, it's still kind of nice. It's Mom and me, sharing a blanket, in a rare quiet moment when all we're doing is enjoying each other. This woman made me. She should get to cuddle me whenever she wants. She spent years with me attached to her side. Why should it be weirder now that I'm more than a couple of decades old?

"I'm sorry we fought," Mom says. Her face is turned away from mine, so it's hard to hear her mumbles at first. I realize what she's said a few seconds later.

"I'm sorry, too," I say. "I love you."

"I love you, too. And I'm really glad you've come home."

I know what she means. She means her home. But I also know what she *means*. She means this can be *my* home, the second I declare it.

"Are you still mad at Gregory?" she asks.

I can't hesitate too long here. I stall with words, choosing them like we're playing three-card monte, because I know no matter which one I pick, no matter how sure I am I made the right choice, it'll end up being the wrong one. "I wasn't mad. I don't know him very well."

"He's my favorite, of all of them," she says, rotating to face me. "He's worried he insulted you. He's not a racist. He's had a really difficult life. His father killed his mother, you know."

"No, I didn't know that."

How the fuck would I?

"Ax," Mom says. Like it's so common to ax another human being that one word is sufficient enough to explain the entire homicide. I let it go because now is not the time to hear that story. Not before I go to sleep, for God's sake.

Mom runs her fingers through my hair, sliding her hand along my forehead. It's incredibly soothing. "I worry about you over there," she says. "My baby out in California."

"I'm fine."

"So far away. Getting as far away from me as you can."

"That's not why I'm out there."

Mom's voice drops to a whisper. "Then why?"

It makes my heart hurt. To even insinuate I'm trying to harm her by living in another time zone, my mother is making me feel like the worst daughter ever. She must know that I'd live here if I could.

If I wanted to.

See? She's still right, even when she's wrong.

"I like it out there, Ma."

"Here's nice, too, Boobs. We have travel agencies."

"I have a boy out there."

Forgive me, Mickey, for using you as an excuse.

"The one who calls you all the time?"

"He doesn't call all the time."

"You're always on the phone with him."

This isn't true. Jami is always on the phone with Charles. I talk to Zack way more often than I have ever chatted with Mickey. I could let this escalate into a bicker, but I choose not to. "His name's Mickey."

"Like the mouse?" She sounds disgusted.

"Like the baseball player. Mickey Mantle?"

Okay, one little lie. You'd totally do the same thing. Don't even look at me like that.

"When do I meet this baseball player?"

"He works at a music store."

Mom's quiet here, which is her way of saying eighteen thousand things, all of which have to do with the fact that someone who works in a music store probably isn't making any money, which means I'm probably going to pay for his living expenses, which was her only problem with Brian, whom she's probably still hoping I'll get back together with because his family lives in Maryland, which means she'd see me more often.

Mom's quiet for so long, in fact, that she falls asleep.

I'm twenty-seven years old and sleeping in a twin daybed with my mother.

You know what this means? My mom finally got her wish. Both of her daughters are living with her. We're lost and lonely, unemployed and running out of money. We now actually need each other to survive.

I wonder if it's too late to call Child Protective Services on her.

Get Away.

Jami needs to pick something up from crappy Charles, and I'm the only one of the three of us who currently has a car. Why Gregory chose me to entrust with his vehicle says a lot about the kind of drivers my mother and sister are.

"Where are we going?" I ask.

Mom's in the passenger side, and Jami's straddling the middle of the backseat, leaning in between us. Seat belts are for pussies, she informed us—this coming from a woman who has been in no fewer than five car accidents.

"The bank," Jami answers.

"I didn't know Charles worked at a bank." Mom sounds so pleased with this new tidbit of information, as if this suddenly gave him a high school diploma. Jami's careful not to have this boy anywhere near the house, so we feed off new facts about Charles like guppies to fish food.

"He does security for them," Jami says, rolling her eyes. "It's one of his part-time jobs."

"Is it hard for him to find full-time?" Mom's trying to make this question sound casual but it's failing. We all know, but won't discuss, how Charles recently spent some time in prison. Not jail—prison. And Jami finally admitted that *recently* means he got out six months ago. And *recently* means that it's not the only time he's been there, just the most recent one. She was vague, promising he never hurt anybody, which makes me think he must have stolen some serious shit. Mom's hoping it was drugs.

Yes, you're understanding that correctly. In the board game of my sister's love life, I'm rooting for grand theft, while Mom's got her money on crack dealing.

Jami tells us about the car she's going to buy herself when she gets a job.

"You don't need a Hummer," Mom says.

"Ma," Jami argues, cool like she's had this line of defense prepared for weeks. "We live very close to our nation's capital. You never know when we're going to be living in a war zone."

"Then please spend the money to build us a bomb shelter. I could use the storage."

Jami snorts in disgust and sits back for the first time since we left the house. We are nearing Charles's bank. "Let me out in front," she says. "I'll just be a minute." I get out of the car and help her climb out of the backseat.

I idle in front of the bank while Jami runs in. Once she's past the glass doors, I turn to my mother. "It's weird we've never met Charles, right?" I ask. "I mean, not nearly as weird as the fact that he's been to prison. He's a felon. We act like Jami said he's a Gemini, but she said he went to prison. That's where bad people go. How can they let him do security when he went to prison? What piece of shit security company does this bank use?"

With a sudden intensity, Mom grabs my knee, hard enough that there's going to be a bruise. "What if they're robbing the bank right now?"

It's crazy, and I know it's crazy, but as she says it, I know she's right. Charles and Jami are robbing the bank right now. The revelation makes my mouth dry instantly.

"We're the getaway car," I whisper.

"Drive away," Mom says.

"But Jami!"

"Don't leave," Mom corrects herself as she lowers her passenger side mirror to get a glance behind us. "But drive away from the door."

I slowly put the car into gear and inch it.

"You're driving too slowly!" Mom shouts.

"I don't know how to do this!" I shout back. "I've never driven a getaway car before!"

"You have to drive faster. Like you know where you're going."

"Where am I going? And how do you know how to drive a getaway car?"

Mom puts her hand on the wheel and urges it to the left. "Go to the other end of the parking lot."

I drive away from the bank, circling the rows of parked cars, until we're hiding behind a Dumpster. I shift the car into an idling gear. "Don't we look even more suspicious now?"

"You're right." Mom sounds all business. She's tucked her casted leg up on the seat. She's got one hand over her face, like she needs to hide herself from her thoughts. "You're going to have to go get your sister."

"Ma!"

She grabs my arm. "She won't know where we are. She'll think we left her."

"What if she robbed a bank?"

"She's your sister!"

That's somehow enough logic to get me out of the car, running wildly across the parking lot, trying to avoid the gunfire I imagine is seconds away from hitting me. I'm run-

ning like a panicked dork toward the bank doors, and all I
can think is that I have no idea what I'm doing, or what my
sister's going to do when she emerges from the bank with
bags of money and I don't even have a gun. How did my sister get messed up in all of this? Why can't she date normal
guys? Why don't we have a getaway plan?

I can hear my mother screaming my name from across the
lot. "Benny!" she shouts. "Come back!"

*Right. Yes, I should go back. Back to the car, where it's safe.
Good idea, Mom.*

I serpentine my way back across the lot, a series of skips
and jumps like I'm dodging lightning as I run toward the little sports car.

*Please let me make it out of this parking lot alive. Please don't
let me get shot. Please don't let me be on the evening news. Please
don't let my sister make us accessories to a felony. Please.*

Mom's in the driver's seat itching to go. "We have to get
your sister," she says. "Even if what she did is wrong, we love
her, and we have to protect her."

It's how I feel, too. I want to help Jami, no matter how bad
her life might get, no matter how shitty the boyfriend. If she
needs to rob a bank today, I need to help her ditch the cops
until tomorrow, and the day after that, and the day after that,
until I drive her to Mexico with a suitcase filled with unmarked
bills. I don't care. She's my blood, and she's everything to me.

I can see Jami standing outside the bank doors. "There!" I
shout, pointing.

Mom guns the gas.

We reach her in seconds flat. Jami is holding a two-liter of
Dr Pepper and a pair of large, worn tennis shoes. "What the
fuck is wrong with you guys?" she asks, her face scrunched
into a furious frown. "You drove off!"

"Get in the car," Mom shouts. "Get in!"

"I call shotgun, then."

What if she has a shotgun?

We all get out of the car, changing positions. Mom crawls into the backseat. I take the wheel again. Jami takes her sweet time getting into the car. She opens up the two-liter and awkwardly takes a sip. "Charles knows I love Dr Pepper," she says. "Isn't he sweet, giving me this bottle for picking up his Nikes?"

"Why did you need his shoes?" I ask, wondering if they're filled with cash, or made of explosives.

"We're playing tennis when he gets off work and he didn't want to have to carry his shoes on the bus. Mom, why are you all sweaty?"

Mom's laughing a nervous laugh, and I'm still too amped to talk.

"What?" Jami asks.

"Nothing," Mom and I say at the same time.

"Jesus Christ, you two are loony."

Mom gives me the briefest of glances in the rearview mirror. We never tell Jami how close she was to getting away with the perfect crime.

Cheese.

I want a family photo. I want to be a normal family, and normal families have pictures hanging on their walls of everyone gathered together, hands resting on each other's shoulders, smiles pasted awkwardly on their faces, hair captured at an unfortunate moment in time, and everybody looks just seconds away from a meltdown.

Since I found boxes of myself in storage exile, I started noticing just how many pictures of Jami were on display *inside* the house. There's one of Jami from her softball years on the bookcase in the living room. A baby picture of Jami holding her favorite doll is in the kitchen, near the microwave. There's one of Dad and Jami jumping on a trampoline. It hangs on the wall at the bottom of the staircase. I found one picture of myself—my high school graduation photo—in Mom's bedroom. If a complete stranger walked into the house, he or she could conceivably guess that a three-person family unit lived there, and there was this cousin—or perhaps an inner-city child they sponsored—one who's thought about, but rarely seen.

I've asked Zack to take the picture. His eyes can't stop roaming around our house. Now that he can see Mom's ceramic collection of miniature dogs, the stacks of random objects at the end of the hallway that I still haven't sorted, the overflow of crap in every bedroom, I wonder if entering my mother's house confirmed his suspicions that she is a crazy lady and the people she loves are even crazier.

"Okay, y'all could maybe sit on the couch?" This is Zack's first suggestion, in the form of a question. He's asking hesitantly because nobody's listening to him. It's the first time I've heard him use the word *y'all*. Perhaps he's nervous.

Jami cannot stop with her hair. First she flatironed it, but then decided it made her face look too round, so she washed it, dried it, and curled it. Declaring her hair hideous, she then washed it, dried it, and flatironed it again. Now she's seriously debating cutting bangs. Right now, for the first time, for our family photo, Jami's thinking bangs. She's walking around the living room with a hank of purple hair between two fingers, bending it back just above the bridge of her nose. "What do you think?" she keeps asking anyone near her. "Bangs or no bangs? Bangs or no bangs?" I tell her not to cut her hair, immediately increasing the chances of her snipping those locks by about 87 percent.

Mom's upset about her pants. She wants to wear a pair of tight lilac slacks. Mom likes the word *slacks* and now, whenever I think of my mother, and then her pants, the word *slacks* comes to my head, too. This means when I'm older and looking for my pants, I'll probably refer to them as "slacks," too. This also means I'll end up calling my jeans "dungarees" and mashed potatoes "mash-poes," just like my father used to, and I fear there's nothing I can do to stop it.

These slacks of Mom's are what she calls her "skinny slacks." The problem is the skinny slacks won't clear the cast on her leg. She has two choices: cut one leg off the skinny slacks or wear something else. This is a decision she's weighing with more importance than the time I cut my forehead at a playground but we didn't know if I was going to need stitches or if the wound would stop bleeding on its own. I remember Mom sitting down to have a cigarette, holding her free hand to my head, and asking me, "Do you feel dizzy?" When I said I felt fine, she said, "Then go play. Come back here if you think you're going to throw up or fall down." There's a small scar just below my hairline that most people never notice. It did heal on its own, but that's probably because I kept my hand clamped to my forehead for the next three days, terrified my brain was going to fall out.

Mom enters the living room holding the skinny slacks. She's not wearing anything but a blouse and a pair of underwear.

"Incoming!" Zack shouts, turning his attention to the ceiling. "Your mom's not wearing her pants. You need to fix that."

"Ma." I approach her cautiously, like one walks up on an escaped bear. "You need to put something on. Zack's here."

Mom shakes the slacks impatiently. "Oh, like he's never seen anything I've got before."

"Ma'am, I am most uncomfortable," Zack says to the ceiling.

"Then grow up," Mom says. "Pretend we're at the beach and I'm in a swimsuit."

Jami's still holding her hair against her forehead when she joins my side. "Mom, I'll give you a hundred bucks if you wear just your underwear for the picture."

"I don't know if I should cut the skinny slacks," Mom says again.

"I don't know if I should cut bangs," Jami says for the millionth time.

I try taking control. "You leave your hair alone, Jami. And Ma, you'll regret cutting those pants once your leg heals. Just wear something else."

"Everything else makes me look fat," Mom says.

"Ma, you're not fat."

"I am fat."

The word *fat* is said in my house more often than any other word. More than *you*. More than *the*. Everything is about the fat. How fattening is this meal, how fat are these legs, how fat did *she* get. Hearing the word that many times in a row, it really can make you feel fat. The power of suggestion. I look over at Zack, who is rubbing his stomach, questioningly. See what I mean? Superhot Zack can't even help but worry about his gut because there's something in my mother's house that makes you feel like you've expanded.

"I'm not sitting on that couch," Mom says to Zack. She's standing next to him, panties and purple cast, arms crossed defiantly. Zack is doing everything he can to avoid looking directly at my mother.

"Okay," he says. "You can do whatever you want."

"I'm going to stand. Sitting makes my thighs look wider than they are."

"Are we all going to stand?" Jami asks. "Because I'm going to change if we're standing."

I have to put a stop to this. "We are taking the picture in three minutes," I say. "You have three minutes left to fret about how you look, what your positioning will be, and how you want to smile for the camera. In three minutes, Zack is going to start taking pictures. Please be ready by then."

I need to leave the room, so I walk straight into the kitchen to refill my coffee cup.

Three short minutes later I am seated on the couch. My mother is standing beside me, Jami behind both of us. It's a little awkward having the couch in the shot; it looks like we're saving an empty space for Dad. Maybe we are, without talking about it, without meaning to.

Jami's cell phone rings. It's Charles, and he wants to have an argument about a video rental. I know this because all Jami keeps repeating is, "It's not my fucking responsibility, Charles. I don't even like *Van Wilder*."

Mom takes this opportunity to hobble back upstairs to her room to change her pants again.

Zack sits down next to me.

"You're not mad at me anymore," he says.

"I wasn't mad."

"So you call all your friends 'asshole'?"

"When they're assholes, I do."

"You look good," he says.

"Thanks."

I don't look at him. I keep my eyes forward. I don't want him to think I'm flirting anymore. One of us should be more responsible.

He slides a handful of my hair off my shoulder. "I've been wanting to do that for an hour."

"Fix my hair?"

"No. Touch it."

We stare at each other for a few seconds. He's grinning; I'm wondering the right thing to say. I could make the excuse to touch his arm, pat his knee, admit I've wondered what that little dip underneath his lower lip tastes like. I have full permission to touch him right now, however wildly inappropriate the gesture, because he's waiting for me to. He'll laugh, pretending it's a big joke, but he's basically waiting for me to touch him.

But aren't I awesome, being so responsible and good? Look at me, standing up, ending this moment of electric current. "I'll go check on Jami," I say.

"You'll be back."

I hate how I know what he means. No, I hate how he knows I know what he means.

When I find Jami she is crying, holding the cell phone away from her face, yelling into the little dots that represent Charles's ear. "Fuck you!" she's shouting. "Don't ever call me again. We just broke up!"

She clicks the phone shut and tosses it aside, burying her head in her hands.

"Jami," I say hesitantly, pressing my fingers to her back. "You okay?"

"No," she says.

"I'm sorry. You want to get out of here? Get something to eat?" Maybe she could tell me more about him and I could understand why she's with a guy she fights with twice a day. I'd like to understand. Is he really attractive? Wealthy? Good in bed? If she's screaming obscenities at him, what could he be saying back to her?

"We're taking the picture," Jami says. "You wanted this picture. We should do it."

"Forget it. Mom's freaking out and you're sad and Zack won't be serious long enough to take the picture."

"Zack likes you." Jami bumps into me.

"He does not." I bump back. We're instantly twelve. I try neither to smile nor blush. I will give nothing away, because there's nothing to give. "We're just friends," I say. I don't know why I don't tell her he's got a girlfriend. Yes, I do: I don't want to see the look she'd give me if she knew.

"Whatever," Jami says. "Let's go take this stupid picture."

Zack decides our final positioning. No couch. Mom's standing behind me. Jami's on my right. Zack moves back and forth, trying to find an angle he likes.

"I'm not going to call Charles until tomorrow," Jami tells Mom.

"Does he still owe you money?" Mom asks.

"You know he does, Mom. That's why you're asking me that question."

"My question is a reminder. Benny, stand up straight. You're making yourself look like you have four boobs."

"Let her slump," Jami says. "It makes her look fatter than me."

Mom says, "It's taking two of you to cover me up, so I don't want to hear it."

They can't have a moment of peace. It's like if they stop talking for even a second, one of them will implode. There's no room for me to jump in. There's no place for me in their practiced dialogue. They have a rhythm, one that involves self-deprecation and condescension, but also a lot of love.

When Jami complains about Charles, Mom reminds her that she's better than anyone she dates. Jami pretends to be insulted by this, but you can hear what the backhanded compliment has done to her confidence. When Mom makes another crack about the size of her ass, Jami immediately counters with a joke about her own. They chat and bicker like an overrehearsed comedy routine. You can't hear anyone take a breath. There is no time for thought. This is the sound of their brains working, out loud, in real time. I don't know how to hear Mom's words and Babelfish them into loving remarks. I marvel at Jami's talent to hear the good through all the criticism, and then dish it right back out in Mom's unique language.

"Why are we taking this stupid picture anyway?" Mom asks. "I don't want a reminder of me looking like this."

"Benny probably wants it so she can forever make fun of us for once being fatter than she is. Taking a picture so it'll last longer."

"If I were Benny, I'd be taking six rolls of film to preserve this moment."

"Benny and Her Fat Family."

From across the living room, Zack gestures for me to come to him. I do.

"We should probably save this for a different day," he says quietly. I've never seen him look so serious.

"What's wrong? Is it your camera? Did I get the wrong film?"

"I don't think I should take this picture. You're going to be able to tell that you're crying."

Dammit. I didn't even know I was.

I try wiping the tears away with the edge of my fingers, to keep my makeup from running, to pull it together and get a grip, but the more I struggle to keep my breath even, the more tears I'm pushing away.

"Tell them to forget it," I whisper, and then walk upstairs. I can hear Mom and Jami happy to be off the hook, unaware that I'm only a few feet away, curled in my old daybed, wishing I knew how to talk to them. No, not *to.*

With.

In Public, Take Two.

I want to break Mom and Jami's code, figure out how to be with them like they are with each other. I want to be a family, not Benny and her family. I need them to think of me as a part of them, not someone standing nearby.

Mom wants to try walking around on the cast more. Her doctor suggested she should stay in bed, so Mom suggested we all go out.

Sometimes no matter what, we end up becoming the exact stereotypes of the women we try not to be. This is my explanation as to why we're at a department store, watching Jami try on a shirt that barely covers her navel.

"Take that off," Mom says. "You look like a hooker."

"Then it's perfect," Jami says, darting back into the dressing room.

Mom purses her lips, but says nothing more about Jami's shirt. She turns to me and asks, "Are you going to try on those slacks?"

I've been holding a pile of clothes, but I've yet to try anything on, as I avoid looking at myself half naked in fluorescent lighting at all costs. "I don't know," I say.

"Jami, let your sister in there."

Jami and I share the dressing room, just like when we were little. This time we have to be careful not to bump heads as we bend forward and take off our clothes in the tiny room. I keep my T-shirt on as long as possible as I lean forward and cover my thighs with my torso, angling my butt into the corner of the dressing room. I'm anxious as I pull the jeans over my knees, wishing I could get into them without having to take off the ones I was already wearing.

"You dress like you're in gym class," Jami teases. "I'm not a lesbian."

"I know," I say. But the truth is I dress this way in front of everybody. I don't want to inflict my nakedness on others unless they're really excited to have me naked with them. Jami isn't blinded by any kind of lust for me; she can mock my flaws without the threat of losing a blow job. "I was trying to give you room," I lie.

"I look disgusting," Jami says, turning in front of the mirror. She puts her hands on both sides of her face. "My skin looks like pizza. Don't even look at me."

She leaves and I hear Mom compliment her outfit. I take this moment to sneak a quick peek of myself in the jeans in the big mirror at the end of the dressing room hallway.

Mom *clunk-clunks* over the second I'm out of the safety of the dressing room. "I like those," she says.

"You think?"

"They make your hips look less wide."

It's a compliment, and it's not a compliment, yet it's still technically a compliment. It takes years of practice to do this. Don't think you could do it on your first try.

"Thanks, Ma."

She takes off her glasses and winces, rubbing her forehead with her free hand, like she's spent the entire day doing back-breaking work.

"Your leg hurting?"

"A little. It's good to be out with my girls." She reaches out and strokes my arm, petting me gently. "Love you, Benny. Don't go home yet."

We haven't talked about me leaving. I haven't mentioned it at all. "Why do you think I'm going home?"

"With all the work you've already done, and my leg getting better, and Zack helping out . . . I can tell you're wrapping it up around here."

"I don't know how much longer I can stay," I say.

Mom is frowning, cleaning her glasses absently. "You're always in such a hurry to get away from me."

"I have to go back to work eventually. One of us has to earn a living."

Jami shouts from inside the dressing room. "I forgot to tell you. I got a job!"

"That's great!" Mom says.

"Congratulations, Jami," I say. "What's the job?"

"Charles got me a job at the store where he works. I'll work the perfume department."

At the mention of Charles's name, I see my mother's back stiffen. "When do you start?" she asks.

Jami opens the dressing room door. "Monday," she says. "So buy me this outfit for work, would you?"

"I thought Charles worked at the bank," I say.

Jami gives me a death glare. "Not anymore," she says.

"How come?"

Jami makes her *tsk* sound. "Shut up, Benny."

I Do.

I'm looking for Mom's ring in the study, sifting through piles of old bills, when Mom finds me.

"It's not going to be in there," she says.

I hold up a stack of receipts and ask, "When did you guys own a boat?"

"Oh, the boat." Mom sits down on the desk, in the one space I've cleared, and shakes her head. "That thing was a mistake from start to finish. Your father had to have it. Wanted to be a fisherman. Thought it would be good to do with you and Jami, going out fishing every weekend."

I have one memory of fishing with my father. He wanted me to put a hook through a fish's eye, a tiny fish that would be bait, and use it to trick other fish to swallow the metal hook and suffocate in front of me.

"That's right," I say. "We did go fishing."

"Once, but you wouldn't stop crying about being a fish killer, and then Jami wouldn't stop crying because she cried whenever you cried, so he drove you both back to me, dropped you off, and I didn't see him until it got dark. He came home with ten fish. We had to eat fish for dinner for the next two weeks. You cried every meal."

"I ruined the boat."

"It took him six months to find someone else to buy that thing. I was glad you ruined it. I hate the taste of fish."

"I thought maybe you'd hide the ring here with the bills."

Mom leans back against the wall, her hair squishing up

around her head. "Your father gave me that ring on a Tuesday night. I remember the first thing my mother said when I told her I was getting married. She said, 'Who gets engaged on a Tuesday?' Your father completely surprised me with that ring."

It occurs to me that I've never heard this story before. Why wouldn't I have asked one of them?

"How'd he propose?"

Mom smiles, her eyes closed. "I was staying over the apartment he had with six other boys. That place was disgusting, and every night there would be a Scrabble game to determine who got to have the . . . well, it was called the Sex Room. But it meant you got to be in there with a girl and nobody else. And that night your father won the Scrabble game."

"This does become about you getting engaged at some point, and not so much about you and Dad having sex?"

"He put the ring on my finger when I was asleep. Then he woke me up, pretending to have a bad dream. Scared the shit out of me. He's screaming that there's a monster and it's the middle of the night and I'm terrified. So I start crying because I'm so scared and think there's a monster in the room." I see tears in the corners of her eyes as she smiles. "I was shaking so bad I had my hand to my chest. Eventually your father had to ask me to count how many fingers I had. He said, 'I want to make sure I'm not still dreaming. If you still have ten fingers, then I know I'm awake.' I started counting, but only got to two."

I have to find that ring.

Unleashed.

Zack's screaming my name from outside.

I run to the front porch, shoes in my hand. "What's wrong?"

"Help."

The meanest dog, the one we call Killer, has broken free from the tree where Jami keeps him chained. He is viciously barking, standing in the back of Zack's truck, where Zack is trapped in the small space between the dog and the back window.

"How?" I ask, cautiously approaching them.

"I climbed in here to get this paint can, and I turned around to find him. He smelled my flesh."

"Don't move."

"I haven't moved in five minutes. Why won't he get bored, Benny?"

"This isn't good," I say.

"I need you to distract him so I can jump off the truck."

"Distract him how? By getting him to eat *my* face instead?"

"Hey, in a face contest, mine would—"

I turn back toward the house. "Good luck!"

Zack's voice turns to a whimper. "Wait, wait, wait! I'm sorry. I'm sorry. Please come back."

Killer is standing rigid, eyes focused squarely on Zack's body. I look around for his favorite toy.

"Where's Kitty?" I ask. Kitty is Killer's stuffed tiger. He spends half of his day licking it like it's his own offspring.

"I don't know," Zack responds. "I think it might be over in the small pen."

The only fenced off dog area that I find endearing is the puppy pen, where four tiny dogs spend their day stumbling over each other, constantly in vicious fake fights. I see the mauled, matted tiger on its side, a tiny, brown mutt taking a nap on its back.

I reach in and gingerly pull the stuffed animal from under the sleeping pup.

"Got it."

"Hurry!" Zack says.

I take tiny steps in Killer's direction, Kitty out in front of me, trying to sound like a lullaby. "Hey, Killer," I whisper. "Look what I have!"

Killer turns and gives me a lazy eye. Then he notices what I'm holding.

"Jump!" I say to Zack, but he's already in the air, flinging himself over the side of his truck like a Duke brother.

"Throw it!" he says.

I toss Kitty toward the tree, and Killer leaps in the air, catching it in his mouth before he or the toy hits the ground.

"I did it!"

My hand has found Zack's. My body is pressed against his as he holds me back, using me to shield himself. "Thank you," he says, his mouth close to my ear.

I detach myself. "Sure," I say. "It was nothing."

"Naw, you saved me. My hero."

He takes my hand and raises it high in the air. It's supposed to be like a victory, like I'm a winning prizefighter. But the metaphor doesn't work here, and it feels like he found an excuse to hold my hand again, and I didn't pull it away quickly enough to show him that I didn't exactly want that.

We're quiet for a few seconds.

"We should chain him," he says.

"I'll call Jami," I say. "This is her job."

"Sorry I bothered you," Zack says, shoving his hands into his back pockets.

"I'm glad you didn't get your face chewed off," I say. "Even though you probably deserved it."

He's still standing there, staring at Killer, frozen in that sexy side-grin when I make myself walk away.

Being Friendly.

I don't know how it started, exactly. I think I was taking something out to the trash, but I ended up sitting with Zack, talking for three hours. A conversation began about music, and then concerts we had gone to, until we're sitting on my mother's porch, sharing our brushes with rock idols.

We talk about college, and stupid relationships. Zack tells me a story about a time in high school he snuck into a girl's room to leave her a note that he liked her. He thought she was at a friend's house, but she was just in the shower. "I can still hear her screaming," he says.

I tell Zack about the time I was dating a boy who kept accidentally calling me "Mom." It would be at the worst times, like in the middle of an argument, or when we were drunk and kissing on the couch. Zack teases me. "After the third time he did that, you should have been gone."

"After the second time, I should have kicked him in the balls."

"You have issues, my friend."

He tells me about his odd jobs while putting himself through grad school, when he was a telemarketer for a company he thought was selling self-help books. It turned out to be a freaky cult that one day asked him to sign over his checking account under the guise of direct-depositing his paychecks. "I still get mail from them," he says with a shiver. "They want me to donate sperm."

"How do they ask you to do that?"

"I'll bring you one of the brochures one day. You'll laugh. It's got a picture of a woman holding a baby and it says, 'She'll never be able to thank you enough.' "

"That is creepy."

Three hours. I haven't sat and talked with someone like that in I don't know how long. The time flew by. The sun set around us and eventually we were sitting in the dark. Mom turned on the porch light and teased us. "I don't want to find you two still there in the morning. You'll be frozen."

"I should go home," Zack says, stretching. "I feel like I just went to therapy or something." He's still squinting from the harshness of my mother's porch light, which is as bright as a policeman's flashlight.

"See?" I ask. "That wasn't so hard, now, was it?"

"What?"

"Being civil."

"I've kept my arms crossed in front of my chest for a reason."

"Don't turn this into something bad," I say. "This was something good, and now you're going to ruin it by insinuating that we were just pretending—"

"We're not pretending anything."

I'm not even sure what he's talking about. I thought it was great we were talking like friends, just enjoying each other's company. I shouldn't have said anything at all. I should have gone inside and let it be what it was. By calling attention to it, I looked like I wanted him to say something about the two of us. Now I'm in the middle of a conversation I didn't try to have.

"It was nice talking to you, that's all." I stand up. My knees creak, and my thighs are stiff from sitting still for so long.

"It is. It always is."

He's smiling at me, and I don't know where to look, because every time I catch his eye I can tell he's imagining this other reality, where there are no other people. It's just the two of us, and the potential. And in that gaze, I am overwhelmed.

"You look sad," he says.

"Yeah, well, sometimes you make me sad."

I'm not going to top that one, so I head inside.

Such a Pretty Face.

As I walk into the grocery store by my mothers's house, the supermarket DJ is playing War's "Why Can't We Be Friends." From coast to coast, satellite radio enjoys taking little digs at me.

I'm standing in the express lane with the three items my mother has asked me to pick up for dinner tonight. There are six people in line ahead of me. The woman at the counter is trying to use a coupon to purchase a single candy bar. The coupon has expired; the woman is contesting the expiration date.

The man in line ahead of me catches my eye. He's older, probably in his forties, a kind smile on his face. He lowers his wiry sunglasses and smirks. "Never fails," he says. "No matter what line I pick, it's the worst one."

"I think that's how it always goes," I reply.

The song changes. It's "C'mon Marianne," by Frankie Valli and the Four Seasons. *"She was a passing fling, not a permanent thing."*

I force myself to stop thinking about Zack.

"You can cut ahead of me," the older man says. "You've only got three things."

"You have five," I say.

"Yes, but you're prettier than I am."

My first response is to be flattered. In fact, I can feel my face flushing. But at the same time my brain hits me with a single thought: *This never happened Before.* Capital *B* in *Before* because I'm talking about my weight loss. Fifty pounds ago, this man most likely wouldn't have offered me his place in line. He probably wouldn't have even turned to notice me, unless I was bleeding heavily from a severed limb.

This has been happening more and more now that I'm an After. I've had men hit the crosswalk button for me, open doors for me, offer to throw out my trash. One older gentleman offered to purchase my coffee at a Starbucks because he decided it was "Be Nice to a Pretty Girl Day."

They're flirting with me. Strangers are taking chances on me, assuming I know how to handle this, that these kinds of propositions have been happening to me my entire life.

"No, thanks," I say to the man. "You got here first."

He seems nice enough, and I'm sure he doesn't mean anything lecherous. He's just trying to get a girl to smile at him. I know that. But it still makes me disappointed in people, how easily invisible I was when my jeans size was in double digits.

It also makes me disappointed in myself, that this attention never happened to me sooner. How different would I be if I were more accustomed to the glances and random acts of kindness from gentlemen? Would I have more confidence? Would I be better at picking boyfriends?

Would I know how to handle Zack?

I wouldn't have been a threat to him before. We probably still would have hit it off and been friends, but he would have talked about his girlfriend sooner, and he wouldn't have pushed me away in anticipation of a problem. I would have just been a friend, a girl who's nice, but absolutely harmless.

Am I now dangerous? It hardly seems fair. I'm exactly the same person I was fifty pounds ago. Right?

"We Need to Talk."

It's easier to ask the really tough questions when you're focused on slicing onions. That way any emotion you might show can be completely blamed on the vegetable in front of you. All sniffs and tears have nothing to do with the topic at hand.

I'm cutting onions while Mom's peeling garlic as I ask, "When did you start seeing Gregory?"

Mom's standing on her good leg, the bad one resting on a stool propped behind her bent knee. She looks like a lazy flamingo. "About six or seven months ago."

"Not before that?"

I say it really quickly and it sits there for a second, punctuated by our alternate chop-chopping.

After some time Mom answers. "Not really," she says. It's too close to the answer I'm dreading. I chicken out.

"How did you know you were ready to start dating again?" I ask.

"Oh, I dated lots of men before Gregory," she says. She laughs at herself. "And after," she adds.

"I meant how did you know you were ready for men again?"

Mom sighs, sounding relieved to have the conversation back to something as fun and frivolous as her sex life. "A woman has needs, Benny."

I hope she can't see my spine shiver. "I meant emotionally."

"I did, too, in a way. People need to connect with each other." She elbows my side, softly. "Connecting."

I elbow her back. "Connecting."

"Like you connect with Zack," she says, her voice slipping into a teasing rhythm.

"Nothing's going on there," I say, hoping my tone will make her stop. "He has a girlfriend."

"And you have Mickey," she says, sounding like she doesn't buy my excuse for a second. "Which one will be around for a while?"

I wipe my nose on my sleeve, knife close to my eye. "What do you mean?"

Mom scoops garlic cloves into a bowl. "Benny, we all know how you treat men."

Maybe "we" all know this, but it's about to be news to me. My last major relationship ended because of his infidelity. The next closest broke my heart. All the other ones after that have been two-week flings who end up having some horrible personality trait, like the one who insisted on eating popcorn in my bed, or the one who always left pubes on my soap, or the one who thought he was going to be on *American Idol.*

"How do I treat men, Ma?"

"Like you're channel surfing." She elbows me again. "I'm trying to joke with you, Benny."

"But you're serious." I put the knife down, because it's probably best if I don't hold onto anything sharp right now.

"When's the last time you let yourself have a real boyfriend?"

"*Let myself?* Like I get to decide when I date someone real?"

"After your father I went through all kinds of men who could have been serious relationships, but I kept them far away from me, like you do."

"I don't."

"Using them for sex, like you do."

I brace myself against the counter. "I don't. And neither do you."

Mom laughs, heading to the other counter. "I'm pouring you a glass of wine. We're talking about this."

"We really don't have to."

But in seconds the glass of wine's in my hand, and Mom's sitting on her counter, wiggling her plastered leg at the knee. We're girlfriends, simply by the change in subject matter and beverage. She seems so much happier to talk to me now that there's no pressure to mother me.

"What's wrong with this one?" she asks. "He doesn't like the same music you do? He wears too much cologne? He has too many fillings in his teeth?"

"Nothing's wrong with him," I say. Other than the fact that he's not my boyfriend at all. "Except he lives in Los Angeles, and I'm here." Or he lives here, but has a girlfriend.

Mom nods. "I thought you were going home soon."

"You said that. Not me. Your leg's still in that cast. And you don't have a car or a job."

"I'll be okay, if you want to go home."

I swirl the wine in my glass, seeing how close I can get it to the edge. "If you want me to stay here, I'll stay. I went to Los Angeles because Brian needed me to."

"You spent two years telling me you *didn't* move to Los Angeles because Brian wanted you to. But because you broke up, now you can blame the move on him?"

"I didn't want to be an actor," I say. "I wanted to make my boyfriend happy."

"Right. I forgot Benny never gets to live her life for herself."

"Not really, I don't." I am careful not to let my voice slip into a whine. "I end up going where people need me."

"Nobody has ever asked you to do that."

"Sure."

Mom stares me down. "I didn't ask you to come here."

"I know."

"And Brian was going to go to Los Angeles. You followed him on your own."

"Are you trying to make me feel better?"

The oven buzzes, letting us know it's ready for the roast.

"I don't want to tell you about Gregory," Mom says. "And I want you to stop asking me."

You know how sometimes you get these weird impulses but you don't act on them because you're aware the consequences are too severe? Like, say you've got a razor blade in front of you. And you know it's ridiculous to take the blade and drag it along your wrist. That doesn't mean sometimes you don't wonder what it would feel like. Would it be so sharp you wouldn't feel anything, and would blood ooze out of your arm like a seam ripping in fabric? Would you see your veins or would the blood be too much? Would the blood be darker than you expected?

What if one day you decide to find out? You don't want to

die. You don't want to do any damage. You're just so curious you can't take it anymore. You're pretty sure you know exactly how it's going to feel, you can even imagine the dizziness in your head as your life drains out of your body. But you have to know if you're right.

So you slice. And as you're dying, your brain thinks, "Damn. I was so right."

That's what this moment feels like. Deadly victory.

I take a sip of the wine, letting the bitter, fruity flavor pucker my tongue as I choose my next words. "I won't ask you anymore," I say.

"Good," she says. "You aren't going to like what you'll hear, so it's best not to go digging for answers." She eases herself off the counter and hobbles over to the oven. "Now help me with the roast."

Confession.

Mom has told Zack that he can come into the kitchen whenever he wants. This is how he was able to find me in my pajamas, huddled over a bowl of half-cold oatmeal. He sits down across from me, his jaw set.

"Hey, I have to tell you something you're going to be really mad about."

"Good morning to you, too."

"I'm not fucking around, Benny. Look at me."

I put down my bowl and lean back in my chair. I will my eyes to stay open, focused. "Yeah."

"I'm married."

He said it, but it must mean some kind of figure of speech or some weird Southern—

"You're *what*?"

"Married. To a wife."

"You said you were in a relationship."

"Yeah, it's called a marriage."

Now I'm standing. "But you knew I thought you meant a girlfriend."

"It shouldn't make a difference, right? You don't like me, remember?"

"Shut up."

He's baiting me. He's telling me this to make me angry. Why am I this angry? I don't fucking care if he's married. I don't fucking care who he is. He's just a friend, so fantastic if he's married. I'm happy for him. I'll send him a gift. Mazel tov.

I ask, "Why don't you wear your wedding ring?"

"I don't want it to get messed up. I love my wife, so I don't want cat shit touching my wedding ring."

"You really have a problem with cat shit."

Zack's eyes widen. "That's it? That's all you've got? I tell you I'm married and you tell me I have a problem with cat shit?"

I picture him at home with a wife, over a candlelit dinner she's made while he's hard at work at my mother's house. She's cooked meat loaf, and wants to hear about his day. He tells her everything he lifted, shifted, mowed, and shoveled, but I bet he never mentions me. And why should he?

"I don't know what you want me to say." My voice sounds raspy, like the morning, like possibly I can make this all be a dream. We're still asleep, and Zack isn't really here. "It's weird you never told me about her."

"I shouldn't have to tell you about her." He's looking at me like I've done something that demands an apology. He's turning us into something wrong again, when we've done nothing. Why is he looking at me like I should be on the floor in tears?

"Okay, I guess you didn't have to tell me about your wife," I say. "But it would have made more sense, before all the flirting."

His cheeks are a violent pink, and his hair is shoved back, wet and angry, like he came here straight from a sobering shower. I wonder if he planned what he was going to say, or if he got to work, saw me through the kitchen window, and was overwhelmed by the need to confess this . . . whatever this is. "I didn't start the flirting," he says. "You did."

"What's her name?" I ask.

"None of your fucking business. You don't care."

"I do, actually."

"Don't. You don't get to know her name."

"Are you angry with me?"

I can't believe how calm I am. I'm really, really calm. I'm sitting here, and you could feel my pulse, and it would be the mellowest beat you've ever touched. Zack's exploding in front of me, all sweat and fury, guilt and frustration. The more he's erupting, the easier it is for me to sit here and watch it. Because it's not happening to me. This is Zack's trip he's on. He can decide all he wants that we've been wrong or whatever, but the reality is we've spent time together talking and nothing else. There's nothing criminal in that. I refuse to feel guilty or get dumped again by someone who was never my boyfriend.

Zack stands to pace the kitchen. "I'm in love with my wife," he says, loudly. "Nothing is going to happen between the two of us."

"I know. I don't want it to."

"Me either."

I'm pissed that he hid his marriage from me. This means he thought there was something about us that's illicit. He made us have a secret, even if I wasn't a part of it. He's been living some kind of double life, and made me an accomplice to something, even if on my end it felt innocent.

Okay, I don't have the most innocent thoughts about Zack. And he doesn't say the most innocent things about me. So. If he told me he's in a relationship in order to get some distance, but now he's telling me he's married because he's feeling guilty over what I mean to him—that means I mean something to him. Which means he likes me. Which isn't the worst news in the world.

This really makes me seem like an asshole. Here. Try this. I want you to think of that one person at your job who doesn't make you want to puke. The one person you actually enjoy talking with when you both end up refilling your coffee cup at the same time. Whoever it is that makes funny faces at you from across the conference table when you're in yet another interminable meeting. Think of that one person who knows you're not a complete loser, the one who sees inside you and treats you like an actual loving, living, breathing creature, worthy of so much more than the walls of your cubicle.

Go up to that person and ask him or her to tell you the nicest thing about you. Just one compliment. Take it in. Digest it. Now you tell me: do you need to hear more? We are all good people and we all hate ourselves deep down in the darkest, smallest, hardest part of us. So when that person who recognizes the glimmer, the essence of you, says something that resonates, when the person you admire shoots a little admiration, there's nothing you can do to resist asking to hear every possible syllable of praise.

This does not make you an asshole. This makes you human.

"This is the dumbest thing," Zack says. "Because I don't want anything to happen with you, and you don't want anything to happen with me, but I'm thinking about you all the time. And maybe it's just me. I don't know. Do you think about me?"

I don't want to tell Zack that he's sometimes in an inappropriate fantasy that involves him pushing me up against a wall, clamping his hand over my mouth, and touching me while he stares into my eyes but says nothing. That's not what he means. And I can't believe I just told you that.

"I don't know," I say, but my breath is quickening from anxiety and I see him watching my chest rise and I know he knows I'm not saying anything because I'm seconds away from saying *everything*, and I'm not too sure what that is. I think about him all the time, but he doesn't have to know that.

"I've never been so stupid in my life." He wipes his face with both hands, pushing the skin around, before running his hands over the top of his head. "Because I'm so married it's like I'm dead," he says. "I've been married ten years. Since high school. She's the love of my life. So who the fuck are you?"

My spoon is stuck in my hardened oatmeal, but I've liquefied. If Zack wanted to, he could drag a finger down my arm and leave a mark, forever, on my body. This is a very weird situation. Zack likes me. He's got a crush. It's understandable, as we've been spending a lot of time together. But there's no way Zack is in love with me. He barely knows me. He might find me interesting, or pretty, or he likes my friendship. But he can't be in love with me. I should tell him that, because he's way more upset than someone with a crush should be. Maybe I should kick him out, fire him, send him home to his wife, and tell him to forget I even exist. Besides, I don't live here; I barely exist here as it is.

Only, I'm not going to say that to him. I'm not going to tell him to go away. I don't know why, but I'm not going to do it. I can't. All I know is I don't want him to be gone. So now, what the fuck does that say about me?

I've waited too long to speak. "Say something," Zack demands.

"I'm sorry."

"Tell me your boy's name again."

"Mickey." My boy, who hasn't called me in over a week, who I'm pretending is my boy so my mother will stop trying to set me up with her boyfriends' sons, is someone I forget exists when I'm talking with Zack. "His name's Mickey."

Zack nods, quickly, like the name was a punch to his chin. "Great. I hope Mickey knows what he won at the carnival." Then he storms out the door, leaving it open behind him. Mom limps in moments behind.

She asks, "Does Zack need anything?"

Seeing my mother's curious face seconds after seeing Zack's guilt-wracked one makes me realize that right now, sitting here, I have become my mother. Or, more accurately, Gregory. I'm Zack's secret, a part of his marriage, and now I know I can't go anywhere near him anymore. Maybe I didn't do anything wrong yet, but I'm not going to give myself the opportunity.

Rivers Cuomo, the lead singer of the band Weezer, has taken a vow of celibacy that has lasted a number of years. I used to think this meant poor Rivers was damaged and sad, that he couldn't handle the emotional strength necessary to deal with members of the opposite sex. I used to feel pity and sorry for the man. But now I know: he's a genius. Rivers knew what I've been telling myself for months now. *This is not worth it.*

Maybe I Shouldn't Be Asking
These Two for Advice . . .

. . . but regardless, I'm going to do it anyway. I'm at a bar with my sister and Amber, who insists on calling herself my semisister, and all I can think about is the conversation I had this morning with Zack. It almost feels like it didn't happen, keeping it in my head like this. I need a little female perspective. I buy the next round of drinks, and keep the girls enthralled during my rehashing of the details.

"Well, of course he's in love with you," Jami says. "You guys only flirt, like, *all the time.*"

"I didn't know he was married."

Jami smirks. "You knew he had a girlfriend, though. And aren't you sort of dating Mickey?"

"No. And Zack and I were never going to do anything. *Are* never going to do anything."

Jami dances in her chair to the music playing on the jukebox, a grinding rap song I've never heard before. Her arms are in the air, elbows like little pointy weapons, flapping all around as she sings along.

Amber leans forward on the table, like she's really letting this soak in. "Did you want something to happen with Zack?" she asks.

"No."

"Did you make it sound like it was?"

"The opposite. We talked about how nothing was ever going to happen."

"Why's that?"

"Because I'm . . ."

I stop myself here because the answer I'm about to give surprises me. I was about to tell her that there's no way he'd ever be happy with me.

Jami offers to finish. "Too stupid?"

"Too insecure," Amber suggests.

"I thought we were kidding around," I say.

Jami says, "At a certain point you had to have known he wasn't kidding anymore."

"No. He calls me Ugly."

"That's terrible," Amber says.

"It's funny," I say, sounding even more ridiculous.

Jami says that men are constantly reading signals from women, even subconsciously. "If you stay outside late talking to him, sit next to him too closely, touch his arm when you giggle—even if you don't mean anything by it, he's going to think, on some level, that you're saying you'd be willing to bone him."

"Are you saying this is my fault?" I ask. "And don't say 'bone.' You sound like a frat boy."

"It's not your fault," Amber says.

"Okay." Jami's still smirking. "But it's *so* her fault."

Amber makes a sound in the back of her throat. "You basically just said if she didn't want to get raped, she shouldn't have worn such a short skirt."

"I'm saying if she didn't want some guy to fall in love with her, she shouldn't have made him get emotionally invested. They're always talking, sharing stories, huddled together at lunch like they have all these secrets to tell each other." She's making it sound like we behave like Mom and Gregory, and it's bothering me.

"It's called being *friends*," I say.

"It's confusing to anyone who has a dick. You need a friend? Call a girl."

"I don't want to call a girl."

"Because you like the attention. You confuse sexual frustration for friendship."

My jaw tightens. "So every guy who has ever been my friend is basically just waiting to get into my pants? And if he's still my friend it's just because he hasn't fucked me yet?"

Jami leans back, hands behind her head. "I think you know exactly how far you can go to make a guy go completely batshit crazy over you, and then you act like it's the biggest surprise in the world."

Amber is still on my side. "All Benny did was be nice to Zack and give him back what he was dishing out. If she didn't reciprocate, he'd be sexually harassing her. But since she played along, she's a tease?"

Jami laughs. "You both can't sit here and tell me it's absolutely shocking that Zack developed feelings for her."

"It's not Benny's fault."

"It's not Zack's fault either."

"I didn't make him do anything," I say. "What if it's because I've lost all this weight? Maybe I wasn't as much of a distraction before, when I was heavier."

Jami laughs so loudly the people at the next table look over to see if one of us has fallen over. "Okay, first of all, you haven't lost *that* much weight," she says. "And if anything, losing some of that ass made you flirt harder because you think you're hot shit, and *that's* why Zack doesn't know what to do with you."

"He's the one who's married!" Amber shouts. "He's the one who shouldn't be flirting in the first place."

"He's married. Not numb. Not blind. Still a man. Still thinks girls are pretty."

Amber rocks her head from side to side, debating her next point. "I mean this in the nicest way," she says, "but it's not like every boy is going to fall in love with Benny just by getting to know her."

"It does sound conceited," I say. "He's laughing at my jokes. Better stop, or he might decide I'm worth destroying his marriage over."

Jami's cell phone buzzes between us on the table. I can see Charles's name on the window. She stands to take the call outside, but leans down for one last remark. "You keep that shit in check, Benny. You look in his eyes, and if he looks back at you like you're made of angels and powdered sugar, you get the fuck out of there or you deal with the ramifications of your actions."

Once Jami's outside on her call, Amber turns to me. "Charles cheats on her," she says. "She's really sensitive about this stuff."

I should have known. Jami's been cheated on before, by quite a few of her crappy ex-boyfriends. Jami is able to find the most fucked-up boy in her perimeter and chain herself to him like she's the only one who can save him from himself.

"Why does she stay with these assholes?" I ask it more to the air than to Amber. But she peers down her bottle, one eye closed.

"I could go on and on about it, but it's pretty simple," she says. "Love makes people fucked up."

Stuffed.

I come home from my run to see that in my absence, Mom and Jami took my car and stuffed it with items from a nearby garage sale. They're unloading boxes and lamps and bags of clothes, carrying them into the house. Mom has found some superhuman strength that lets her carry things while staggering on that cast.

I lose it.

I yank things out of their hands, tossing them back onto the lawn. "No!" I shout. "I've worked hard to get this place empty."

"Benny, stop yelling." The dogs are barking all around us, wanting to kill me, howling with the frustration of not being able to go further than their leashes and fences.

"Take it back or throw it away, Ma. Right now."

Mom's wrestling another lamp out of my grip. "I need this," she says.

"You don't need another lamp."

"It's for your bedroom."

"I don't want it."

Jami lights a cigarette and watches us, leaning against the house. "People are watching you guys," she says.

"That's it, Ma," I say. "This is the end."

"End of what?"

"The trash. The dogs. The cats. The lizards. This house can be clean in a matter of weeks, but you keep finding ways to stuff it with more shit."

"You're not getting rid of my dogs," Jami says.

"Everything goes. And you two are going to act like normal human beings."

Wow, I sound like my mother.

"Benny, this isn't your house. You don't get to decide what happens." Mom picks up a bag of dish towels I threw to the ground. "We need things, and we don't have a lot of money. The garage sale saves money. You would know something about the value of a dollar if you had to live through the Depression, like my grandmother did."

"I'm living through a depression. *Yours.*"

She drops everything to the lawn. "You," she says. And then that's all she says. I watch her brain go apoplectic. She wants to hit me. That's the look right before we'd get spanked.

"Ma, come inside," Jami says, grabbing my mother's shoulder. "Benny, go run."

"I just got back."

"Go again. Get out of here."

"I'm serious, Jami. The dogs have to go."

"You have to go," she says. "When are you going to hear it? How many times do we have to say it? We didn't ask you to do any of this. You aren't helping."

They're wrong. The house is cleaner. My sister has a job. I'm going to find my mother's ring. If I weren't here, they wouldn't even have a way to get to the store.

Jami pulls Mom inside. I drive the car to Goodwill and dump out the contents.

Blood Is Thicker Than Charles.

That night my cell phone rings. It's Jami. Her voice comes in choppy through sobs. "Come . . . get me." A shuddery wail. Then: "Charles."

She gives me directions while I'm still on the phone, jumping into the car. I don't know exactly where I'm headed, but at the end of this drive I'll be saving my little sister from some kind of bar brawl. This much I know.

There's a girl singing a punk version of "Why Don't We Get Drunk" as I enter the dark club. There's spray paint on the walls, smoke in the air, and the floor under my feet is sticky. I squint against the neon lights from the beer ads on the wall. I'm searching the bar stools, looking for Jami.

She's tucked into a chair in the corner, almost hiding behind a bottle of beer. There's sweat on her forehead and her hair is pulled back, secured with a pencil. A single strand of purple snakes down her forehead toward her nose. She won't look at me. Her tongue ring darts out from between her lips.

"Jami. What's going on?"

"How come Mom can have all these guys and I can't find one who will love me? I mean, Mom's great. But she's got three. And I've got half a guy. Not even. He's not even half a guy. I hate Charles so much."

And in one quick motion she's on her feet and in my arms, crying. "Please get me out of here," she says. Her body is trembling against mine. I want to pick her up like she's a little monkey, but she feels so heavy, the weight of everything in her head keeping her feet locked to the floor.

"Come on, Jami," I say. "Let's go."

"He's an asshole, Benny," she says. "He's such an asshole."

A guy grabs my wrist, his biceps bulked up so severely it looks like he's got popcorn balls trapped beneath his skin. "I'm glad you're here," he says. "I told her she had to call somebody to come get her. She said you're the only person who really loves her."

"She said that?"

The guy keeps his eyes on Jami, who's bent over the table, grabbing her purse, out of earshot. "She was throwing up at the time," he says, "but yeah."

"Thanks for making her call me."

"She's a great girl," he says. "Too bad she's seeing that douche."

I never catch the bartender's name. In the car, Jami tells me what happened. She wasn't supposed to go to the bar tonight. A friend of hers called to tell her that Charles was there with another girl. When Jami showed up, she expected Charles to apologize, to toss the other girl out on her ass and make sure Jami knew he regretted his mistake. Instead he asked Jami to please leave them alone; he didn't want to embarrass anyone publicly. Jami, true to form, sat at the next table with six shots of tequila lined up in front of her, and did shots while she watched Charles with his clueless date. The other girl didn't know who Jami was, even when Jami pegged the sixth empty shot glass at the girl's skull.

"Oh, my God, Jami."

"I missed," she says. "Unfortunately."

"Then what happened?"

"Charles told me I was a sick, twisted bitch, and he left. With her." Then her body doubles over again in tears. She is howling next to me, her hands clutching her face. I know she's heartbroken, humiliated, and in the deepest of sorrow. But still, I can't shake this feeling of relief. I hope he's out of her life.

Maybe this will be the time Jami has had enough. She'll realize she's better than the men she decides to fix. She doesn't need to be jobless and broke to be in love. There are men who haven't gone to jail or prison, who don't break any laws at all, who can look at Jami and see she's worth everything. Or maybe she'll look in the mirror tomorrow and see that she's perfect all by herself, without a male project, without someone else who's so fucked up he demands every ounce of her attention. I want Jami to cry everything inside her out until there's nothing left of Charles, until he has faded into a bad memory, a past mistake. If there was a way she could cry until everything changed, I'd drive this car for days and weeks, waiting for her to catch her breath, look forward, and never look back.

She's quiet about fifteen minutes later, as we round onto my mother's street.

"You okay?" I ask. I slow the car down, willing to go another circle around the neighborhood.

"Yeah. Thanks." She opens her cell phone and pushes a button. "He'd better fucking be home," she says.

Gregory's House.

Are you wondering why nobody's talked about that last fight, the one in the front yard that all of our neighbors witnessed? The answer is simple: because we won't. Mom and Jami will pretend they never said such things, and I'll act like I don't care that they said them, and everybody will go on as if that day never happened. It's much easier than trying to figure out which one of us needs to apologize the most.

"Does Gregory have any guy friends?" Jami asks as we sit cramped in the sports car for a few seconds while Mom fixes her hair for the third time. We're parked in Gregory's driveway.

"He does," Mom says. "But I don't get involved with them. How would that look? All those men and then me."

Jami says, "Yes, don't sit at a table with five men, Mom. What a slut."

"How's the hair?" Mom asks.

"Puffy and stiff," Jami answers. "Just like you like it."

It's the first time I've been to Gregory's house. It sort of feels like I'm going on one of Mom's dates; Jami and I are the accessories to her date outfit. Jami and I both tried excuses to get out of this meal, but Mom wasn't having it. She said it was important to her.

Once inside, I can smell chicken roasting, garlic simmering in butter, and the yeasty smell of fresh bread in the air. There's jazz music playing. The walls are a brown, mustard color, with dark wood beams and bookshelves that go to the ceiling. There are touches of antique decorations—trunks, suitcases, and stacks of old books. If I ever get Mom's house clean, I hope she lets Gregory do the decorating.

Mom asks us to take off our shoes at the doorway. On the small shelf waiting for my sneakers, there's a picture of my mother. It's weird to walk into someone else's house and see my mother's face smiling at me. I've never seen this photo before. She's leaning forward on a railing, head tucked at her elbow, like she's posing for a professional shot.

"That's the only picture I've ever liked of me," Mom says, putting her hand on my back. "Gregory took it. Don't I look happy?"

She limps toward the kitchen, calling out to Gregory, using a nickname I don't understand. Did she just call him "Pud"?

Jami is sitting on the bench beside me, one shoe still on. "Hey, is it weird for you that Mom has a boyfriend?" she asks. "I know we deal with it all the time, but sometimes it really hits me that Mom likes some other guy who isn't Dad." Her eyes are watery, and turning pink around the edges.

"Jami, please, if you do this now I'm going to start crying, too."

She angrily pushes her hands over her eyes and sighs. "I know. I know. Fuck. Fuck. Fuck." She punches her thighs with both hands. "Stupid."

"You're not stupid."

"All of this is stupid. What the fuck are we doing here in this Pottery Barn–looking house?"

"They asked us to dinner. You haven't been here before?"

"Yes, but I try not to. I like seeing Mom so happy, and I like Amber fine, but I don't want to play house with them. This isn't my family."

Jami seemed so cool, I thought I was the one being ridiculous about not wanting to run into Gregory's arms every time I saw him, not wanting to think of him as my new daddy.

"I know we should just get over it," Jami says, her voice raspy as she tries to keep it quiet. "Mom's dating. Lots of men. She's going to. She's allowed to." She touches the frame of my mother's picture. "Are we fucked up?" she asks.

"What do you mean?"

"The other morning. You made us sound fucked up."

"I'm sorry."

"Mom just likes going to garage sales. And the house is messy, but it's not like we're dying of black mold. And my boyfriend sucks, but that's not your problem."

"It is my problem if I—"

"Forget it," she says, standing up. "I'm sorry I brought it up."

Her face changes as she puts her wall back up. Jami clicks her tongue ring and shouts toward the kitchen, "Gregory, I'm already pissed about how much food I'm going to eat tonight."

Gregory's in a green apron. His bare feet slap on the hardwood floors as he shuffles around the large island in the center of his kitchen, multitasking dinner preparations. My mother sits on a stool, watching him, enjoying her glass of wine.

"You should take Benny to see out back," she says. "She'd like it."

"What is it?" I ask.

Gregory gives me a rare smile. Proof he has teeth. "I'll show you," he says, putting out a hand I don't take. What am I, six?

I can hear Mom, Jami, and Amber cackling back in the kitchen as I follow Gregory out of his house and into his backyard. He points to a pair of slippers with hard soles. I slip my feet into them.

His backyard is dark and wide. The sound of crickets is louder than our feet crunching through dirt and gravel. Gregory's got a flashlight and leads us down a winding path to a large shed. He doesn't say anything as we walk. I don't, either.

The shed is sturdier and larger than it looks from the path, and once inside he turns on fluorescent lighting. It's a workroom, and as it floods with greenish light I see large, metal figurines twisting toward the sky.

"Did you do these?" I ask. Gregory nods.

They're tall, skinny, sturdy figures that are part human, part animal. Each one is frozen in play, dancing, running, tangled up in each other in celebration.

"They're amazing."

"This one's your mother," he says.

My mother's statue is round and made out of a different metal from the rest. It gives off sparkles of light. He's tied bits of ribbon and string along the bottom swirls, so she appears to be wrapped in a rainbow of energy. It's as delicate as it is strong.

"It's beautiful."

"Thanks." He nods at the one next to it. "Can you tell who that one is?"

The jangled mess of wires, twisted metal, and pieces of shattered CDs glued in mosaic along the base is unmistakably the tangible representation of my sister's attitude.

"What's that poured down the side?" I ask, pointing to the thick, dark line.

"Ink," Gregory says. "I'm proud of that one. She hasn't seen it yet. It's for her birthday."

"She's going to love it."

At dinner, Amber takes the spotlight, telling gossipy stories about her latest temp job. Gregory stays quiet, but listens intently to his daughter's every word, as if he needs to pay attention for a surprise twist ending. Mom takes her turn telling embarrassing stories about Jami and me. We let her go, interjecting only to correct factual errors.

Jami leaves the table at least three times to take calls from Charles. Mom doesn't stop her, even though I can tell Gregory's disappointed and mildly insulted. Mom raises her hands to show she has no control over Jami's rudeness. "She's too old to spank," she jokes. Gregory looks at his daughter. They share an "I'd slap her" smirk and go back to their desserts. Mom doesn't see this exchange.

Jami returns this last time apologizing. "It's so much easier to talk to him for two minutes than to deal with him being angry later."

"I can't handle clingy guys," Amber says like she's bragging.

"He's not clingy," Jami protests. "He works all the time, so we don't get to talk that often."

Mom says, "You're always on the phone with him."

"For, like, three minutes every time! It takes all day for us to have a single conversation."

I stand to clear my plate. Gregory shakes his head at me and I sit back down.

"I don't mind," I say.

"I wanted to ask you a question," he says. "You never talk about Los Angeles. Do you like it out there?"

"I do." I fiddle with my fork, feeling on the spot. "It's sunny and warm, and there are lots of weird people all around, which is comforting because it means I'm never the weirdest one in the room. And I like driving everywhere and needing a map. Everybody needs a map because it's so big, so I don't feel bad when I get so lost. Everybody's lost."

"Sounds lonely," Gregory says.

"I think Los Angeles is superficial," Jami says.

"Did you just say that while playing with your tongue ring? I'm sorry, it's hard to understand you through your amazing nonconformity."

Mom gives a warning. "Girls."

"What made you move out there?" Gregory asks. I know he's trying to get to know me better, but he's about to unleash a lot of my mom, right here on the table. She'll just vomit it out all over the pretty centerpiece.

"Benny couldn't wait to leave our house," she says, never missing her cue. "She followed some boy all the way to California. The Actor. She thought they were soulmates and he was going to be famous and they'd have fancy homes and she'd never need me again."

I make the long story short. "And then he cheated on me and Mom was right."

"I liked him," Mom says, emptying the last of a wine bottle into her glass. "He was really cute."

"Seriously hot," Jami tells Amber, her voice dropping to a somber tone, like I'd somehow screwed up my marriage to George Clooney.

Gregory asks, "Did you move out there before your father died?"

"Yes. Just before," I said. "His death was unexpected."

"Yes, I know," he says. "My parents died unexpectedly, too."

Then it's quiet because I don't really give a shit how his parents died, and apparently neither does my sister. Mom said there was an ax and now they're dead. I'm sure it's a fantastic story but it has nothing to do with my father, so it's not really going to be any kind of bonding moment, Mr. Not Dad. Thanks for the chicken, but maybe you could stop trying to get to know me, okay?

Gregory says, "I knew him, you know."

Jami stands, gathers all the plates within her arm's reach, and walks out of the room. Mom excuses herself and follows.

"I didn't know that," I say. "Mom never said. She hasn't said a lot of things about you. Some things I've had to figure out on my own." Now Gregory and I are staring at each other. I can't tell if he knows what I mean, but I'm pretty sure I've jostled him a little.

"I have to pee," Amber says, and then she practically runs from the table.

"I cleared the room," Gregory says.

"Dead Dad discussion isn't usually the best thing over strawberry shortcake."

Gregory nods in a sad kind of agreement. "I met him once at a company picnic. He loved you very much. I met all of you at that picnic, actually. You and I played with a softball. Do you remember?"

My chair makes a yelping noise as I push it back from the table. I don't say another word as I grab my purse and shoes. I walk barefoot to the car and sit there, waiting for my family, my real family, to join me. I don't remember meeting Gregory back then, but the image of us tossing a ball while my dad watched makes me sick.

This is when I fantasize doing something that might not be nice, but would be for Mom's own good. Like getting all of her boyfriends in one room. Let them meet each other. Let's get it all out. Hell, I'd have Charles over, too. And Zack.

It would be fantastic. All of these men in one room so I can tell them what's really going on. I'd deliver one big speech with so much drama and passion that they'd understand they're wasting their time with us. Mom would have to see what it looks like to have all of her men in one place. Jami would have to compare Charles to Zack, who would be sitting right next to him, and certainly wouldn't take any of Charles's shit.

Sure, Mom and Jami would be mad at first, because nobody likes having her secrets out in the open like that. But if Mom's going to pick Gregory to be her favorite, then she might as well stop pretending that she just met him somewhere recently, that he swept in all of a sudden and became this man she loves. If she wants me to trust him, then she needs to tell me that he's been in my life for much longer than she's ever admitted. She needs to look me in the eye and say, "I loved this man when I said I loved your father." If she can say that to me, to Jami, and to all the men in her life, then maybe I'll be willing to listen to Gregory, and let him be a part of my life. But as long as he's a tertiary character in her love life? A dirty secret she hides in the garage? Then fuck him.

Let's Go Home.

Mom can't stop apologizing the entire ride home. She drives, which makes me realize how close she is to getting that cast off. Good. I can't wait to get out of here.

Jami calls Charles on her phone. I sit in the backseat, crying as quietly as possible.

"I don't know why he said any of that," Mom says. "Maybe he had too much wine. Maybe he thought it would make it easier for you to get to know him, if he made it seem like he had a history with us."

"Tell him to try a different tactic," I say, my nose stuffed. I sound like a little kid.

Jami starts talking to Charles on her phone, loudly. "That sucked," she says. "The food was good, but then he talked about Dad in front of Benny, and you just don't do that."

After she got off the phone, I asked why she made it sound like I'm the one who has the problem.

"Because," she says, "if someone even mentions you had a father you flip out like that person killed him."

"You were the one crying when we got there." I'm ratting her out, but I don't care. "You said—"

"I said I don't like being reminded constantly that Mom has a boyfriend. That's not the same thing."

"Yes, it is."

Mom is staying quiet, but I can only imagine how bizarre it is to hear your daughters discuss you like you're not right there.

"You act like Dad was so sacred that nobody's good enough to talk about him," Jami says. "We don't talk about him around you. You never bring him up. It's frustrating."

"I don't do that."

Mom pulls into her driveway, her shoulders leaning away from us. "I want you two to promise me you'll never fight like this about me after I'm dead," she says.

All fighting stops as Jami and I picture our dead mother, whom we killed by being horrible daughters.

She's really good. You have to admit.

She's not done. "I've come to terms with the fact that I'm probably never going to be a grandmother. This means all I have is my memories of you two girls. I won't bring you to Gregory's again. It's too hard on both of you to see me in a relationship. I should have thought of that."

"But—" Jami doesn't get to finish her protest.

Mom goes in for the kill. "I think Benny should go back to Los Angeles. And Jami should start looking for another place to live. I need my independence. I want to see my boyfriends without feeling guilty. You two need good jobs and should find nice men. Go get married and be happy. It's wrong to keep you here any more."

She opens the door and leaves.

After a few seconds, Jami asks, "Did Mom just kick me out?"

"And ask for a grandkid?"

Mom's in her bedroom with the door closed by the time we enter the house. Jami gives me a quick hug good night.

"Maybe I'll see you tomorrow," she says. "If you haven't already flown back to Los Angeles."

"Yeah. If you haven't already started living out on the street."

"She drives me crazy, Benny," Jami says. "She really does."

I search the office, the kitchen, the junk drawer, the address book, and even Mom's purse, but I can't find Paul's number. Her cell phone is up in her bedroom, so I can't check that until tomorrow. It occurs to me while I'm searching for information that I don't know anything about Dave. Did Mom say he lived in Philly?

My fantasies of ruining my mother's secret love life are disintegrating as I realize how hard it'll be to pull off, not to mention the fact that I don't know if it'll accomplish what I want. I'll only succeed in making my mother even angrier with me.

Maybe Mom's right. Maybe it's time for me to go back to Los Angeles and forget about this place.

I Can't Believe This . . .

. . . but I'm about to smoke a cigarette. I'm going to sneak a cigarette, to be exact, in my mother's backyard, because I've been avoiding her all day after last night's tantrum.

The neighborhood kids have erected another makeshift shed, covered it in graffiti, and have been using it to hide stolen bottles of beer and wine. I found a pack of Marlboros (half were damp and ruined) and grabbed a pack of matches from the box of hundreds I found in the basement. I can't explain the size of the box or why it was sitting underneath sixteen cans of aerosol upholstery cleaner. How my mother's house hasn't burned down is beyond me.

Crouched like I'm thirteen and skipping school, I light my first cigarette in close to six years.

Not one cough. Just pure cigarette bliss. It's wrong how right it feels.

"Sexy."

It's Zack, and the grin on his face shows he's happy to have caught me in this position.

"You want one?"

"Yep."

He taps the cigarette against one of the wooden beams, tamping it down before he lights it. "Haven't had one of these in years," he says.

"Still tastes good, doesn't it?"

"It's one of the best things I've ever put in my mouth."

He kicks some dirt aside with his dark, scuffed boots, and takes a seat next to me, folding his legs up close to his chin. "What's happening?" he asks casually, as if this was the office where we worked every day, as if we happened to meet at a coffee shop, or on the street.

"Nothing."

"Just thought you'd take up smoking?"

"Maybe."

"I normally hate the way girls look when they smoke, but it looks cute on you."

I sneer at him. I cannot believe I sneer, like a teenager. It feels like we really did skip class to smoke cigarettes in the fort behind my mother's house and we're not supposed to be here, it's completely forbidden, and therefore much more fun. I keep expecting him to pull one of my pigtails, to pop me with a rock from his slingshot.

But we are *adults*. This is stupid and—somehow—thrilling.

"So, I have something to tell you," Zack says. "After this cigarette, I plan on keeping my distance from you."

As I turn to face him, my feet make scraping noises along the grit and gravel on the wooden boards. "This is all in your head," I say. "You and me. You keep making it into a bigger deal than it has to be."

"If you say so."

"I had no intentions with you."

"And I still have no intentions with you. Doesn't mean I shouldn't be careful around you. I keep trying to find reasons not to like you. I keep hoping I'll come back here to find you ugly again."

"You don't have to worry. I'm going back to Los Angeles."

"Oh." And here his voice gets quiet and he says, "Shit."

It starts to rain outside, and I already know we're going to sit in this shed for as long as we can possibly take it.

In the Dark.

That night I walk into my mother's bedroom. It smells like my childhood and it makes my throat close up just a little bit.

"Ma?"

"What is it, Boobs?" No sign that I woke her.

"Do you really want me to go back to Los Angeles?"

She clicks on her bedside lamp. She stares at me from within the small circle of yellow light around her face.

"I want you to do what you have to do."

"I'm still trying to find your ring."

"It'll turn up. Everything lost gets found in some way or another."

I sit at the edge of her bed, right by her cast, which Jami has attacked with a black Sharpie so it now reads, KICKING IT OLD SCHOOL.

"Ma, can I ask you a question?"

Mom closes her eyes and waits.

"How did the house get like this? Why is there so much stuff everywhere? Where did it all come from?"

"I don't know," she says. "It just happened. I needed things."

"Why do you still need things? Why get more?"

Mom reaches up to turn off the light. "I'm having Dave over this week," she says. "It would really help me out if you weren't here. Jami's going to stay at Charles's. There's a nice hotel just one exit further down the highway. I could call them for you, if you'd like. Make you a reservation."

"No thanks," I say, backing out of the room. "I'll handle it."

Watch how fucking far I can go, Ma.

Decisions.

"Window or aisle?"

The woman behind the counter at the airline has asked me a question, but her fingers are flying across the keys as if I've already given her an answer.

Aisle would be nice. I like sitting on the aisle because it guarantees I'll have at least one armrest. I can cross my legs without my knee getting crushed by the back of someone's seat. I like having space around me, my entire side free of another person.

Of course being on the aisle has responsibilities. I'll have to deal with the cart that can come by and smack my elbow when I've fallen asleep. And I'm in charge of doling out pretzels and drinks for my row, waking people up and asking if they want anything. I'm the one who has to get up all the time for whatever the other two need. Plus there's double the chance of getting talked to by a stranger, with rows on either side of me.

So the window's good, because I could lean against the plastic or glass or whatever it is and take a nap. People leave the window person alone. I don't have to feel guilty for turning on my overhead light, or for putting down my tray table. It's like having a fort, the window seat. I can choose to stare out the window and hog it all I want. That's what people expect from the window person. They leave you alone and mostly ignore you.

But then it's going to be a long flight, so if I have to get up and use the bathroom, I've got to bother everyone, including waking them. It can get a little claustrophobic, all crouched in the window seat. Can't move around or stretch your legs at all. It's like being put on a shelf.

"Ma'am?" The attendant's voice is loud, impatient. "Aisle or window?"

"Um, aisle?"

Her fingers fly again. "All we have is middle anyway," she says. "Sorry I asked."

L.A. Woman.

My apartment is exactly how I left it. In fact, it looks nicer than when I left. There are flowers in a vase on the kitchen table, which is free of the normal piles of mail and receipts I normally keep there. There's a smell in the air of something sweet and girly.

I don't remember having curtains before.

Grace enters the living room bent forward, pulling her damp hair into a towel.

"Hi," I say.

She jumps, yelps. "Oh, my God. Did you knock?"

"I used my key," I say, sounding like an idiot. Of course it's not my apartment right now. What was I thinking? "I'm sorry."

"It's okay," she says. "I know you're freaking out."

"I've called you a million times. Where have you been?"

Her cheeks are pink and I can see her neck is damp. She must have just gotten out of the shower. "I was out of town," she says. "Visiting home. And I forgot to bring my cell phone. I totally flaked. And when I got back, I was going to call you, but I couldn't find your number and anyway, I'm really sorry. You didn't fly all the way back here for me, did you?"

"Not exactly."

"Oh, Benny. I hope you didn't. I'm so sorry."

"It's okay."

She flops down onto the couch and holds a pillow in her lap. "I've kept your place nice, right?"

"It looks great," I admit.

"All your mail is in the top drawer of your dresser, and I renewed your newspaper subscription, because it was going to lapse." She's staring at me with this squint that lets me know she's thinking about asking me something I can't predict.

"What?" I finally say.

"Are you going to see Mickey?" she asks.

I'm trying to figure out why she would know about him. I didn't mention him before I left, did I? "How do you know Mickey?"

She bites down on her lower lip with all of her front teeth and pulls her nose so high she looks like she's expecting me to slap her. "Because I talk to him sometimes. He calls here."

"He does what?"

"He's a really nice guy," she says. "He called here once to check on your place because you asked him to, and we ended up talking."

So that's why I haven't heard from Mickey lately. He's been dating my subletter.

"Oh," I say. "Well, that's interesting."

"Don't be mad," Grace says, extending her long legs across the coffee table. *My* coffee table. She looks so comfortable in my home, with my things, with my Mickey, that I feel like I've been replaced. Upgraded to a newer, younger, taller model.

"I don't know what to say," I admit. "You guys don't do it on my bed, do you?"

"Nothing's going on," she says. "I've never even met him in person. We talk about you."

"Me?"

"Yeah. At first I thought it was a little weird, the way he'd ask me questions about you when I don't know you. But then we started figuring you out."

"What do you mean?"

Grace laughs, pushing a hand through her hair. She rests her elbow on the couch. "You were our puzzle. Mysterious. He knew a little about you, and I knew what your things looked like, and we started trying to solve you."

I'm feeling a little dizzy, so I fall into the armchair. "I don't really understand. You went through my things?"

"Not really. Not at first."

"Uh-huh."

She proceeds to tell me how this happened. He had called

to check up on the place for me, but on a night when he'd had too much to drink, and the next thing Grace knew, Mickey was telling her all about me, and how he was thinking about me even when he didn't want to. Grace was curious about the woman whose home she'd been living in, and proceeded to describe my apartment to him. Suddenly hours had passed, and she was going through my yearbook, describing my senior photo.

Grace points at my bookshelf. "I read him all the books you have. We tried to figure out which one was your favorite."

Curiosity gets the better of me. "What'd you decide?"

"Pride and Prejudice."

"No. *Brave New World.*"

"Damn. I owe Mickey ten bucks."

A number of questions fight inside my head. "How long has this been going on?"

"We talked about you maybe three times," she said. "Until we both felt a little guilty for invading your privacy."

"A *little*?"

"If it's any consolation, it came from a really nice place. He likes you a lot. Seems to hate that he does, but he does."

I know that feeling. I also didn't know that Mickey had that feeling for me. Not exactly, anyway.

"How long are you in town?" Grace asks.

"A week."

"Oh," she says, looking disappointed. She looks around my place. "Do you want me to sleep on the couch?"

I'm staying with Jane, but I don't tell Grace this yet. Let her squirm a little for going through my things.

"I don't know what I want," I say. "Will you excuse me?"

I walk over to Mickey's.

When he answers his apartment door, he doesn't register

shock. He sort of nods a little, licks his lip, and asks, "Decided you're in love with me?"

His hair is longer, getting shaggy around the ears. He's clean-shaven, and there's a nick on his chin that looks like it took a long time to stop bleeding. I look him over, changing my memory of him into what he really looks like.

"Are you stalking me?" I ask.

"I haven't talked to you in weeks," he says.

"I just spoke with Grace."

His face actually turns white. "She wasn't supposed to tell you anything," he says.

"Well, she did."

"Man. Girls can't stop talking."

From inside the apartment, I hear a woman's voice calling Mickey's name.

I can't contain the snort that comes out of me. "You're busy."

"No," he says. "Wait here." He disappears back inside. I hear the tones of their conversation, but not their words. He's explaining something. She's upset, indignant, probably offended, but he is firm.

He's kicking this girl out for me.

She's blond, with her hair in two braids, wearing a shirt that exposes her taut stomach muscles. Her super-low-rise jeans skim a tattoo on her lower back of a purple butterfly. She looks me over before she says, "He's all yours."

Once she's down the street, headed toward her car, Mickey says, "You owe me for that."

"Whatever," I say. "I just saved your ass from Hep-C."

Mickey pulls me in for a hug. It's unexpected, and fills my lungs with everything, with him. I haven't been held in forever. I bury my face as deep as I can into his chest, smelling him, letting everything else go.

"Didn't mean to ruin your evening."

"You didn't. I'm stalking you, remember?"

We go inside. He gives me a drink, and lets me talk. I tell him all about my mother, her boyfriends, the fights we had. I tell him about Jami, and how I worry about her even though she doesn't want me to. Mickey listens as he holds my hand, his thumb stroking mine.

"And I lost all this weight," I say. "I've never told you this, but I lost a lot of weight right before you met me, and it makes everything weird and different."

"How much did you lose?"

"Enough that I don't want to tell you. But it makes me think of myself differently, and somehow it changes the role in my house. My dad's gone, and my weight's gone, and now Mom and Jami treat me like I'm someone else. I want to help, but they won't let me."

Just before my tears can start, Mickey puts his mouth on mine. I'd forgotten just how perfect his kisses are. His hands embrace my face, covering my skin from chin to temple in warmth. His teeth graze my lower lip and my entire body begins humming to the rhythm of his breathing. It's a mind eraser. Powerful, and something I'd like never to stop doing.

He pulls back and smiles, observing me. "Yeah, I still got it," he says.

"You sure do."

"I didn't want you shit-talking yourself."

"What a good way to shut me up."

He takes me to bed, and shows me all the other things he's still got.

Later that night, at dinner, I take mental snapshots of the way he's got one hand holding his plate, the other hand gesturing wildly with a fork as he tells me about the time a porn star backed into his car, how it was almost physically impossible not to make a joke using the words *rear-ended*. I'm soaking it all in, his eyes happy and bright in the candlelight, the way his knee is pressed against mine under the table, making sure we're still touching in some way, even though we're in public. I can smell him on my skin, on my wrist when I wipe my mouth with my napkin. My body is still aching from his on top of mine, little pains I know will turn into faint bruises I will welcome.

It's so good to see him, flesh and blood, loud and hilarious, right in front of my face. It's important to see him smiling at me, absorbing me. This is what I let myself forget about. This is the stuff I pushed aside.

This is the stuff that scares the crap out of me.

I'm going to disappoint him. Maybe not right now, maybe not even this week or this month, but there will come a time when I'm going to say something or do something, and he'll never look at me this way again. How he looks at me will change, because I will change. I will become flawed, imperfect. I will become just like any other girl he's ever been with. I will morph into the same old thing.

We're back at his apartment, sitting on his porch, staring at the twinkling lights that stretch across Los Angeles, when Mickey lets go of my hand. For reasons I cannot understand, I suddenly begin telling him about Zack, how I'm dealing with a man who isn't mine, who somehow became a part of my life. I tell him more than I've told anyone. In fact, I probably tell him too much.

"Wow," Mickey says, when I come up for air. "Jesus, Benny."

"Yeah."

"Why did you just tell me about that guy?"

"Zack?"

"I don't give a fuck what his name is. Why are you telling me about him?"

Mickey has his feet on the porch railing. He's pushing his chair back, angling dangerously on two legs, rocking as he tries to balance.

"I don't know," I say.

"Are you telling me about him because you want me to be the bad guy? Make an ultimatum? Him or me, so you can go back to him and break it off without feeling guilty?"

"There's nothing to break off." My voice sounds hoarse and small.

"Then are you telling me this to make me angry?"

"No."

His chair lands hard on all four feet as Mickey grabs his bottle of beer. "I'm really not interested in playing games." He stands and stretches. I have to lean my head back to see him. He's above me, looking over my head, staring at the city full of people who aren't me. "I know we're not anything, but I thought maybe we were going to be something."

"I don't know if we can," I say.

He starts picking up our wineglasses from the small table between us. He's cleaning, which is so dismissive and aggressive I start cleaning, too, just to have something to do with my hands.

"I'm sorry," I say, putting the cork back into the empty wine bottle. "But you told me about the girls you were seeing, so how is this different?"

"Yeah, you're right," he says. "You're right. This isn't different, Benny." His voice cracks on my name. I see his stomach struggling to control his breath. "Go back to Virginia. Go back to your apartment. I really don't care anymore, Benny. You win."

Bottom.

I can see Virginia out the airplane window. It doesn't feel like home. I'm almost out of money from Dad's savings, but I'm still not ready to go back to Los Angeles. Things with Mickey are ruined, my family is a mess, and I'm wondering what exactly I'm supposed to do next.

In the minutes before our descent, when my iPod's battery runs out, I begin imagining my funeral. This is what I do to prepare for the plane crash I'm always sure is seconds away. I picture my funeral, in a very solemn, dark church. My mother's crying into a handkerchief. My sister looks shell-shocked. A boy with a shaved head holds her hand. Something sad is playing, preferably by the Beatles.

But that's not what I focus on when I think about the funeral. That's the backdrop. What I focus on are the people who want to speak, who stand behind the podium with a ball of Kleenex in one hand, who flip through pages of notes they can no longer get through now that people are listening.

I try to picture the line of speakers, and what they'll say about me.

Are they thoughts of love? Admiration? Does someone break down during the word *special*?

There are people in attendance who hardly know me at all. There's Gregory and Amber.

My Hollywood friends wear big, dark sunglasses, and talk about how skinny I got, and how I was nice on the inside, too.

There's Zack, with his wife, whom I picture small and

beautiful, sitting in the back corner. Zack weeps, but will not speak. In fact, he will not speak of me ever again.

Back at his apartment, leaning his chair against a wall as he stares into the dark night, is Mickey. He doesn't come to my funeral. I can't tell if he's crying. I can't tell what he feels.

I really hope this plane doesn't crash. I'm not done yet.

Déjà Vu.

If Mom and Jami are surprised to have me back in their house, they say nothing about it. I was gone for the week, like Mom requested, but nobody's asked me where I was or how my past seven days have gone. How does this family forget someone exists as soon as she walks out of the room?

That night I find them both in the kitchen. It's almost midnight, and they are sharing a chocolate cake, still in the bakery box. They are giggling with each other, high on sugar and gossip. When they see me, they quickly hush their conversation.

"What?" I ask.

At the same time they say, "Nothing."

You know who this used to happen to all the time?

Dad.

It should be easy enough for me to pull up a chair, grab a fork, and dig in with them. Shouldn't I want to be a part of this? What is keeping me stuck in the doorway, watching these women drag their forks through the icing, their eyes frozen on each other as they keep their secrets behind their sly grins? Why can't I ask them to let me in?

If I joined them, stuffed my face with sweets and attention, then everything would go to hell. I know myself well enough to know that this wouldn't be one midnight snack, one girl-bonding evening. This would be the start of the chain reaction. By excusing myself once, I'd start letting myself get away with everything. Soon I'd stop exercising, telling myself I've been so good over the past year that a few weeks off won't hurt anybody. I'd treat myself to non-diet Coca-Cola, whole milk, and real, melted butter on my popcorn.

I'd sit down with them and I'd never leave. I'd eat and eat and eat until the three of us felt fat and disgusting and then we'd finally all be equal.

My father was a great cook. One of my favorite things about summertime was his grilled steak. I remember a Saturday afternoon when it was just the two of us—Jami and Mom must have been out shopping together—and we were going to have a big meal, Dad and his older daughter. He let me help him prepare everything as we talked about how excited I was to start the sixth grade. I could run for student council, work on the yearbook, and go to the sixth-grade dances.

I set the table for the two of us, pulling out candles we'd used when company came for dinner. That was the day my father taught me how to open a wine bottle, how to know when the steak was ready, and told me about his first girlfriend in the sixth grade. Her name was Suzie, as all first girlfriends seem to be named, and she broke up with him on Valentine's Day because she wanted to be his best friend's valentine instead.

I remember giggling hysterically as I finished my meal, one hand clutched to my stomach, which was filled with good food and cramping from laughing all afternoon. Dad had fallen quiet.

"What's wrong?" I asked.

He shook his head, and looked at the table. I followed his

glare, staring down at my empty plate. "You really ate all of that," he said. His fork came into my vision, hovering over the pools of steak blood and scraps of potato skin. Everything inside of me scalded hot with shame. I didn't know I wasn't supposed to finish my meal.

"Oh," I said.

"I didn't want to say anything to you, Benny. I kept thinking you'd get full on your own. I waited. But you didn't. You ate all of it. Your mother . . ." He meant my mother had been right all along. I was a fat monster who couldn't see that a steak that big was meant for grown-ups. Not me.

"I'm sorry," I whispered, looking right at his face, desperately needing him to make eye contact.

He didn't. Instead he stood from the table, his eyes turned away from me. He gingerly placed his napkin beside his plate and said, "Do the dishes."

It's this memory that comes to mind as I watch my mother and sister share stolen, forbidden food because this is the very behavior that got me into trouble in the first place. Food is what made my parents argue over me. Fat is what kept me from being everything my parents wanted.

This memory, combined with watching my mom and sister have yet another moment where I'm just not included, fills me with rage. I am tired of feeling like I have to apologize for wanting to be a part of this family. If they don't want me, if I'm always going to be a disappointment or someone to ridicule, then I will go out fighting. I will shake this place up and make them have to admit that they needed me here, that they were wrong to make me feel unnecessary. Invisible.

I want to be included.

I want someone else in charge of the order, the structure, making sure everybody's doing what she's supposed to be doing.

I want my dad.

Guess Who's Coming to Dinner.

While Mom and Jami are busy giggling, I find both of their cell phones and take down every male phone number I can find. I'm having this boyfriend dinner, and I'm having it tomorrow tonight. It may not be the kindest way to deal with my mother's indiscretions, but subtlety does not work in my family.

I'll have everyone over, and we'll get it all out. That's what Dad would do. He'd call a family meeting, at the dinner table, where we hate the food and the conversation even more. This family has gotten smaller, and now there are so many insignificant additions that I'd like everybody to step up and take some responsibility.

I invite Paul first. He's surprised to hear from me.

"Your mother told me she was in Phoenix," he says.

I'm getting better at lying on the spot, particularly when it comes to my mother. "She came back early and we're having a birthday party for my sister."

Jami's birthday is in a week. I'm sure she wouldn't mind the early celebration, since she'll be getting a room full of drama as a gift.

I leave Charles a message on his voice mail, which only plays a Linkin Park song, which makes me hate him even more.

When I reach Gregory, he sounds confused. "Why doesn't your mother invite me herself?"

"I'm planning the night," I say. "I wanted everybody to

get together, so we can talk about some of the problems we've been having. You know, smooth some stuff out."

Hey, I didn't have to lie to Gregory. All of that was some version of the truth.

"I know you don't like me," he says. "You don't have to pretend."

"After tomorrow night," I tell him, "nobody will have to pretend anything anymore."

Mom and Jami are in the living room, watching a DVD.

"Is Dave still in town?" I ask.

"Yes, he's visiting his family tonight."

"I was wondering if you'd like to have him for dinner to-morrow. I'll cook. I'd like to meet him." Still all true state-ments.

Mom smiles. "That would be nice of you, Boobs."

I head to the kitchen to make my grocery list for Fuck You Chicken.

I call it that because *Chicken Gregory* didn't have the same ring to it.

Endgame.

The next afternoon I walk out back to find Zack standing on the shed, clipping branches from the large oak. Scattered on the ground beneath him are empty beer bottles.

"I don't know if it's better that the bottles are yours or the neighborhood kids'," I say.

Zack doesn't look at me. He just keeps clipping, silently.

"I came back," I say. "I guess you can see that."

More clipping. Branches slide off the roof of the shed to the ground at my feet. He's ignoring me, so I turn to leave. That's when Zack speaks.

"What for?" he asks.

"What?"

"What'd you come back here for?"

"I'm still trying to figure that out," I say.

Zack raises a fist and punches it slightly in the air. "Good for you, Benny."

"What's wrong with you?"

He leaps from the roof of the shed and lands in front of me. I don't know how his ankles didn't snap. He's got a look that makes me take an instinctive step backward.

He gets close. I can smell the sweet and salty taste of boy on his skin.

"Do you love me?" he asks.

I wasn't expecting the question and my body goes into autopilot. My brain is trying to keep up, but my mouth knows I have to answer.

"I don't know," I say, surprising myself. "No."

"What if I said I loved you?" he asks. "Now do you love me?"

"No."

"Bullshit." He takes another step toward me. "Do you love me?"

"You don't love me."

"That's not what I asked."

"That's my answer," I say. "I can't, so I don't."

"But you do."

"I don't."

"Fuck you. You do."

My head is spinning and I'm trying to catch my breath. I was going to find out if he was even interested in talking to me and now here we are wrapped up in a very serious question and I feel like any answer is the wrong one. Something happened to Zack while I was gone. He stopped kidding. If I ever tried to blow this off as some kind of game, this is the moment where Zack has proven to me that this is real, and not something he's going to belittle anymore.

"I'm sorry," I say. "You asked me to stay away. I shouldn't have come back here."

"But you did." His voice drawls as it gets lower, deeper, primal. "All right, Benny. I'm tired. Let's end this. You want to find out if we love each other? Then you're going to let me kiss you."

"No. You're ridiculous."

"I'm sick of wondering. Aren't you?"

His body is millimeters from mine and he smells like lust and dirt and I am just one person. I wasn't expecting this; I don't know what to do with it. I can answer all of my questions right now, here where nobody can see us. I can push myself into him and see what happens next. But if I do, there's no undoing it. It will have happened, and there will be ramifications.

"Zack," I say, because in times like these, we resort to clichés. We resort to starting our sentences with each other's names.

"What do you want?" he asks slowly, each word having the same weight. His eyes are locked on mine. Big, green, and waiting for my answer. "You think this'll work? You and me and fuck the rest of the world? Because if we're going to do it, let's do it right now. Kiss me and seal the deal. It'll be on. It'll be *so* on."

I can't feel the lower half of my body. My brain is screaming for me to run away. My gut says to stick around, see what's about to happen. It doesn't matter what those two sides are arguing, because it's as if my feet have never learned to take a step.

"Is it worth it?" he asks. "Will I be everything you've ever wanted? Because, Benny, I'm warning you. If this happens? You'd better be a fucking gift from God. You will end my life, and I'll have to start over. With you. But I'm thinking that might not be the worst thing that could happen to me. Now, what do you think about that?"

There is no time to think, to plan, to prepare. There is nothing but this exact second, and I have no idea what to do.

There's sweat on Zack's forehead. "I'm not a little boy," he says. "I don't do things halfway. You will be consumed. Devoured. Do you understand?"

I think I just nodded.

"If we kiss, you can't take it back. You can't change your mind. Your life will be permanently . . . altered."

I can't remember the last time I took a breath.

"You control what happens next, Benny. This is all your decision. And it boils down to one simple kiss."

My mouth is open. I can feel myself swaying, gently, in shock. Everything in me screams, *"MOVE!"*

His fingers graze my wrist.

And I take a step back.

My lips join themselves, my tongue running over them briefly to prove they touched nothing but each other. My mouth opens, and I hear my breath. One of the dogs begins to howl. I jump. Zack doesn't.

He's just staring at me, slowly nodding. He looks impressed. He also looks wounded.

"There you go," he says, his voice a shocked whisper.

Who Wants Dinner?

I put the leaf in the dining room table. This has always meant one thing in my family: company's coming. As I'm waxing the dark pine, I try to imagine the look on my mother's face when she sees all of the men in her life around one table. I know she will be angry. This much I'm prepared for. I wonder if she'll choose to deal with them first, or me.

Paul arrives, holding a huge bouquet of flowers. He's got a big toothy smile that makes me feel sorry for him. There's something about his silence that creeps me out, but the happiness on his face from being anywhere within the general vicinity of my mother shows me that his intentions toward her seem good. He just wants to be my mother's boyfriend. I shouldn't have all of this resentment toward him. The poor guy probably didn't even know my name until a few weeks ago.

He sits nervously in the living room, knees bouncing, the cup and saucer in his hands chirping as he trembles. "Dinner smells great," he says.

"Thanks," I reply. I watch him sip his tea, keeping his eyes on the flowers he's brought for Mom. I put them in some water and they're now the centerpiece of the coffee table. I'm happy to have added some breakables to this intervention.

Gregory arrives next. I introduce him to Paul by name only. They shake hands and sit across from each other. Gregory is looking at me questioningly, but I just shrug my shoulders and make an excuse to check on the chicken.

While I'm in the kitchen, Jami enters. "What the hell is going on in the living room?"

"We're having a dinner party," I tell her. "For your birthday."

Jami turns her face to the side, but keeps her eyes on me. I've just confused the hell out of her. "What did you do, Benny?"

"I thought we'd have a little talk," I said.

My sister, who is quick enough to understand in a millisecond not only what I've done, but why I've done it, says, "You gave me drama for my birthday."

"I hope it fits okay," I say.

"Benny, this is going to be awesome. And horrible."

"I know."

"Can I sit next to Gregory?"

"I thought you'd rather sit next to Charles."

At the mention of her shitty boyfriend's name, Jami jumps up and down. "I'll go set the table," she says, and skips out to the dining room. Jami's excitement makes me feel slightly less like a dick.

Only slightly.

Party of Seven.

I'm at one end of the table. Jami took the seat to the left of my mother's empty chair, at the other end. Paul and Gregory are seated next to each other, keeping their eyes on anything that's not each other.

Jami has gone all out on the table setting. She put out Mom's good china, and the food is waiting in our best bowls, the steam trapped underneath glass covers. It's quiet except for the clank of the grandfather clock in the foyer, counting down the seconds.

Jami pours everybody a glass of wine. "It's supposed to be a party, remember?" she asks. But the look on Gregory's face as he turns to give Paul another once-over lets me know he's starting to figure things out.

I hear the front door open. Mom's talking to Dave. "I smell chicken!" she says.

She walks in, her cheeks windblown and pink. Dave looks like a tan Frank Sinatra and has both of his hands on one of her arms, like he led her to us. They stop, midstep, the smiles on their faces freezing into that hardened confusion when the brain is working faster than any other part of the body, faster than the heart, which has taken to panging outside the chest.

"Hi," Gregory says, all full of energy, puffing up. "We're having a dinner party."

Mom takes only the slightest of hesitations before *clunk-clunking* to her chair at the table. "Well, fun," she says. She gestures to the empty seat. "Dave, sit here."

There's a knock on the back kitchen door. "I'll get it," Jami says, scooting out of her seat. "It's Charles." She grabs the back of her chair with both hands and leans over, kicking a foot behind her. "Please nobody say a word until I get back."

My mom is staring at me from across the table. All the men between us blur. I don't see any of them. I only see Mom, her face just a little slack, her eyes on mine. I can tell she's realizing I'm not quite the person she thought I was. Maybe she's wondering what she ever did to me that would make me put her in this situation.

She's right. I may have had a sick glee about seeing this in action, but now that it's here in front of me and I'm about to watch Paul get his heart broken, Dave figure out he's nothing but some kind of long-distance booty call, and Gregory realize my mother has secrets even he didn't know about, I am feeling not just guilty; I'm feeling a little regret.

Jami returns. "Not Charles," she says, disappointed. "It's Zack."

Zack walks over to my mother, leans down, and gives her a hug. "I didn't get an invite to your party," he says.

"I wasn't aware we were having so much company," Mom replies, her eyes still on mine. "Benny organized this shindig."

Jami scoots another chair between hers and Dave's. "Come sit, Zack. There's plenty. Right, Benny?"

"Yeah." I'm wondering why he's here, if he's going to tell me what else he's figured out about the two of us.

Zack hasn't looked at me yet. He puts his hand out to Paul. "Hey, I'm Zack."

"Paul."

"And how do you know everybody?"

"I don't know," he says.

Mom stands up. "All right. Benny is having fun at my expense. But I'm glad you're all here. This is something I should have done a while ago."

Zack sits next to Jami. Dave grabs the extra chair leaning against the wall, slides it over to the table, and eases himself into his seat.

Mom smiles. "Gregory, Dave, Paul, I'm seeing all three of you. I care very much about each of you individually, and what you do for me as a group. I'd like to keep seeing you. Please don't be upset."

It's quiet for only the briefest of moments. Then Mom scrapes her chair back and sits down. "It smells great, Benny," she says. "Do you want to start serving?"

"I have a question." This is from Gregory. "How long?"

Mom's scooping mashed potatoes onto her plate. "Well, maybe they can answer that. Paul, how long?"

Paul jumps like an unprepared kid called on by a teacher. "Since we met, or since we fell in love?"

"I'm asking you, Tina," Gregory says. It's weird to hear my mother's first name spoken out loud. "How long have you been seeing these men?"

Dave reaches over to pour himself a glass of wine. "We're not in love," he says. "I just see Tina when I'm in town, or when she comes to visit."

"We're good friends," Mom says. "Gregory, I'm sorry you found out this way, but we never said we were exclusive."

"I thought we were." This isn't from Gregory. This is Paul talking. I turn to see tears rolling down his face. His voice, however, is calm. "I thought you loved me," he says.

"I do love you, Paul," she says. She reaches over and rubs Paul's forearm, but quickly, like she's trying to shake him into her way of thinking. "I love all of you, in your way."

Gregory is fidgeting with his napkin. I can see his fingers trembling. "Why didn't you tell me?" he asks.

"Pud, I—"

"Don't," he interrupts. "Don't call me that now."

"Fine," Mom says. She takes a sip of the wine Dave has poured for her. "I'm sorry."

"You're damn right you should be sorry."

Paul stands up. "Excuse me," he says. "I think I've been mistaken."

It's a strange exit line, but it's a good one. Paul turns to shake my hand. "Sorry I won't be staying for dinner, Benny," he says. His skin is soft and his fingers feel small in my hand. He's wiping his face with his napkin, looking absolutely lost.

"I have to go," he says. "Good-bye, Tina." He's talking to my mother, but he's looking at me.

"Paul," Mom says. "Please don't go. Hear me out."

"Okay," he says, and takes his seat again. Zack laughs, then quickly covers his mouth with the edge of his fist.

Dave clears his throat. "For the record, I never thought we were exclusive. I see other women. You know that, right, Tina?"

"I don't care," Mom says. "Gregory, do you want to hear what I have to say?"

Gregory nods, but he's staring at Dave. Nobody's looking at whom they're speaking with. It's like a bad art house film.

Jami gives an uncomfortable laugh. "This is really trippy."

"I was faithful to my husband for thirty years," Mom says.

"Oh, really?" I say.

Mom looks at me. "Yes," she says. "I was."

I look at Gregory. "You sure about that? Gregory?"

"You don't know what you're talking about, Benny," he says. "Your mother's talking."

"You don't get to talk to me like that," I say.

"Shut up." Mom has just said to me the two words forbidden in our house. You never get to say "shut up" to anybody. It's worse than the worst curse words. In our house, "shut up" is akin to slapping someone across the face. My mother has just said it, and not quietly.

"I was a very good wife," she says. "I stood by my husband through everything. But I'm older now, and I don't want to have to live the rest of my life with just one person. I'm through with monogamy. It leads to boredom. I lost myself in a marriage, and I'm happy to be my own person again. I refuse to feel bad about that."

Now she's looking at me, straight at me. "Paul and I go dancing, and he makes me feel like a teenager. With Dave I can have a good time with no strings. We see each other only when we want to. He's my boyfriend." She turns to Gregory. "But you, Gregory, are my rock. You're my best friend."

She sounds like she wants to be finished. She picks up her fork and holds it just above the plate, poised for her final thought. "I hope you can all understand that I need you. I love each of you, and there's no reason to be jealous of each other. There were others, but now it's just you three. I'm sorry you had to find out about each other this way, but at least now I don't have to feel like I'm keeping secrets from you."

"That's great," Gregory says. "But it doesn't work that way, honey."

"It's been working fine," my mother says.

"What about us?" My voice finds the words before I realize I'm saying them. "How long were you keeping secrets from us?"

Jami says, "I knew about everybody."

"But I didn't. I had to find out. I found letters."

"Those are none of your business," Mom says.

"What was my business, then? When you guys got in that car accident, you took a week to tell me. You both hide things from me. And this house! Why did your house get like this?"

"I won't feel guilty for making myself happy." She gestures toward the men with her head. "That's why everybody's here."

"But it's miserable here," I say. "The dogs. The mess. You don't have a job. You can't live like this."

"I *do* live like this!" She's trembling, her face blotched in angry, red welts. "This is my life, Benny. You came here expecting us to fall to our knees, thanking you for saving us. 'Oh, Saint Benny! You are so generous and wise!'"

"Stop it," I say.

"You can't boss us around. I got enough of it from your father when he was alive. I refuse to get it from my daughter.

The week you were gone, everything was back to normal. I don't like that I was happier when you were back in Los Angeles, but at least we could breathe again. You weren't here to throw away our things, or make disapproving faces, or call our boyfriends and have them over for dinner. You make us feel guilty for who we are, and I'm not going to let you do that anymore."

"Yeah, you're right, Ma. This is all my fault." I sound like I'm fifteen, indignant and hormonal.

Mom's found her old voice, too, the one that gets weary from having to deal with me. "No, Benny, you're right. I'm a horrible mother. I've got one kid who can't move out and another who thinks I'm a loser. I tell you I love you all the time, but that's not good enough for you."

"It is good enough, Ma." I can feel myself weakening.

"You don't need me. You haven't needed me in years."

"Of course I need you. You're my mom."

"Yeah? Well, try treating me like one, for once."

Paul stands up again. "No, I'm still going to leave. I was right the first time." He looks around the table, pausing to smile briefly at Jami. Then he says, "Good-bye, Tina. You just broke my heart."

My mother doesn't move an inch as Paul makes his way out of the dining room, down the hall, and out of her life. It is only when the door slams shut that she jostles, her eyes closing shut.

"Well, now that you've alienated two daughters and a boyfriend, you only have Dave and me," Gregory says. "How much easier that will be."

Dave has finished his glass of wine. "Can someone pass the bread?" he asks.

"I think you should leave," Gregory says. "Tina and I have some things to discuss."

Mom puts her hand on Dave's arm. "I'm sorry," she says. "But he's right. I knew you could handle this, but this has all taken Gregory by surprise."

Dave sighs, reaches back and stretches, his shirt riding up over his stomach, revealing a massive amount of hair around his navel. "Should I go upstairs?" he asks.

Gregory is on his feet so quickly that Jami, Zack, and I stand as well. Zack looks ready to break up anything that might start. "Greg," he says. "Be cool."

Mom pats Dave's arm. "I think you should find a hotel tonight. I'll call you."

I cannot believe how calm my mother is with them, when she was just practically screaming at me. I've never seen her like this before. She's someone else entirely.

Mom looks at me like I've just burned her house down. "I'm through talking to you," she says. To my sister she gives a gentle "Good night, Jami."

Gregory heads to the living room as Mom ushers Dave out the front door. Jami, Zack, and I are left at the table, looking at the mostly untouched food.

Zack laughs, his hands covering his face. "Jesus Christ," he says. "What is with the women in this family?"

Jami says. "I'm just sitting here."

"You get *one,*" Zack says, his finger raised between us. "One guy. If you're lucky. You get one man who loves you and is willing to do anything to make you happy. But you women, you think you can just take little pieces from everybody and build them up into one gang? That's not how it works."

"Look who's talking," I say.

"It's all making sense now," he says. "You only wanted some of me. That's why you didn't kiss me. That's why you don't want me to change my life. It's not about me; it's about what you need from me."

"No," I say. "It's not." Because even if it is about him, it can't be.

Jami tries to interject. "Guys?" she asks. "Do you want me to leave?"

Zack doesn't acknowledge her. "You can sit there and say you're not in love with me," he says. "That's fine. I get it. You're stubborn and to admit you feel something is like admitting you're wrong or doing something wrong. But I see how you look at me. You make time for me."

Just because I care about him and can't seem to stay away from him, does that mean I'm in love? If he says it often enough, will it somehow turn true? That's not how it works, is it?

"It doesn't matter what I feel for you," I say. "Don't you see I'm doing you a favor? You're getting off easy."

I can tell Zack isn't getting what I'm saying, so I turn to Jami. "If someone tells you he loves you, but he's married, what would you do?"

Jami mulls this over, like she's got money riding on the answer. "If I felt nothing for him, I'd tell him to get the fuck away from me. But if I loved him, and he wasn't planning on leaving his wife for me, and he just wanted me to know something like I won a consolation prize? I'd set his car on fire. And then I'd find his wife, and I'd make sure she knew about me. And then I'd probably stalk his job. Until he apologized."

"Why would you do that?" Zack asks.

"Oh, I'm always crazy when I'm in love," she says, clicking her tongue against her teeth. "When I think about how much I love Charles, and how much he treats me like shit, I want to rip his balls off."

"Seriously," Zack says. "There are some crazy bitches up in this house." He stands. "Waste of my fucking time," he says. He grabs my shoulder and leans down, his face inches from mine. If he's going to kiss me, he'd better do it right now, and he'd better do it right.

"I hope you do fall in love," he says. "So hard you can't breathe. When that guy comes along who makes you so messed up inside you'd rather kill yourself than spend a second without him? I hope he treats you like shit. Then you can see what it's like to love someone who pretends they have no interest in you."

"You have no idea what I've felt," I say.

"Neither do you."

"You don't love me," I say, for what feels like the millionth time.

"Well, congratulations," Zack says. "You've finally convinced me."

The edges of my vision go black, like I can only see a small tunnel as I stare at the table. My throat feels thick. I don't say anything.

It's only after Zack's out the door I hear my sister crying.

"I'm okay," I say.

"Not you, stupid," Jami says between sobs. "I really thought Charles was going to be here."

Zack's right. There is something seriously wrong with us.

There You Go.

Mom and Gregory take their discussion up to the bedroom. I can hear them talking all night. I have the same feeling in my stomach as when I was little and in trouble, waiting to find out what my punishment will be.

In the morning, I walk out back, hoping to find Zack, wanting to fix this, to get him to stop being angry with me.

There's writing on the backyard shed. In bold, black, shaky lettering, different from any graffiti I've seen before, it reads:

"I AM NOT YOUR PROBLEM."

I feel horrible. Worse than horrible. It feels like I've swallowed shards of glass and my stomach is spinning them around, whirling them into different organs. I miss Zack, and I don't want to. He should be gone, free of me.

This feeling I have, this yearning and sorrow, this is the exact feeling I don't want to call love. Because if it is? Why the hell do we do this? This doesn't make any sense.

Why has evolution let us down? Thousands of years ago if something was dangerous to our bodies, we'd find a way to change our instincts, our bodies, our language, to keep each other and ourselves safe. We stand upright. We have thumbs. We have eyelashes and eyebrows. Human beings change their internal and external structure to shelter themselves from harm. So why do we still let ourselves feel this misery?

I am constantly nauseated. I can't eat. I can't sleep. I am aging years by the second. This isn't love. This is serious illness. This is when I should see a doctor.

Or, at the very least, a therapist.

I hide out in my bedroom. It has the only closet I've yet to go through in the house, so I throw myself into it, boxing up all the sweaters and men's suits that fill the rack. Underneath a stack of various versions of Trivial Pursuit, I find a cardboard box sealed with tape. It's got my handwriting in blue pen across the top. "DO NOT OPEN," it says. "BENNY'S THINGS."

I drop to the floor and pull the box between my legs. I rip the tape and open it. The smell of baby powder mixed with

Obsession hits my face. Instantly I'm back in high school.

I find a yellow spiral notebook on top. I've scribbled band names and peace signs all along the cover. Inside are geometry notes. Good thing I saved this.

There's a shoe box sealed with tape underneath a T-shirt from my rarely discussed Latin Club semester. Inside the shoe box, I find pictures of myself.

My fat pictures.

There are at least one hundred photographs of my face, arms, and torso—parts of me torn from other photographs, my companions and family members gone from the picture. I've removed myself from the memory and stored myself here, in this box of shame. There's a folded sheet of loose-leaf paper. I open it to find my handwriting: "Dear Benny. You are fat. Love, Benny."

My mother didn't hide these; I did.

It looks like I was planning a collage of my worst moments, all thick thighs and chubby cheeks. There's me blowing out birthday candles. There I am at an amusement park, my shoulders sunburned and my hair sweaty, plastered across my forehead. I have my arms around someone who is no longer a part of the photograph. I find several pictures of my stomach, one where I've written in blue ballpoint pen across my waist: "GROSS." How much time did I invest in this box, and why don't I remember doing this? It's like finding a scar on myself and not knowing how I got it. I certainly have the aftereffects of this project, but no recollection of inflicting the damage.

At the bottom of the box, I find the tiny pink journal I had in the fifth grade. This was during the time Dad was home and Mom was working at the bank.

The first entry in the diary is dated January first, of course, where I boldly declared I would write in my diary every single day of the year, chronicling my growth as a pre-teen. The next entry isn't until the end of March.

MARCH 25. DEAR DIARY.

I had a half-day at school today. Dad was in bed when I got home. He said he was sad, so I went to sit with him. Mom works late at the bank and Dad misses her even more than I do. That's what he said. And when I asked why Mom has to be so late at her job he sounded like he was crying. He told me I'm a good daughter and we talked about what we should have for dinner. I got scared because I could tell that he was sad and I don't want him to be sad. Jami spilled an entire box of cereal on the kitchen floor and Dad didn't get mad at her. I'm so sure! She's so lucky. I love Patrick Hart. Please don't tell anybody, Diary.

Lylas, Belinda.

My parents were sad, so I was sad. My mom was gone and my dad was lost and I started eating. This isn't to say my parents are to blame for my weight problem. It just means I'm starting to figure out the time line of my own unhappiness.

"I need you to take me to the doctor."

Mom's standing in my doorway. The sound of her voice makes me gasp. The diary tumbles to the floor, and I'm on my feet in a second. "What's wrong?"

"Nothing," she says. "I'm getting my cast off."

"Ma," I say, trying to figure out what to say while the words are coming out of my mouth. "I'm sorry about last night."

She shakes her head. "I don't want to talk about it now. I'm still angry with you."

"What did Gregory say?"

"He dumped me." Then she looks down at the carpet. My mother has finally run out of words. I've done this to her.

"I'm really sorry."

"Well, I shouldn't have lied to him. Or rather, I shouldn't have kept all of the truth from him. I thought I was protecting him."

"He's just mad, right? He'll come back. He loves you."

Mom grabs the doorknob, as if to brace herself. "Sometimes that just doesn't matter," she says. "I'll meet you in the car."

Painkillers.

Mom gets her cast off, only to find the cut she got from dropping the knife on her foot so long ago has gotten infected. Her bones have healed, but her skin has turned a disarming purple and green color, with angry streaks of darkness radiating out, looking almost as painful as it must be.

"I guess I had that coming," she tells me. "It's been hurting for weeks, but I didn't want to say anything. I was worried they'd make me keep this on longer. I just want my life back."

The doctor writes her a prescription for pain medication, and orders her to stay off her foot.

Back at home, I help Mom to the couch and set her up like she would when I was home sick from school—lots of pillows, all the remote controls, a stack of DVDs, and some chicken soup. I'm trying to be careful around her. Everything I do is an apology.

"At least the painkillers will make my heart stop hurting," she says.

"Oh, Ma."

I put in one of her favorite old movies. A few minutes in, I notice she's crying.

"You okay?" I ask.

"This movie's so old," she says. "Like me. I'm so old."

"You're not old."

She reaches out and pulls a strand of my hair.

"Ow!"

"Look at this," she says, her eyes straining to focus on me. "This is a gray hair."

"It is not. Watch your talkie."

"It's gray. I'm old enough to have a daughter with gray hair."

"Stop talking about me getting old." I settle back into my couch groove and try to focus on the movie, where Cary Grant is muttering something charming.

"You know what I figured out?" Mom says, her voice getting lower, her slack muscles making her speech slur. "I was afraid of Gregory. I thought if I loved him back like he loved me, then he'd leave. He'd leave or die. I lost him once before, and I didn't want to do that again."

She's talking about the letters. I can feel my fingers start to tremble as I ask, "Lose him, how?"

Mom closes her eyes, swallows hard. "I knew it was real when I loved Gregory so much I felt like nothing I could do would ever be good enough. People die and go away; it doesn't mean it's not real love. There are all kinds of ways to love someone. Gregory loved me in a way I'd never been loved before. He waited for me."

She pauses for a long time, one hand frozen in the air from when she was gesturing.

"Ma?"

"I miss Gregory," she says, and then falls asleep.

Mea Culpa, Non Pater.

The drive to Gregory's is confusing. There are all these turns and dips I'm not prepared for in his little sports car. I can tell I'm repeatedly grinding the gears. I know I should feel guilty for causing damage to his car, but each time the car shudders, it feels indescribably justified.

I find him in his workroom.

"Hi," I say. "I need to apologize."

Gregory's bent over Jami's statue, gingerly trying to shift it onto a wooden plank.

"Here," I say, joining him. Together, we lift it easily.

"Thanks." He turns away from me, putting his focus on a workbench. I can tell he's just keeping his hands busy.

"I shouldn't have done that," I said. "It wasn't nice of me."

"No, I suppose it wasn't," Gregory says. "You were mad at your mother. I get it."

"She really misses you," I say.

"What do you think of Jami's statue?"

The finished product is a towering mass of metal, found objects, sparkles, and power. There's something new about it every time I look.

"Do you think she'll like it?" Gregory asks.

"I know she will."

"I'm going to drop it off at your house, but I'm not going to come in. You give it to her for me, for her birthday tomorrow, would you? Sort of a good-bye gift. Your sister's a nice girl."

"I wanted to tell you why I had the dinner party," I say. "I think I found some letters. From you. From when I was little?"

Gregory's face goes through several changes as he stares at me. First he's confused, and then I notice the smallest jump of the skin on his forehead, his scalp sliding back. I can see his brain putting together the past few weeks, realizing why I've been behaving as I have. "Jesus," he finally says. "We're not having this conversation without a drink."

We go inside and perch awkwardly at his kitchen island, both of us tracing the lines in the wood with our fingers.

"Man, you scare me," he admits.

"Me?"

"You make me feel like I'm about to be in trouble. My knees are actually shaking right now."

I don't know if I'm supposed to apologize for that.

"It was easier meeting your sister, because she's so like your mother. I felt I knew how to talk to her right away. But you're different."

"Not really."

"Yes, you are. I feel like you know all my secrets."

"I know some of them."

Gregory nods, peeling at the label of his beer with his thumbnail. "Your mom helped me through a rough time," he says. "When my parents died. It was in the news, people were calling my house, asking me to go on television. It was a bad scene. I found them. Dad killed my mother and then did himself. No note. I don't know why."

"Wasn't it with an ax?" I ask. "How did he do it to himself?"

"It wasn't pretty," he answers.

We all have these moments when we feel our problems are so enormous and massive we'll never be able to crawl out from under them, but I have never had to even entertain the notion of finding my slaughtered parents, knowing that one of them did all the carnage.

"I had just gone through my second divorce," he tells me. "I started working late, because nobody could bother me at the office. And your mother would sit in that break room and listen. I'd talk her head off, late into the night, about all kinds of things I hadn't thought of in years. Not just about my parents, but myself, old relationships, places I'd traveled. She has a way of pulling a story out of you. You know?"

"I do."

"I guess it's only natural that I started having feelings for her. She made me feel. I don't like feeling anything, but she made me feel like everything I was feeling was okay. So I thought it'd be okay to feel that I was in love with her."

He leans his forearms on the counter, pulling his body tightly against the wood, as if to protect himself. I notice his hands, and how he fidgets in a way that looks like he's constantly checking to make sure he still has all ten fingers.

"What'd she say?" I ask. "When you told her."

"She tried to stop me. She told me that once I said something, I couldn't take it back, and it would permanently change our relationship."

I flash back to Zack and me in the backyard, how I was recently given the same warning, but from a man who wanted to put his mouth on mine. I've been so sure what my mother and Gregory went through was nothing but wrong, and now here I am not only identifying with their story, but I've got way too many similarities to have any right to judge them.

Gregory wipes his palms across the countertop. I can see traces of his sweat on the wood. "But I'm stubborn," he says, "and when I want to say something I'm going to say it. So I told her that I loved her. She stood up, put her hands on her hips, and said, 'I'm really going to miss our talks.' I didn't see her again for almost fifteen years."

I'm trying to imagine my mother, who would have been just a little older than I am, hearing a man confess his love for her in a break room of a bank. She's got two kids at home and a husband, she's trying to make a living to raise a family, and with three little words, she decides to quit her job and never see this man again?

At first it sounds very heroic, that Mom didn't want anyone to come between her marriage and her family. But she must have felt something for him, too, or this doesn't add up. Just because someone has feelings for you doesn't mean you quit your job and go back to raising a family. It seems so rash.

So, I understand. You can fight it, you can rationalize it, and you can pretend to ignore it, but you can't stop love. You can't help whom you bond with, and the need we have for each other. All you can do is try to handle it with respect, and ultimately do the right thing. Mom and Gregory weren't trying to hurt anybody when they fell for each other. But Mom knew she'd made a commitment, and went back to her home. Zack keeps beating himself up for having feelings for me, and because of that he needs to know if I'm reciprocating enough to do something about it. But I don't want him to. Just like my mom wanted to keep her family together, I don't want to be the reason Zack loses everything he's made of his life.

If I get to decide what love is, for myself, in how I want to love others, then I can keep the kind of love I have to offer from being destructive. I know it can work, because it's what my mother did, so many years ago.

"You sent her letters," I say. "Because she told you to go away."

Gregory covers his face. "I always thought she burned them the second they arrived. I never thought she'd keep them."

"She didn't tell you she still had them?"

"No. She must have kept them to remember how much she hated me for making her have to walk away. She warned me, but I didn't care. I wanted her to know I loved her. She needed to know she made me feel those things."

"She didn't stay gone."

Gregory looks me in the eye. "I lost a lot of time not being with her. Years I can never get back. Years I would rather have spent with her."

"Those were years she was with me and my family," I say. "I know you needed her, but we needed her more."

I watch this sink in for Gregory. He nods. "I can't believe you found those things," he says. "You must think I'm a scumbag."

"I did. I don't think she kept them to remember why she told you to go away."

Gregory looks hopeful. "No?"

"No. I think she kept them because she loved you, and didn't want to forget what she meant to you."

His throat clicks as he swallows. Just above our heads, there's a wall clock humming.

"When your father died, she tracked me down and called me. Said she was in so much pain that she started thinking about me, that I was the only person she could think of who knew about the kind of pain she was feeling. I told her to start talking, and I listened."

"When was this?"

"Years ago. I think your father had been gone for about six months. She didn't know what to do. Didn't know where she should live, or what she should do with all of his belongings."

Gregory's telling me things I already know. Mom barely moved in the months after Dad died, living off his life insurance policy. I never knew what it was that made her suddenly get out of the house, put on clothes again, and look for a job.

"You really helped her," I say.

"I just listened. She did all the hard work. It's probably my fault she started collecting all that crap in her house. Every time she felt better about buying something stupid, I encouraged her to do anything that made her smile. I know she hid everything in the basement and the garage for a while, but I guess it got out of hand this year."

"She probably felt guilty about seeing everybody, and just couldn't stop buying."

"Or she really likes having boxes of weird shit. Some people need lots of things."

"Did you start dating right after that?"

Gregory shakes his head. "I was worried she thought I was trying to take advantage of her. Then I realized I'd gotten my wish, to have your mother back in my life, and I was wasting it. So I invited her to come see me in person again. Scariest question I've ever asked. I knew it would change things between us if we saw each other again, once the safety of the phone was gone. We still waited a long time before we got together. I thought I had waited out all those other men she distracted herself with. I didn't mind. Because I was sure when she finally came to me, if she did, that it'd be forever. I'd be done." Gregory stretches out his legs. "I guess I was wrong."

"You weren't."

"I'm not enough for her."

"You are," I say. "I think she's scared."

"Well, so am I."

"Come talk to her. Work it out. Will you take that statue to my house now?"

"You just called it your house," he says.

"That's weird, isn't it?"

He laughs. "Yeah, a little."

"Gregory, I'm going to be a wreck until you two get back together."

He nods. "Well, this is all about you, isn't it?" His voice is deadpan, but I know he's joking. He reaches out his hand, and this time I take it. "Come on," he says. "Let's go see if your mother still wants me."

Surprise.

That night, Gregory and my mother stay up in her bedroom, talking. I'm in the living room, waiting for Jami, who hasn't been home in days. She called three hours ago, to say she was borrowing Charles's car and is on her way home. It is almost two in the morning, and there is still no sign of her. So, here's where I tell you about regrets, because when we wait up all hours for someone we love to prove that they were just being idiots and not lying in a heap of bloody bones in a ditch, we tend to think about ourselves.

I regret never sneaking out of my house. I never did it growing up. Not once. Never skipped a class, never climbed out of a window, never had to find a way back into my home when I saw that my parents were awake in the living room at an hour when they'd normally be fast asleep. That was always Jami's job. She took on the role once she figured out I was too busy being the Good Kid. Jami was a natural at being the Bad Kid. Mom and Dad would be so furious with her blatant lies and obstinate breaches of their parental rules that they would have no idea how to punish her. They'd constantly change their minds. It would go from being grounded for two weeks to getting all of her CDs taken away to losing her television privileges to getting a stern warning. All in one day. They knew that no matter what they did to punish her, she'd either make up enough excuses and lies that they'd repeal the sentence, or she'd be so miserable during her home incarceration that they'd let her go to the mall, and once she was gone for an afternoon it was as if she had never been grounded in the first place.

She knew how to play them against each other, too. Jami can find your button, your most sensitive area, and she pushes it until you're begging her to leave you alone, until you're apologizing to her for whatever it is you did to her that made her do that bad thing. You're the bad parent. You're the bad sibling, the bad teacher, or the bad boyfriend. Jami can get anyone to feel guilt over her mistakes. She's such a good person at heart you refuse to believe she's capable of some of the things she does. You also assume she wouldn't have done it if she didn't need to. Then you feel bad for not loving her enough, for not giving her enough.

I hear her car crunching through the gravel driveway. My heart begins whipping up an angry monologue. I run outside. I'm running, like when we were kids in trouble, and I've got to tell Jami so we can come up with the perfect excuse so she doesn't get grounded.

"Where have you—" is all I get out before Jami's whipping her head toward me, indignant, a lit cigarette dangling from her lips.

"I had to wait until Charles was done with his car," she says.

"Jami. You should have called. Mom made carrot cake."

You know, because it's really all about the *carrot cake.*

"She still up?" Jami looks up toward my mother's bed-room window. The light is on.

"She's talking to Gregory."

"Good."

"Why do you do this to her? Don't say you're on your way home if you're not."

Jami slams the car door and practically throws her back against it. "I have a lot of shit going on," she says. "You don't know anything."

"Tell me."

"I don't want to tell you. I shouldn't have to just *tell* you. You should ask. You never ask about my life."

"Jami, just apologize."

"Sorry, *Dad.*"

"I'm not Dad."

"No. Dad at least knew he made mistakes. You think you're perfect. It was easier dealing with Dad. When he judged us, at least he felt guilty about it. He wasn't always perfect."

One night at the dinner table he said his only regret in life was having a family so young. Another time he dared us to try to survive without him. "You wouldn't make it a month," he said to my mother. "Just try it."

Memories of my father are flooding my head, images I'd forgotten, of him angry with us, drunk with depression, frus-tration, and disappointment. When I told him I was moving to Los Angeles, he said, "When you come back here in a year with nothing, don't say I didn't warn you."

"What good does it do to remember the bad stuff?" I ask Jami. "Who's that helping?"

"Me," she answers. "If I don't remember the bad stuff, it's too sad that he's gone."

"Is that what you and Mom do with me?" I ask. "Since I'm far away, you both focus on my bad parts?"

Jami looks like she wants to shake me. "Get the fuck over yourself, Benny."

"Tell me what you want, then, Jami!"

We're shouting in the front yard in the middle of the night like white trash yokels, making the dogs bark all around us, and I don't care. If we're going to do this, I want to do it out here, in public, where everybody can see.

Jami tries to push past, but I grab her elbow. "Let go of me," she says, her voice in the same whine she used when we'd wrestle as little girls.

"I can't," I say.

"Why?"

"Because I'm afraid you're going to die."

It came from nowhere, but it's the truth. It's what I'm always thinking. It's in the pit of my stomach every time the phone rings late at night, every time Mom makes a sigh first thing when I answer. I'm always convinced Jami has been killed in some kind of gang warfare, died in an accident caused by another shitty boyfriend, or is officially a missing person. It's what keeps my heart both frozen and at a distance from her.

"I'm not going to die." She wriggles her arm from my grip and rubs it, a scowl on her face. "You're so dramatic."

"Do you want to live with me? Come out to Los Angeles?"

"Hell no," she says. "You're worse than Mom."

"Then what can I do?"

"When are you going to get it? I don't want you to *do* anything."

She storms into the house, leaving her purse on the ground in front of the car. I take it inside and leave it at the bottom of the staircase.

And Now There's This.

An email from Mickey, all in lowercase, the way we write when there's nothing but true emotion behind our words, when we are speaking from the smallest, most vulnerable place inside ourselves.

subject: very late (in many ways)

benny. i don't think i'll see you again, so i need to tell you some things. you want to be everywhere. i just want you in one place. here. and I can't ask you to do that for me. you are your own person, and your life is what you want to make of it. but before i came to this conclusion, before i decided to save my last shred of dignity, i had to get really drunk. that was last night.

i got shit-faced drunk and projected our future together. i saw us old, eighty-something and wrinkly faced, holding hands and looking out over our grandkids and great-grandkids, and i looked over at you and smiled, so happy about the life we created together. you looked back at me, and you were crying. you were not crying tears of happiness. they were tears of regret. i saw our future, and you were thinking about your past.

you deserve to know that i love you, more than i ever intended to, more than i ever thought i could love someone whom i admittedly barely know. it's the dumbest love there is, love that doesn't come back to you.

i'm not a quitter. this isn't quitting. it's self-preservation. i know you understand that one. i've learned that much from you. you are the most stubborn person I've ever met. the only thing i don't understand is that you never fought for me. when i said good-bye to you, you just took it. i know after i hit "send," that'll be the end of this. why was i not worth fighting for?

why didn't you want me to wait for you? what's wrong with me? why wasn't I good enough?

getting drunk made me realize i'd been putting off dealing with my own shit, getting wrapped up in you. so I'm going to go deal with my shit. just remember there's a guy in los angeles who is glad to have experienced the whirlwind that is you, if even for the briefest of moments. i have no regrets.

that last sentence was a complete lie. i have a lot of regrets. but that's not for you to care about anymore.

mickey

So I Write This:

I'm sorry.

I told you this would happen. I knew it was dangerous. I knew this would hurt. I knew you would leave, eventually. They all leave. Men leave, boys leave, dads leave. I wasn't beautiful enough or good enough. It wasn't that I didn't fight for you, it's that I wasn't worth the fight. I can't have you. I can't want you. I can't have can't have can't have what is wrong with me and why don't I just go home and fix my fucking life and leave all of these people alone? How many more people have to tell me to go away before I GET IT? I am only making everything worse for everyone. I need to make myself invisible and figure out why I can't stand the sound of my own voice. You got lucky, Mickey. You got out before any real damage was done. I'm sorry. I'm sorry. I'm sorry, and I love you, too.

But I don't hit the SEND button.
I hit DELETE.

The Day After.

It's oddly quiet in the morning as I wake up without hearing the normal bustle of the house. Mom's bedroom door is still closed. Jami's is open, but she's not in her room. Even the dogs are silent.

Downstairs in the kitchen, Jami has her face in one of her arms, draping herself across the table. In the morning sunlight, I can see new streaks of blue in her hair. Perhaps that was what was so important last night.

Standing next to her is Gregory's statue. She's got one hand on it, her thumb rubbing the metal like she's making a wish.

I make myself a pot of coffee and force myself not to say anything to her. I will not have the first word. I know Jami is doing the same thing.

Gregory enters, dressed for work. "Your mom's foot is bad today," he says. He opens a cabinet and pulls down a medicine bottle. "I don't think she should stand on it. It hurts too much. I'm going to give her these, so would you check on her every couple of hours?"

"I will," I say. I hand him a cup of coffee. Little milk, little sugar—Mom said that's how he likes it. He nods a thank-you as he takes a sip.

"I'm going to call her doctor today. I don't like how it doesn't look any better and she's not responding to the antibiotics."

"I could call," I say.

"Don't need you to." Gregory stops in his tracks and looks over. "But if you really wanted to . . ." He trails off, catching himself. "I mean, if that's what you'd like."

"It's okay," I say. "I don't need to call the doctor."

"Good, because I'd really like to talk to that guy."

Gregory looks at the back of Jami's head and then at me. He raises one side of his mouth. I shake my head. He nods, lifts his cup of coffee again, and heads back up to my mother's room as Jami makes a purposefully audible sigh.

I slide into the chair across from her as I tear into an un-toasted bagel, my fingers ripping the bread into tiny pieces. I hear Gregory come back downstairs. "Bye, girls!" he calls from the front door before leaving.

Jami says, "I'm sorry." She leans back in her chair, but her head's down, facing her lap.

"Me, too."

"No, I mean I'm sorry."

I put down the bagel. My hands are too heavy. "Me, too. Do you want to go check on Mom?"

"I can't," she says, lifting her head to look at me for the first time this morning. She's got a black eye. Purple, really, in a blotch underneath her right eye, like a smear. The corner of her eyeball is blood red. Tears fall down her cheeks like some-one's poured water over her head. "I'm sorry," she whispers.

Nobody touches my sister. Nobody hurts my sister and gets away with it.

"Where is he?"

"I don't know." She's lying.

"Jami. Where is he?"

"Work."

"Bank or store?"

She looks away, covering her eye with one hand, gingerly touching the swollen, purple welt. Finally she says, "Store."

Up Chuck.

You always hear people talk about their blood boiling, but until that moment happens to you, it's really a vague notion of what it's like to be that angry. I am that angry.

My knuckles are gripping the steering wheel so tightly I can feel blisters forming on my palms. This is what sports cars are made for—driving as quickly as you can, as furiously as you can, to go kick some no-good, motherfucking ass.

You can talk trash about her. You can cheat on her. You can convince her to loan you cash. You can sell her shit at a pawn shop. You can even harass her cell phone three times an hour. But if you touch a hair on my baby sister's head, your ass is getting scrambled.

The car lurches to a halt in front of the department store. It practically tosses me out the door. I have to force myself to take the keys out of the ignition, because I want to leap from the car, arms out, shooting through the air like a she-beast until I land on the jugular of that asshole.

I know which one he is by how fucking stupid he looks. He's so small and weak, I almost feel bad for what I'm about to do to him. Charles has no idea I'm coming toward him as he stands behind the perfume counter. He's long and skinny, with ridiculous green hair in wild spikes around his head. He looks like a carrot.

He spots me immediately, and my eyes must be wild because he's startled. He jumps in place, taking a breath. He seems to know exactly who I am, and that makes me proud to be Jami's sister. She must have told him about me.

"She fell," he says, first thing, the excuse coming out of his mouth before I've even introduced myself. "I didn't do it."

"Get out here," I say, walking toward him at a steady clip, ready to leap that glass counter in one smooth motion if he doesn't listen to me.

"Call security," he says to the openmouthed, fake-goth, skinny girl standing to his side. She nods, mouth still agape, and fumbles for the corded phone in front of her.

"Get out here," I say again. But now I'm at the counter. "I'm going to kick your ass, so let's do it where you aren't near so many breakables."

Charles tries taking a step backward, but my reflexes are faster. I snatch him by the shitty tie, twist it in my fist and pull him to the glass between us. I hear his forehead hit the counter with a satisfying smack.

"Shit, woman," he says. His voice is strained and choked against his collar. "You don't want to do that. Ask Jami; it was all her fault."

I hit the back of his head with my other hand. It doesn't hurt him more than it hurts me, I'm sure, but I don't know what else to do. There's security coming toward me to escort me out of this building or arrest me, and I really didn't plan further than this moment. In my head Charles was going to cower, apologize profusely, and then shoot himself in the skull. I didn't actually picture myself abusing a perfume counter man in public.

I want to twist his neck, smash his nose in, grab his hair and slam him into the glass counter until it shatters. I want to cause his death, but more than that, I want to hear the sound of his life ending in my hands.

People are staring, merchandise hanging limply from their

crossed arms, as Charles struggles to get away. He suddenly remembers he has fists of his own, and reaches up to slug me. I catch one fist with my free hand and pin it back behind him.

I'm bent over a counter, Charles's head at my crotch, holding one of his hands awkwardly to his spine, and I don't exactly know how or when this game of Twister will end. I've stalemated myself.

"You stay the fuck away from her," I say. "You don't call her, you don't go see her, and if I ever find out you've touched her again, I will kill you."

"Benny!" It's Jami, breathless, running up behind me. "Let him go."

"Let me go, bitch," says Charles.

But I can't let him go. I can't move. Everything feels locked.

I feel a body behind mine, hands urging mine to let go. I let myself melt away from Charles, assuming security has finally come to take me to some kind of mall jail.

But it's not a security guard holding me back. It's Zack.

"Okay, Benny," he says, his mouth close to my ear, soothing me like I'm an angry dog. "You did good. Let go of him."

Slowly, and with an amazing amount of regret, I drop Charles. He immediately flings himself to the far end of the counter, away from me. His tie's twisted and there's a red mark on his forehead already starting to swell. The goth-girl puts her hands on his arm, protectively.

Zack takes my hand.

"What are you doing here?" I ask him. "You don't have to be here."

He gives me his side-grin. "Your sister told me you were fixing to kill somebody. Couldn't miss that. I'd pay money to see that."

"Your family's full of lunatics!" Charles shouts at Jami. Now that he's out of our reach he's brave.

Jami picks up a heavy-looking purse from a nearby display and throws it at his head.

Zack squeezes my hand for a second, and then lets go. He reaches Charles in what seems like one motion. "Next time it won't be a girl coming here to kick your ass. Benny would have inflicted a lot of damage, but you won't come back from what I'll do to you. Understand? You stay away."

"Yeah," Charles says, his lips curling into his mouth. I see the welt forming red and angry on his forehead, and it makes me happy.

The actual security guards are approaching, so we leave the store and walk quickly to the car, not looking back.

"That was awesome!" Jami shouts, dancing at my side like she wants to see it all happen again. "You guys were totally my bodyguards!"

I'm shivering. Zack has me by the arms, hugging me from behind as he leads me to his car. "That was sexy," he says. I can feel his body trembling against mine.

"Shut up, Zack."

"I'm serious. Hot."

"Shut up, Zack."

"I'm not kidding. Now I'm *really* in love with you."

"Leave her alone," Jami says, softly. "The superhero needs her rest."

Looking Better.

The house is almost clean. There are no more stacks of news-papers. There are no more hallways lined with boxes. My mother's basement has been cataloged, organized, and cleaned to an impressive sheen. Every closet is in order. Even the videotapes in the videotape room have been alphabetized. I have spent the past week doing nothing but banging this place back into shape.

My mother isn't as happy about it as I thought she'd be. She's standing in the doorway of the dining room, watching me dust the third china cabinet, when she gives a heavy sigh. I'm able to read sighs like a second language now. I've become fluent in Exhale.

"What's wrong?" I ask.

Mom leans on her cane. She's using it again while her foot's still swollen. "I sold my Betsy Wetsy doll for two hun-dred dollars."

"Ma, that's great!"

"I guess. I'll miss her."

I've taught my mother how to sell things on eBay. Once she realized she could get rid of stuff as easily as she once bought it, she quickly took to the site. Now all the unnecessary crap she refused to part with has started paying her bills. The mailman comes every other day to haul off more packages sent around the country. My mother's shit is now your problem. Whoever bought that electrical nightmare of a lamp that was made out of a coconut? No take-backs.

Gregory appears at my mother's side. He kisses her on the cheek and rubs her shoulders. "The place looks great, Benny," he says. "It smells like lemons in the kitchen."

"It's amazing what cleansers will do."

Gregory laughs. "Hey, I wanted to tell you I just got back from the store."

"Okay. Thanks."

"I'm not finished. I was standing in line behind an African American, a Hispanic, and an Asian."

"Were you at Benetton?"

The joke is lost on them. Mom is waiting for me to say something else.

"What?" I ask.

Gregory stammers for a second. "I just wanted to make sure I said all of those right."

They're both looking at me like students waiting on a grade. I realize Gregory must have done some research, or at least read a book, on more politically correct terminology. "That's perfect," I tell him.

"Thanks. But the cashier was a real Wop."

They laugh like Gregory's channeling Lenny Bruce as they head back into the kitchen.

My family. Full of comedians.

My Sister Is Tough. But Only So Tough.

There's someone at the door. I am in my bed, listening from upstairs, as Jami answers. I don't recognize the voice of the woman who has just entered our house. I find something presentable to wear and change out of my pajamas before heading down.

Jami's at the kitchen table with a notebook in front of her. She's talking to a young woman who's sipping from one of our coffee mugs.

"And how long have you been at your current residence?" Jami asks her.

The young woman tucks a strand of dark hair behind her ear and answers, "About a year. I've recently changed jobs and I'm going to be home more often. I wanted to wait until I'd be a good parent."

Jami sees me and smiles. "This is my sister, Benny," she says.

The young woman turns to me, putting out her hand. "Daisy," she says. We shake.

"I just wanted some coffee," I say. Jami goes back to her notebook, and I make the slowest cup of coffee ever as I linger nearby. There can't be a good reason for whatever interview is happening in my kitchen.

Jami asks Daisy a few more questions about her home, the size of her house as well as her property lot. After a few minutes, they stand up and head out to the backyard.

I stand at the window and watch Jami as she braces herself against the porch rail. Daisy is down by the dog fence, falling in love with one of the boxers.

Fifteen minutes later, Daisy drives away with the dog my sister once named Bitch Slap riding in her backseat.

Jami turns to me, her lips trembling, her nostrils flaring, her eyes rimmed in heartbreaking purple. "Well," she says, forcing herself to smile. "One down."

Following My Head Line.

I give Mom her pain pill and help her up to bed before I start cleaning the kitchen. It's the last room that needs a good overhaul. I start with the refrigerator, working from the back where peaches have become gardens of mushy repulsion.

I hear a clamor out back, and my brain gets distracted. Zack comes here every day, but has been staying away from me. Even though he stopped me from murdering Jami's ex-boyfriend, I know he's still angry with me.

I want him to know that he's not the only one who was hurt by what the two of us never did. I have a lot of questions, and most of them involve finding out what I was supposed to do with the situation we were in. Life doesn't have the best timing, but things that are supposed to happen will happen when they're supposed to.

Funny, I think I sounded like Mickey just then.

Sometimes people love each other, but that's all they can do is feel love. It might be because they live far apart. Or there's a war. They're married to other people. They're cousins. They're gay cowboys. A while ago I read a news article about a Japanese princess who gave up her throne to marry a "commoner." It went on to mention that while she's learning to cook and will have to buy groceries, their new "common" life is cushioned by her $1.2 million dowry. Bitch is still a princess. Just doesn't have the throne. Not the same as giving up your life for someone in the name of love.

Zack's leaning against the shed, kicking empty beer cans into a trash bag.

"Those kids won't stop," he says. "I don't know how your mom's going to get rid of them."

"I have an idea," I say.

I run to the garage and quickly return with two sledge-hammers. "We're going to destroy the shed once and for all," I say.

"I really like your new violent streak."

"Hey, Zack. I'm going to tell you something that will start out like a compliment, and then won't sound like one for a while, but then will end nice."

Zack plops down on an overturned milk crate and pulls out a cigarette. "Can't wait," he says. "Look, I'm a smoker again. Thanks for that."

"When I first met you," I start, "I thought you were going to be somebody completely different from who you turned out to be. I don't know how I would have survived these past few months without your company. You have a twisted sense of humor, and you made me feel really pretty, and I'm flat-tered you wanted to be my friend."

Zack nods. "But."

"*But* . . . you really fucked with my head. We were just going about our lives, doing our own thing, and then you un-leashed all these emotions on me, things I wasn't prepared for. I just didn't know how to handle them."

I squat down across from him, tottering. God, don't let me fall over during this speech.

"The more I thought about how you were feeling, the more I convinced myself that it couldn't be one-way. I had to look inside myself and think about whether or not I had feel-ings for you, too. And I guess I did. But I didn't want to."

"Gee, thanks."

"I *can't*. You have a wife. And I don't live here. And a thousand other reasons that all say you and I may have a very interesting chemistry, but there's nothing we can do about it. It's like you're this brick wall I keep slamming my head against."

"I'm eager to hear the compliment part again," he says, squashing his cigarette on the underside of his boot.

"This . . . in its weird, twisted, awkward, incredibly inappropriate way . . . is a form of love. Impossible love. It feels like it means nothing to tell you that I love you, but I don't know how else to say it."

Zack takes it all in, shoving his face against his folded arms as they rest on his knees. He's pulled up into himself, looking so small. He clears his throat. "My turn?" he asks.

"You don't have to say anything."

"I know I don't. I'm asking if I can. For once, I'm asking your permission, since you seem to think I 'unleash' all these things on you."

"You do whatever you want."

"Thanks." He rolls his eyes, stands up, and dusts off his thighs, like he's some kind of cowboy. "I'm going to tell you something that—in no particular order—will be a compliment, will probably crush you, and will piss you off. But don't say anything, because I'm going to finish with something that will make you laugh."

"I won't remember all of that."

"Shut up. It's my turn."

I take my seat on the milk crate. Zack looks like a lawyer addressing his own private jury. I am the witness, trying my best not to perjure myself.

"You're a hell of a woman. I mean that in all the ways I can. When I met you, I thought nothing. Nothing of you at all. If I turned my back to you, I couldn't even tell you what color your hair was. That's how little I noticed you."

"This is how you start a compliment?"

"But you kept coming around," he says. "Just hanging out, staring at me, obviously crushing on me. It was disgusting. Pathetic. And I started wondering, 'What does she see in me?' And the more I thought about it, the more I was thinking about you. And then one day—I think you were helping me carry one of your mother's nineteen thousand useless storage crates—I just looked at you across from me, and I was looking at your face, and your eyes, and then you went into the house, and I was still thinking about you. Then I cleaned out all the drunk kids' beer bottles and I was thinking about you. And then I had to haul trash to a Dumpster and I was thinking about you. And then I was at home, thinking about you. In my car. At the store. On my iPod. You were everywhere. Everywhere. You just exploded all over my brain and oozed into everything. You made my life a mess. I wanted to hate you for that. But I couldn't. Because you didn't do anything. It was all in my head. It wasn't real. I mean, it was real, but it wasn't real. It's all real; it's very real. But it couldn't be real."

"You're really starting to lose me."

Zack stops pacing. "When I approached you, when I put it all in your hands and let you decide, instead of kissing me, what did you do?"

"I stepped back."

"You stepped back. And why do you think you did that?"

"I don't know."

"Because you're a smart girl." He answers his own question right away. Ladies and gentlemen of the jury, is this badgering the witness?

"Did you want me to step back?"

"I knew you'd step back," he says. "You passed a big test. I forced you to make a decision—something you hate to do.

And boy, did you make one. Big time. *Quickly.* Jumped back like a bunny when you had to make a call."

"What if I hadn't?" I ask.

"You did."

"Zack. What if I hadn't?"

"Then I would've stepped back."

I squint, waiting for him to contradict himself. "Really."

"I didn't want to kiss you, Benny. I had to. Do you understand the difference?"

"So we were playing a game of chicken?"

"I won. No, yeah, actually, I lost. Anyway, you didn't want to kiss me. You ducked."

He's making it sound too simple. "It's not that I didn't want—"

"You made the right decision. You did the right thing. I knew you would."

I'm not used to Zack agreeing with me. "You told me I was wrong," I say. "I don't like being wrong."

"I know you don't."

"You're wrong. Standing here, with me. Talking like this. This is wrong. I don't want to be wrong. I don't want *you* to be wrong."

"See?" Zack asks, smiling. "You're wrong sometimes, like right now. Or when you convince yourself that what we have isn't real. Or how you came out here to put your family in order. You were wrong to butt into their lives, and it was certainly wrong to tell me that we were all in my head. But I know why you said those things."

"I had to."

"Because your heart is never wrong." Zack laughs at himself, and then continues. "Look, when I leave this crazy house at the end of the day and go back to my real life, the one with my home and my family and everything I've worked for? I'm so happy. Relieved. I get home and see my wife and kiss her hello and just want to do a little dance because I'm so proud of myself. I resisted you. You resisted me. That means we really don't want to hurt each other. We're not selfish. We're good."

"I don't feel good."

"Because this part sucks. This really sucks. Saying good-bye? Never fun."

"Good-bye?"

Zack crouches down to his knees so that we're face to face. "Can I take your hand?"

I nod. Zack stares at my right hand for a second, as if deciding his approach. He slides his hand, palm up, into mine. He turns my hand over in his and looks at it for a second. He smiles.

"What?"

"Just looking."

"Do you read palms?"

"No."

I point into my hand, tracing the crevices. "This is the heart line. The head line. And that there is the life line."

Zack quickly smacks my palm with his free hand. "Don't change the subject. Don't you like the subject? You should; it's you." He gives my fingers the smallest of squeezes. His thumb runs across my skin. "Focus with me, Benny."

I look into his eyes. He's locked on mine. "You gave me my life back. You didn't ever have it, but you could've. It might have been wrong. A huge mistake. But it also could have been everything right." He catches himself. Shakes his head. "Jesus, the shit you make come out of my mouth."

"Go on."

"You're a very smart girl. You're good. You're too good for this place. You shouldn't be here. You should be in La-La Land. Where everybody's beautiful and tan and eats soy puffs or whatever-the-fuck. Big cups of juices from the land of Jamba. I want you to wake up to dolphins flipping and Keanu Reeves at your Starbucks and fake tits everywhere."

"Zack, I think a little of your dream just crept into mine."

"You keep making the right decisions. You know how; you just have to make them."

I've never thought of it this way, but I understand what he's saying. I make decisions, but tell myself other people are forcing me into them. I'm here with Zack right now because I want to be. I'm in Virginia because I want to be with my mother and my sister. I even moved to Los Angeles because something over there was calling me. If I'm so smart, why didn't I figure that out on my own?

Zack's still got my hand. "What do you think of all that talking I just did, pretty girl?"

"I don't know. You never call me pretty."

"Sure I do."

"Calling me 'not as ugly' really isn't the same thing."

"You're a very pretty girl. And I love you. But so what?"

This time when he gives me that side-smirk, my heart cracks in half. I force myself to smile. "So what and who cares, right?"

He nods. Then: "So if my wife dies, I'll call you."

"Oh, my God. That's not funny," I say, but I'm laughing.

"Benny. Have we learned nothing from your mother?"

"Stop. That's terrible."

"My wife's never going to die. One day she'll just get sick of me. And then she'll kill me."

We smile at each other again. I look down. "I don't know what to do," I say. "We said all that, but I don't know. I don't know anything."

He squeezes my hand again. "Let me tell you what I do know. Every day I come over here to work, and sometimes we have a drink or whatever and we have a few laughs. But you know what the best part of my day is? The ten seconds before I knock on the door. Because I let myself think I might get here and you'd be gone. I'd knock on the door, and you wouldn't be here. You just left."

I take a moment. A real moment of calm and rational thought before I ask, "Did you just quote the end of *Good Will Hunting*?"

Zack bites the inside of his cheek. "See? You're too damn smart for this place. Get the hell out of here." He leans back, hands on his hips. The cowboy. He says, "But first I need you to help me sledgehammer the shit out of this shed."

We go to town on this piece of particleboard and scrap wood, taking turns whacking it, shattering the shaky structure to the ground. We jump on the shards until there's nothing left but a pile of giant toothpicks.

"Did you get a splinter?" he asks.

I look at my palms. "I don't think so."

"Let me see."

He grabs my right hand and kisses my palm where the life line splits.

Coming into Focus.

I give Mom a pain pill right before I run her a bath, listening to Zack's truck pulling out of the driveway. I run to my bedroom window to watch him drive off.

I miss him desperately. I don't have his phone number. I don't know where he lives. He's gone. It feels like I freed a dog off his chain. He's going home, to a place where he's loved, and I don't have to worry about him. There will always be our time in my mother's mess, and nothing will change that. I suppose I got my wish. We had a beginning and an ending without the middle. It could never be anything more. It will have to be enough.

It has also made me feel ready to head back to Los Angeles. Things are falling into place here, clicking into their own groove that has nothing to do with me.

The bathwater's ready. I give Mom a pain pill and help ease her into the water. While she's soaking, while the tap's still running and the water's only halfway covering her legs, I take the moment to change her sheets.

Her room smells stale, like someone's ill. Mom's been spending most of her time sleeping and her foot still doesn't look much better. Gregory is coming to stay with us tonight, but he won't be here for another couple of hours. I want to make Mom as clean and pretty as possible for when he joins her.

I'm fluffing the pillows, ready to head back into the bathroom, when it suddenly hits me, a voice screaming inside of my head, hysterical and terrified.

You already gave her a pain pill.

In fact: I think you already gave her two.

I'm running but it still takes forever to get to the bathroom. Mom's hunched over on top of herself, face inches away from the water.

"Mommy!"

I put my arms under hers and try to lift her. She's so heavy, small, and naked in my arms. Her head flops back, out cold.

Holy shit. I've finally done it. I've accidentally killed my mother.

"Mommy, wake up."

I turn the water to cold and hit the drain, still holding her against me. I'm splashing cold water at her, weakly, helplessly. I start calling for help. There's nobody. Jami's gone. Zack already left. Gregory won't be here for hours.

Maybe you gave her four pills. How many did you give her before you were talking to Zack? Then another when you got back? One now? Or two before? Two just now? Too many. It doesn't matter how many. It's too many.

I scream and lift my mother with everything inside of me. Somehow her body rounds the edge of the tub and falls on top of me. My mother is wet and naked and the water's running and my head's humming and I have to get to a phone.

I wiggle out from under her and stumble around the house. The only thing not in its place is the cordless phone. Why did I have to get her a cordless phone?

I page it and run from room to room, finally finding it on Jami's pillow. I call 911. My fingers are shaking; I barely get the numbers right.

The ambulance is on its way. They suggest I try to get Mom to throw up.

Hauling her to the toilet is even harder than getting her out of the tub. I have to make her be upright. I have to get my hand in her mouth. I have to do all kinds of things I don't understand how to do. I'm not even aware I'm doing them. My body is moving independently of my mind because my mind can't stop screaming at me, blaming me for this. I am praying for the first time in my life. I am offering myself up to all of the gods of this planet and universe to take me and make me suffer, just let my mother be okay.

I hear sirens screaming. I hear my sister's voice. She has beaten the ambulance and I don't even remember calling her. Then there are people everywhere, in uniform, with radios and machines that beep and things that are trying to save my mother.

Jami pulls me away. She holds me as I cry. She's crying into my hair. We are wet with bathwater and tears as we watch the men and women surrounding my mother, bringing her back to us.

It's going to be okay.

It's going to be okay.

Everybody's going to be okay.

Okay.

Mom's already got her hand reaching out to me when I enter her hospital room.

"Benny," she says, her voice scratchy from all the tubes and nonsense I've put her through. "Come here."

I'm crying into her stomach, on my knees, sobbing so hard I don't know if I'll ever stop. "I'm so sorry," I keep saying. "I'm so sorry."

Mom shushes me, soothing the back of my neck with her hand. "I'm okay," she says. "I'm okay."

"I'm so stupid."

"It was an accident. And I'm okay. You didn't kill me."

"What if I had?"

"But you didn't. Come here."

I climb into the bed with her. She has her arms around me and I spoon myself against her side. My breath is shuddery. Mom tries to rock us, the best she can, from flat on her back.

"I'm sorry," I say again.

"Are you going back to Los Angeles?" she asks.

"Yes."

"Good. I'd hate to take out a restraining order against you."

"Ma." More tears.

"I'm kidding. Please, Benny. We have to laugh about this a little."

"How about later?"

"Deal." She reaches over and turns off the television over our heads. It's quieter, but not silent. I am aware of the business around us, in the hallways, in the next bed over. "I have to tell you something," she says.

"Okay."

"The car accident. It was my fault. I fell asleep at the wheel and hit the guardrail."

I push myself up onto an elbow. "You fell asleep?"

"I made Jami promise not to tell you. I didn't want you to be mad at me. But I've been furious with myself ever since. I almost killed your sister."

"How did you fall asleep? Why? Are you okay?"

"It was stupid. I had gone to get her from Charles's house late one night when they were fighting. I'd been asleep when she called, and it was so late. . . . I'm lucky nobody died."

"Yes."

"My point is everyone fucks up, Benny. We all make mistakes. People almost kill each other. It doesn't mean they want to, or they mean to. We make mistakes." She touches my face, smoothing my hair down. "And I wanted to apologize to you."

"Why?"

"Because I was afraid of what you'd think. It's why I didn't tell you for so long. But now I know you wouldn't have been mad at me."

"I'm as mad as you would be if I had told you the same thing."

Mom smiles. "You're parenting the parent."

"Something like that."

"Time for that to end. That's why you need to go home."

I nod. I know she's right. I rest my head on her shoulder. "You're grounded, you know," I say.

"Absolutely," she says. "I'm sorry I yelled at you at your dumb party."

"I'm sorry I threw that dumb party. It was out of line."

"I needed someone to make me wake up. If you hadn't, I wouldn't have let Gregory in like I have. It's nice being with just him. I've got to tell you, I was getting pretty exhausted keeping all of those men happy."

"Gross, Mom."

"I wasn't talking about sex."

"For once."

Her eyes go distant, the corners of her mouth turn down. "I was thinking about something before you got here," she says. "I don't know if you remember this; it's so stupid."

"What?"

"You were just starting high school, and you needed a new pair of jeans. You didn't fit into any of your pants anymore. Your waist had grown . . . too large. I bought you a pair from a catalog."

I hadn't remembered, but now I do. They were an embarrassing dark indigo color, the absolute wrong color to wear in jeans at that time, like they were made at home, with my mother's sewing machine. They were plus-size, and had a patch on the behind that read, "Cutie," which was all the more horrifying. The waist came up to my navel, making me a fanny pack away from looking like the most fashion-challenged tourist. I remember standing in front of the mirror in hysterics, my face swollen from crying, begging my mother to let me find another pair of jeans.

"There's nothing I can do," she had said. "These are the only pair of jeans that will fit you now that you're so fat. If you don't want to wear these, you'll have to lose some of that gut."

I take my mom's hand. "I remember the jeans, Ma."

"I'm so sorry," she whispers. "I was scared you'd grow up to be a heavy woman, and I didn't want you to have to go through the things heavy women have to go through. I always want your life to be easy."

"It was hard feeling not good enough for you two."

"Of course you were good enough."

The hospital bed creaks under me as I shift into my mother's frame. "No, Ma. I wasn't. You both wished I looked like something else."

Mom shakes her head, frustrated that I don't understand her. But I do understand her. I just don't want to. We can't change what happened, but we can forgive each other for not being compassionate.

"Your dad would be so proud of you," she says, and the sentence turns into a sword that slices from my throat all the way down until I am destroyed.

She strokes my hair, her voice low and soothing like when I was little and she was trying to calm me down after a bad dream. "I know it's hard without him, Benny. It's hard for all of us. And I'm sorry you feel excluded sometimes. We don't mean to. We're all trying to be okay without him, and grief can make you selfish. We love you just as much as you love us, and we all love Dad and miss him just the same. There is no contest."

"No winners," I say.

She looks me over, like she just realized how much older I've gotten. "You look really good," she says.

My arms curl in, covering my body. "Thanks. It was hard work."

"I can tell."

"I'm not done. I'm going to lose some more weight, I think."

"I'm not talking about your weight. I mean, you look great, but that's not what I mean. I mean you look happy."

"I'm miserable."

Mom chuckles. "No, the second you decided to go back to Los Angeles, that's when you started to look happy. There's something back there, isn't there? Someone? Mickey?"

"No. He's not my boyfriend. I hurt him, too."

"I've never subscribed to that 'Love means never having to say you're sorry' bullshit. In fact, love means you always get a chance to say you're sorry. When we love someone, we always want to forgive them."

"I'm sorry about a lot of things right now," I say.

"You can only fix them one at a time."

I snuggle into the crook of my mother's neck and let myself feel like I'm small and young. I close my eyes and pretend it's a long time ago, and everything in my life is still ahead of me, waiting for me.

Mom pulls back her head and kisses me on the bridge of my nose, like she's always done. "You are perfect," she says.

Found.

In a box of my father's things, I find my mother's engagement ring. It's in a smaller box nestled next to my dad's set of keys to the old house, a keychain from his college alma mater, and a picture of Jami and me at the beach when I was about seven.

Mom and Gregory are in the backyard, planting bushes.

"Take off your gloves," I tell her. She does.

I place the gold band in the palm of her hand. She stares at it, the light zinging beams from the diamond onto her face, covering her skin in tiny rainbows of dazzle.

"Thank you," she says.

"Put it back on," I say. I glance up at Gregory, who is smiling. He nods at me, winks.

Mom holds the ring between her thumb and forefinger. She lifts it toward me. "Finders keepers?"

I shake my head. "It's not mine."

"Then you can have it when I'm dead. I'll put it in the will."

"Ma? I don't want to talk about you dying ever again."

"Too soon?"

"Way too soon."

Mom puts her ring back on. Gregory congratulates her and gives her a kiss. I head back inside. I've got packing to do.

Luggage, Not Baggage.

Jami helps. She puts one of her old dolls in my suitcase. "To remember me by," she says. Her hair is now a color yellow normally reserved for Skittles.

"I don't need a doll to remember you."

"Take it anyway. It's creepy. And I have something else."

She hands me a gift, wrapped in tinfoil. I rip open the silver metallic paper. It's a framed photograph of Jami, Mom, and me. We're in the kitchen, seated around the table. Mom's laughing at something Jami has just said to me. My face is frozen in a shocked grin. Jami's hands are in the air in mock innocence. I'm holding a coffee cup. We are all in our pajamas.

"Where did you get this?"

"Zack took it. The morning you made us take that stupid picture. Remember he was snapping his camera before we started getting ready? He said this is the one that's really us. It's good, isn't it?"

It is. It's a moment that is purely my family, my new family. My mom laughing, my sister being outrageous. And Zack's just on the other side, just out of my reach, watching me.

I love it.

"When did he give this to you?"

"He mailed it last week. Said to wait until you were going home."

Somehow, I knew he'd get the last word.

"I'm going to come visit you," Jami says. "As soon as this job starts paying me regularly." Jami got a real job at a restaurant, waiting tables at a college diner. "I can't wait to see what Los Angeles looks like."

"What if you never want to leave?"

"Then I hope you've got a big apartment. If I move there, Mom's going to start living on your couch."

"Bite your tongue."

She does, clicking her tongue ring against her teeth purposefully to give me shivers.

"I'm really glad you came to visit," she says. "I missed you."

"I missed you, too."

"And I'm already missing you again."

"Same here."

She pulls me into a hug. We don't let go for a while.

"I like knowing you're over there," she says. "Far away in Los Angeles, living your own life. I like that we're so different. It reminds me that I can change everything, whenever I want to. And one day I'll leave Mom's house, and part of that will be because you've shown me that I can."

It's the nicest thing she's ever said to me.

And Now . . .

. . . here I am. Sister. Daughter. Not a Girlfriend, or the Other Woman. No longer miserable. I'm Belinda Benny "Boobs" Bernstein, and I live in Los Angeles.

At the airport, I request a window seat. I want to watch Virginia fade away in the distance, getting smaller and smaller. I want closure.

In the air, I once again picture my funeral. This time it's a small wake, held in my mother's kitchen. Everybody's there, having a huge meal, swapping stories about my life. They shed tears and laugh loudly, making fun of the dork I was as they miss the woman I became.

Then I project further.

I see a small ceremony in my mom's backyard. She's promising herself to Gregory. It's not a wedding, not a marriage. Just a promise. Jami performs the ceremony. Amber hands them rings, and Mom promises to never take hers off, no matter what.

I see my sister fall in love with a man who wants nothing more than to be her best friend. She moves into his place, for a change. She goes back to school. She becomes a veterinarian. Eventually, her boyfriend becomes her husband. Her life is filled with laughter.

I see Zack and his wife, with kids all around, as he builds a deck in their backyard. He has a dog. He has a swimming pool. He looks incredibly happy.

Then I see Mickey, sitting on that porch he talked about in his email. He's staring off into the distance. When he looks to the side, at the chair to his right, there's a woman there. I realize there's a chance she might not be me, and it's not okay.

I Want. I Need.

Grace has already cleared out of my place by the time I get home. It feels empty. My apartment seems to be missing something. I don't mean it looks like something has been taken. I mean the walls feel like they're wishing there was something more inside them. My apartment feels lonely.

I suddenly have the strongest desire to own a plant. Not a big one, just something small and leafy that will be mine to take care of, that needs little from me other than companionship and water. Something I can ignore for days on end, but will still respond to me when I pay attention.

I go to the local nursery and I find exactly that. I name him Rupert. He's got a few sturdy leaves and one heavy stalk that promises to bloom into something. Maybe Rupert is more girl than boy. I don't care. He's right now the most important thing in my much smaller life.

Once I have Rupert, I then want a couch where I can sit and spend time with him. I need a table where Rupert can live, boasting hearty leaves that sprout with each passing month. My apartment seems happy to provide a roof to protect Rupert, a sink that runs water that will feed him.

And this is how I go about rebuilding my home. I buy sheets and towels. With a drill I buy at the Home Depot, I hang artwork on my walls. Something for Rupert to look at. I acquire a bookcase, pots and pans, a new, bigger television. It looks like I live here. More important, it looks like I'd choose to live here.

I call Wendy at the travel agency. I ask for my job back. Turns out the girl who's been in my chair has an online poker addiction, and Wendy's been waiting for me to call.

"When can you start?"

"Soon," I say. "But first I need you to book a trip for me."

I hear her nails clicking against her keyboard. "One last hurrah before you're back?" she asks.

"Something like that."

"Where to, Miss Bernstein?"

"Paris."

"Ooh-la-la. How many people?"

"Just one."

"I've always wanted to go to Paris," Wendy sighs. "Just so I can say to somebody, 'We'll always have Paris.'"

I have one thing left to do before I go. I dial a number from memory.

I ask Mickey if I can take him to a parking lot.

What I love about him is that he doesn't ask why I need to drive him to a mostly abandoned parking lot. He doesn't ask my intentions, or demand explanations. He only says, "Of course."

In the Backseat.

When I finally finish explaining my mental state over the past couple of months, Mickey is silent, staring at his hands folded in his lap. I watch him trace the star tattoo on the back of his hand with one of his fingers.

"I didn't think I'd see you again," he says.

"Really?"

He cracks a smile. "No. I figure that's what I'm supposed to say. But I always thought I'd see you again. I just hoped when it happened it didn't hurt."

"Does this hurt?"

I want to touch him, but I don't know if I'm allowed to. I want to put my hands on his head, touch his hair, and feel his skin on mine. Instead I watch the pulse in his neck, the little flickers of life in his body as he thinks everything over.

"I'm really sorry," I say again. "I wasn't ready for you."

"How do you know if you are now?"

"I don't, I guess. But every mile the plane grew closer to

Los Angeles, the more excited I got. And it wasn't because I was going home. It was because I was going to see you. Then I got here and I wasn't sure if I was allowed to, if I could. So I focused on myself, got my shit together. But I couldn't stop thinking of you. There were all these things I wanted to show you, to tell you. I wanted to listen to music with you and see movies with you. Stupid things, like I wanted to see our feet next to each other propped up on a coffee table while we watched a movie."

"I bought a bottle of wine for you," he says, grinning with embarrassment. "I saw it and wanted to see you taste it."

"I heard a Jeff Buckley song that sounds like I wrote it for you. I wanted to play it for you. I mean I wanted to learn how to play the guitar so I could play it for you."

"I saw a girl the other day I thought was you. I followed her for fifteen minutes. I thought if I wished for it hard enough, she could turn into you."

"Maybe she did."

Now he looks at me. "Maybe she did."

"I never stopped looking for the red cars," I say.

"I never stopped hoping you'd see them."

He leans toward me, hesitates for only the slightest of moments, and then kisses me.

It feels like a reward. A gift. My body calms for the first time in as long as I can remember. Everything unclenches and I can breathe and it doesn't feel like I'm too late.

Mickey waited for me when I was impatient with him, scared of him, angry with him, ignoring him, and when I didn't know why I needed him so much. We tried to push each other away, trying to keep the other one safe. We never left each other's heads, even when other people took the focus. I may not have been aware of it—in fact, I probably would have denied it—but I was waiting for Mickey, too.

We're in the backseat and we're kissing and I think I just finally realized what love is supposed to feel like.

I'm terrified.

But something inside of me says it's going to be okay.

Up Close and Personal
with the Author

FIRST QUESTION: IS YOUR MOTHER STILL TALKING TO YOU?

Why Moms Are Weird is a work of fiction. Any resemblance to actual people, living or dead, is purely coincidental. My mother is a fantastic woman who loves me very much. She even once saved a man's life when he had a heart attack on the highway. My mother would like me to remind you once again that I am a creator of fiction, and she has always encouraged my vivid imagination, which creates scenarios that are in no way close to the actual truth. At all. (I love you, Mommy!)

WHERE DO YOU COME UP WITH YOUR COMEDIC SCENARIOS?

While writing *Why Moms Are Weird,* I was working on a failed pilot for the Oxygen network (*Nothing Up My Skirt*: shout-out to my Boggle partners). Then I was on a variety show for Comedy Central (*Mind of Mencia*: shout-out to my NedLos homies) and ended the year working on a (now-cancelled) sitcom for ABC (*Hot Properties*: shout-out to my CoffeeBot peeps). On nights and weekends, I worked on the book. I'm very lucky that not one of my wonderful coworkers tried to strangle me, as they had every reason to try to shut me up.

Working in comedy almost twenty-four hours a day means my brain is asking at every moment, "Is this funny? What about this? Is this funny?" A horrible experience with low-rise jeans at a West Hollywood boutique results in a comedic essay for my website, pamie.com, which in turn finds its way into a script, sketch, comedy show, or—in this case—novel. My entire day is fodder for someone else, and at times it can leave me feeling just a little vulnerable.

SOME PEOPLE HAVE A TENDENCY TO THINK, WHEN THEY WALK INTO A BOOKSTORE, THAT EVERY SINGLE PUBLISHED AUTHOR IN THERE IS JUST A WRITER. BUT YOU HAVE TO HAVE SEVERAL JOBS BEFORE YOU CAN WORK FULL-TIME AS A FICTION WRITER. WHAT ARE SOME OF THE OTHER JOBS YOU'VE DONE TO SUPPORT YOUR NOVEL WRITING?

The joke among my friends is that I always have five jobs going at any time. This, for the most part, is true. I've been a personal assistant (a job at which I was apparently horrible), a transcriber for reality television (a job at which I wanted to kill myself), and wrote English dub scripts for Japanese Anime (a job that made people want to kill me). I tend to turn in six W-2 Forms come tax time, and I often have to file for three different states. But that's what I'm going to do to avoid sitting in a cubicle again, having to answer the phone, "Thank you for calling customer support. Can I have your problem number, please?"

YOU ARE NOT A FORMALLY TRAINED AUTHOR IN THE SENSE OF GOING TO GRADUATE SCHOOL FOR AN MFA. SOME SAY THAT IS ESSENTIAL, WHILE OTHERS FEEL THAT HIGHER EDUCATION IS A WASTE OF TIME. DO YOU THINK THAT YOU ARE IN THE MINORITY OF PEOPLE WHO HAVE BEEN ABLE TO SUCCEED AS A WORKING WRITER WITHOUT THE BENEFIT OF HIGHER EDUCATION, OR IS REAL-LIFE EXPERI-

ENCE MORE IMPORTANT IN THE KIND OF WRITING YOU DO?

Oh my God. I went to college, for Pete's sake. You make it sound like I barely finished grade school. ("Defensive!") I have a BFA in acting, which helps with writing more than you might realize—I hear voices in my head and they talk to each other. That sounds crazy. Well, okay, I'm a little crazy. You have to be to want to be a writer. Do you know how much time I have to spend all by myself? A lot. It's not pretty.

What was the question? I actually spent a little time thinking about graduate school for playwriting, and then I thought, I'd just be impatient, and end up putting on my own plays, anyway. Which is what I ended up doing. And my student loans are much less terrifying, as a result.

WHAT HAS BEEN THE DIFFERENCE IN YOUR WRITING PROCESS BETWEEN WRITING YOUR DEBUT NOVEL AND WRITING YOUR SOPHOMORE NOVEL?

Trying to figure out what a second novel should feel like. I struggled for some time learning the difference between story and voice. While I tried to find a new way to tell a story, struggling with tone (how much satire, how much drama, how much comedy), my editor helped me understand the importance of keeping my writing sounding like me. It was an important lesson, and one that makes me very grateful I've got such a patient, smart woman reading all these words.

Actually, what's funnier about writing this second book is what was the same as last time: I finished both novels while collecting unemployment. That's the circle of life for a freelance writer.

WILL THERE BE ANOTHER BOOK IN THE "WEIRD" SERIES, OR DO YOU FEEL YOU'VE REACHED THE END OF THE LINE WITH THIS? DID YOU EVER THINK BACK IN YOUR EARLY BLOGGING DAYS THAT YOU'D TURN

YOUR THOUGHTS INTO WHAT WOULD BE A WHOLE FRANCHISE?

Is there going to be another "Weird" book? That entirely depends on other people, including the ones who buy (or don't buy) this one. I'm not worried about coming up with another story; I just have to hope someone wants to read it.

There's no way I could have guessed that my website would have turned into this. I've said it before, but it's still true—pamie.com has changed every single thing about my life, from where I live to what I do to the man I'm married to. If I hadn't started a Geocities page back in 1998, I have no idea where I'd be living or who it would be with, but I know I'd be a completely different person. Man, am I lucky I'm such a geek.

Never buy off the rack again—buy off the shelf...
the book shelf!

Don't miss any of these fashionable reads from Downtown Press!

Imaginary Men
Anjali Banerjee
If you can't find Mr. Right,
you can always make him up.

2cool2btrue
Simon Brooke
If something's too cool to be
true, it usually is...

Vamped
David Sosnowski
SINGLE MALE VAMPIRE ISO
more than just another
one night stand...

Lethal
Shari Shattuck
She's got it all: Beauty.
Brains. Money.
And a really big gun...

Turning Thirty
Mike Gayle
27....28....29....29....29....
Let the countdown begin.

Just Between Us
Cathy Kelly
The fabulous Miller girls
have it all. Or do they?

Lust for Life
Adele Parks
Love for sale.
Strings sold separately.

Fashionably Late
Beth Kendrick
Being on time is so
five minutes ago.

Great storytelling just got a new address.

DOWNTOWN PRESS
A Division of Simon & Schuster
A CBS COMPANY

Available wherever books are sold or at www.downtownpress.com.

14185-2